SOMETHING STIRS

SOMETHING STIRS

A NOVEL BY

THOMAS SMITH

CEMETERY DANCE PUBLICATIONS

Baltimore

❖ 2022 ❖

Cemetery Dance Publications
132B Industry Lane, Unit #7
Forest Hill, MD 21050
www.cemeterydance.com

ACKNOWLEDGMENTS

THERE ARE ESSENTIALLY three types of people who read the acknowledgements portion of a book: those who are in it; the terminally curious; and those who like to say, "I read the whole thing from cover to cover." So, if you're in one of these groups, here we go.

It has been said that no one writes a book alone.

That's not entirely true. You do *write* the book alone. Just you, the keyboard, and a head full of ideas (hopefully). But that's about the only part of the publishing process you go through alone, and that's a good thing because once the manuscript lands on the editor's desk, a lot of people begin working their magic to make it the best book it can be. So, on that note, I want to take this opportunity to thank Kevin Lucia and the Cemetery Dance staff for taking a book that was pretty good to start with and making it much better.

Lisa W. Cantrell was the first "real writer" I ever met. Thank you for taking a fledgling writer under your wing all those years ago, showing me the ropes, then showing me where the monsters live. You wrote me into one of your books, and I have tried to return the favor here.

7

I met Joe Cherkes at NECON years ago and he gave me my first job as a columnist for HAUNTS magazine. Later, through editing one particular short story until it looked like it was bleeding to death, he taught me a lot about what makes a story work. And for the last thirty plus years, he has taught me even more about friendship.

Writer and editor Kathy Ptacek was the first person to tell me, "A writer writes. It doesn't matter if it's a book, a coffee mug slogan, a short story, or a bumper sticker. A writer writes." We've been friends ever since.

And to Kathy's husband, the late Charles L. Grant, I owe more than I can ever say. Charlie was my mentor and then my friend for well over two decades. The finest compliment I've ever received was his comment, "Damn, I wish I'd written that," when he bought one of my stories for an anthology. Then again, in true Charlie Grant fashion, he brought me back down to earth with, "But you need to lose five pages of dialogue." One of the finest writers of my (or any other) generation, he was the undisputed master of what has come to be known as quiet horror. The title of this book is a tribute to Charlie (I hope) since I "borrowed" it from him. I am only sorry he didn't get the chance to read it. But Kat did. And that's good enough.

Thank you to Craig Shaw Gardner, who introduced me to NECON, treated me like a true colleague from the first time we met, and gave me some very valuable information about what it takes to become a professional writer very early in my career. He probably doesn't even know what an impact he had me and on my writing back then. But he, Tom Monteleone, and a handfull of others showed me through their example and encouragement what true class is, and how it should be a integral part of who we are as professional writers.

But most of all, I thank God for more things than this book could ever hold. I am truly blessed, and I thank Him for that fact every day.

"Within, its walls continued upright, bricks met neatly, floors were firm, and doors were sensibly shut; silence lay steadily against the wood and stone of Hill House, and whatever walked there, walked alone."

SHIRLEY JACKSON, *THE HAUNTING OF HILL HOUSE*

Whenever the evil spirits saw him, they fell down before him and cried out, "You are the Son of God."

MATTHEW 3:11

For Paul, Kim, and Dani. Some of my favorite people.
And always, for Melanie.
You believed in me even when I didn't. I love you.

PROLOGUE

THE HOUSE LOOKED down on Pike's Crossing like a headmaster observing a group of unruly schoolchildren. It stood silent, watching the town from the top of Grant's Ridge through glittering leaded glass eyes.

Errant patches of moonlight played along the roofline, then disappeared. A weather vane, more for decoration than any real purpose, pointed west, then east. In the woods beyond the back yard, nocturnal creatures stirred, scavenging for food and scouting new scents carried on the night air.

A field mouse scurried across the clearing between the woods and the relative safety of the space beneath the deck, its dash for freedom cut short by a sharp-eyed owl. Talons lifted the dying rodent as lightning arced across the flannel sky.

The night groaned in the wake of the coming storm. Rumbles of thunder echoed and died away, replaced by more of the same. The house stood in dark relief against the darker sky, illuminated by sporadic celestial fire.

Hours earlier workmen had collected their tools, climbed into their vehicles, and sped away toward the coming weekend. Soon electricians would come to run the wiring, then the crew would be well on the way to wrapping up the project and handing the keys to the developer.

But for now, the house was content to hold its silent vigil over the town below.

And inside, something stirred.

SHADOWS TWITCHED and writhed across the floor, given life by two large flickering candles. Three figures huddled together along a partially constructed knee wall. They watched a solitary figure at work in the center of the room.

Rodney Hardwick checked the circle on the floor. Satisfied that it was as close to perfect as he could draw it, he put the wide-tipped marker in his pocket and placed a series of glass votives around the circle. Next, he took a box of kitchen matches from his shirt pocket and scratched a match across the side with no results, repeated the action, and snapped the wooden shaft.

A half-muted snicker skittered through the gloom, and was cut short when Rodney looked up. Robin Davis met his gaze for a second, then looked away. Rodney tried a second match and the head sputtered to life. The flame flickered, caught, then he lit the candle in the first votive. Flame danced on the wick, eddied by unseen currents, and settled itself into a dull glow.

"This is so cool." Myra Webb giggled and folded her legs up under her. Kenny Randall, sitting just to her left on the plywood subfloor of the living room, shushed her as Rodney lit another match.

"Don't tell me to *shhhh*," she said and punched him on the arm.

"Quit it," he said, rubbing the spot where she hit him.

"Both of you just shut up." Rodney glared. The flame burned slowly toward his fingers, then found flesh. He felt the bite of the flame, but didn't show it. He just shook out the match and pulled another from the box.

"Do you want to do this or not?" he asked, the new match poised above the rough striking surface. "It's up to you. But you'd better decide right now. Either get serious or go home."

Kenny hunched forward and looked at the floor. "Sorry Rodney," he said. "This is all just a little creepy."

"Yeah," Myra said, more subdued than before, "go ahead. We just got a little carried away." She looked at the candles scattered on the floor. "I've never been to a séance before." The three sat back against the wall and watched as another match sputtered to life and deposited a portion of its flame on the remaining candles. Robin drew her knees up to her chest and wrapped her arms around her shins. Everyone was still.

Skeletal shadows born of candle flame writhed and twisted on the walls in a macabre tableau. The sputtering of burning wicks produced a bizarre rhythm for their dance.

After repositioning the candles, the older boy reached into a duffle bag at his feet and took out a handful of what appeared to be small, irregular twigs stripped of their bark. The trio watched in silence as he brought out three copper bowls, a plastic sandwich bag filled with a mossy substance, a black medallion, and two smaller black bags.

He removed the marker from his pocket again and connected the candles with a series of straight lines. The resulting form was a five-pointed star within a circle. Each candle marked one point of the star.

"I've seen that symbol," Myra said. "It's called a pent-something. Pent… penta…"

"Pentagram," Rodney finished for her. "It's called a pentagram." He put the medallion on and placed the bowls into position. He took the mossy substance from the plastic bag, and placed it in the first bowl. The twig pieces went into the second. The third remained empty.

Robin spoke for the first time, her voice a faint whisper. "When we tried this at camp all we used was a Ouija board. We didn't do anything like this." She pulled her knees in tighter to her chest and watched Rodney arrange the items from his bag.

A whip crack of lightning threw jagged shadows across the room. Kenny flinched but said nothing. The girls inched closer to each other, drawn together by the hollow echo of thunder.

Rodney pulled a mottled brown book from his pocket and fingered the worn cover. The movement of flesh across aged leather made a rasping sound. "Well this is not summer camp, and we are not reaching into the great beyond trying to contact Elvis." He looked at the three friends, his eyes as dark as the storm outside. "We are not trying to talk to some dearly departed cloud of gas from the other side, and we are not playing around with a Ouija board." He opened the book and ran his fingers over the first page, savoring the brittle touch of the paper.

Myra broke the silence. "I thought you said we were going to form an occult circle."

"We are," he said, still engrossed in the book.

"Well then, do we really need all this?" Her voice sounded small in the open construction of the house. "I mean this all seems like a bit much just to have a little fun. You know, chant a little and get creeped out."

"You're right. It is." He turned a page. "And that's not why we're here. This is about more than getting a little creeped out. This is about changing your life."

"And how do you plan to do that?" Kenny asked.

The older boy stopped reading. "By conjuring an entity."

"By doing *what?*"

"We're going to conjure an entity." He looked at the wide eyes staring back at him.

Robin shook her head. "You've got to be kidding."

"I'm not kidding you, or anyone else." He spat the words, his disgust obvious. "Do you see this?" He held out the book. "I have been looking for this book for over a year. It's a book of spells, and we're going to use it to call up an entity that will do whatever we want. Then we're going to make it work for us."

"Are you out of your mind?" Robin scooted away from the circle. "You're talking crazy now. And besides all that, where could you find a book like that around here?"

He grinned and waggled the book at her. "You can find anything on the Internet."

"Look," she said, "it's one thing to tell spooky stories and fool around with some stupid board game, but this is different. This is just plain wrong."

"What's wrong about it?" Rodney asked, moving toward her. "What's wrong with getting some of the things we want for a change?" He looked at Myra. "Wasn't it you who was complaining that you couldn't go to that arts camp in Virginia because your foster parents can't afford it?" Myra nodded but said nothing. "And you," he said, turning his attention to Kenny. "You could have been first string on the baseball team this year, but the principal's kid got the call. And everybody in school knows you can out-pitch him on his best day. But you didn't see very much time on the mound, did you?"

"Yeah, well nobody said life was fair," Kenny mumbled. "And why are you complaining? At least your folks are rich. You're the one with the trust fund and the big fancy house."

"Oh really?" Rodney squatted next to Kenny. "Let me tell you about my trust fund. I can't touch it until I'm twenty-five years old. Not one nickel. And if my folks don't approve of what I want it for, then I still can't touch it. Not while they're alive." Shadows and anger played along the hard edges of his face. "As for the big house, oh yeah. I live in a huge house with a pool, a game room, and a sauna. And my folks are quick to point out that they bought the house, which means they also make the rules.

"You would think with all their money they would want me to have a car. But no. They say if I want a car, then I have to get a job and save the money to buy one like they did when they were my age."

"So what?" Robin asked. "Everybody wants something. And sometimes, no matter how bad you want it, it either takes longer than you planned, or it doesn't happen at all. That's just life.

"Besides," she said as she looked back at the pentagram, "even if this is possible, it's still wrong. It's…" She looked to her friends for support, but found only confusion. "It's evil."

"Well nobody is keeping you here. You can leave if you want to." Rodney pointed toward the door. "But if you do, you just remember to keep your mouth shut. You were still here tonight, and we are all witnesses. So that means if anybody finds out about us, they find out about you."

Robin looked at her friends once more. "Look, fun is fun, but this is just plain wrong. Come on; let's get out of here before things go too far." Neither of them made eye contact with her. "Please, come on now." Their silence was her answer. She started to say something else but stopped before she could utter the last plea. Instead, she turned and ran through the maze of framed walls and sprinted out the front door.

"You just remember to keep quiet," Rodney said to the slamming door. He looked at the remaining members of the group. "Anybody else?" Kenny glanced toward the front door, then shook his head *no*.

Myra looked at the design on the floor. A shadow touched her shoe, wavered, then explored spots along the outer edge of the circle. "Let's go for it," she said, then smiled. "Who needs her?"

"Kenny, go outside and get the other bag off the porch." Rodney opened the book again and searched the pages. The younger boy made his way to the front door. He paused, fingers just making contact with the new brass door handle.

Rodney glanced up from the yellowing pages. "Are you going out to get the bag or not?"

Kenny gripped the handle but didn't release the latch. "Maybe this isn't such a good idea. I mean, what if somebody comes up here? What if we get caught?"

"What if I walk over there and smack you?" Rodney closed the book. "The house isn't even finished yet, so it's not likely somebody is going to come up here at midnight to look at a half-built house." He glared at Kenny. "We've already had one baby go home. Are you ready to make it two?"

"I didn't say I wanted to go home. I just think we need to think this through a little more is all. I mean, this isn't what we were expecting. It's... it's just not..." Kenny looked to Myra but still held the door handle.

She shook her head.

"Kenny, I've had about enough of you. Now either bring that bag in here and sit back down, or bring it in here and go home. But either way, you go out there and get that bag before it rains. I don't want it getting soaked."

Kenny glanced at Myra once more. Her lips smiled at him, but her eyes were a thousand miles away.

He sighed, turned the handle, and walked toward the coming storm.

DEPUTY STEVE Hughes nudged the Chevrolet Caprice onto Highway 55 one last time. He sighed, wishing he was still in Cricket's Diner having a piece of apple pie and a fresh cup of Helen's coffee instead of chauffeuring the cooling coffee around in a travel mug wedged in the car's cup holder.

At least he'd had the chance to stop in long enough to get a refill before he made his last patrol of the night. Good thing too because he had been rolling nonstop since his shift started. If it wasn't the Claytons fighting too loud and disturbing the neighbors, it was Pete Hammond's alarm going off at the hardware store for the umpteenth time. One of these days he was going to write him up if he didn't get the piece of junk fixed. Or better yet, buy a professional system from a real security company instead of relying on the temperamental system he had cobbled together from parts scavenged from his store shelves.

Two drunks, a cat in a tree, a stranded motorist with a dead battery, and two prowler calls were the highlights of his shift. The first call turned out to be Beth Collins's husband coming back early from a business trip. He had forgotten his house key and tried to slip the lock on their French doors with a credit card. His effort not to wake Beth backfired.

The prowler call from Mamie Hendricks came right on schedule. She had prowlers at the same time every Wednesday and Friday night. Eleven thirty, regular as clockwork. Poor old thing just wanted some attention. She'd been all alone in the family's home place as long as he could remember. Like so many of her generation, she was accustomed to the familiar and didn't want to let it go, even when it lost its familiarity. So, he checked for prowlers twice a week, talked to Mamie for a few minutes more, then headed into the remainder of the graveyard shift.

Just another thrilling Friday night in Cherokee County.

He watched the town flow past on either side. Courthouse in the town square, library, men's clothing stores, women's boutiques, Quarter Moon Café, Trish Arnold's Art Gallery, the old post office building. It all drifted by, a hodgepodge of new and old, trendy facades and patina-touched landmarks from bygone days.

Tonight, the town was both familiar and strange.

He turned right just beyond the square and drove toward the outskirts of town. In another half hour his shift would be over and he would head home for the weekend. Just a quick drive toward Grant's Ridge, about a half mile beyond the house, and then he could head back to the station.

That's what everybody called it.

The house.

Charles Monroe started construction on the modern stone and glass structure before he ever had a buyer. When anyone from town asked why he would take that kind of risk in a slow housing market, he just smiled and told them that the house on Grant's Ridge would be a buyer's magnet once it was finished.

Normally the sight of the house was a welcome reminder that his shift was almost over.

But normally the house was dark.

WORDS ROSE and fell in ancient rhythms. Myra swayed to the meter and cadence as the words washed over her. Her eyes were open, but focused on something far beyond the room in which they sat. Kenny, normally reserved to the point of being shy, grunted in time to the rhythm of words that were little more than guttural noises to his ears than true words. Something in the sound and force of the words caused his fists to clench until his nails cut into the palms of his hands. Unaware, he rocked back and forth violently, completely caught up in the animal extacy of the moment.

Rodney uncapped a vial of thick reddish-brown liquid and poured it into one of the bowls. He lit the mossy-looking substance in the second bowl and continued reading from the book. The words beat a tattoo on the air, rising and falling in tandem with the wind outside. At the height of his recitation, he poured the liquid from the first bowl over the burning substance in the second and resumed his reading.

The flames licked greedily at the thick liquid as it sizzled and popped. The resulting copper smell left little doubt as to what it was, but neither participant acknowledged the thought or speculated on the substance's source.

Outside the storm churned. Lightning ripped through the clouds, unleashing peals of thunder that shook the windows in their frames. Inside the air thickened and pressed in around them. Sounds lengthened and distorted like reflections in a fun-house mirror. The trio appeared oblivious to all but the sound and rhythm of the ceremony.

Rodney closed the book and repeated the words he had memorized for the ceremony. He tossed the book aside but kept chanting while he reached for the bag at his feet. It moved and shifted in his hands and he fumbled with the drawstring holding it secure. The bag shuddered and something inside hissed.

"What was that?" Kenny blinked and looked for the source of the noise. Rodney continued the incantation and worked on the knot that stood between him and the final sacrifice, the blood sacrifice, that would make the ritual complete.

"Rodney," he said again, this time with more force, "what was that?" The older boy ignored him, his voice rose and fell in a dark singsong rhythm while he continued to struggle with the bag and its contents. He stood in the center of the pentagram and gripped the cord below the troublesome knot. His forearms bulged with the effort to snap the cord. Kenny's question went unanswered.

Outside the wind intensified, hissing through dry leaves and clicking the wooden fingers of an ancient oak together like the rattle of dead men's bones.

Myra swayed to the rhythms swirling around her. Kenny sat stiff, fists clenched in his lap. He was afraid to move, though he wanted desperately to run from the room. He couldn't understand the words, but something about them made him uneasy. They sounded wrong.

Vile.

And he did not want to know what was in the bag.

What had started out as a lark was turning into a nightmare. Kenny opened his mouth to say something and the words died in his throat. The expression on Rodney's face killed his last reserve of courage.

Rodney's eyes were blank. Two blue pinpoints of light in an otherwise dark visage. He was no longer in control, that much was obvious, and it was equally obvious he didn't care. His lips moved and his gestures became more animated, but his eyes were blank.

Vacant.

Dead.

The words of the chant, spoken in a language that was old when the earth was still new, reverberated in the air. They rolled and tumbled through the gloom with an almost tangible impact. The air was thick and every breath Kenny drew felt like he was breathing through dank cotton.

Around him, the house seemed to shrink in on itself. Shadows pooled in the corners and the light cast by the candles advanced and retreated with each flicker of the flames.

He looked toward the front door again, hoping for the courage to break away and run. *Oh please dear Lord...*The words tumbled through his mind as much a silent scream as a prayer. *Please...*

Myra weaved side to side as if enraptured by the guttural cadence of the chant. Her movements mirrored Rodney's. Their eyes were locked on one another, and Kenny was little more than the spectator of a *danse macabre.*

What?

A flash of light brought Kenny out of his fugue and illuminated the cut glass panels on either side of the door. Then it was gone.

More lightning, he thought. But there was no accompanying thunder. He listened a few more seconds. Just wind. But if it wasn't lightning, then what… The answer hit him like a fist.

Headlights.

Someone was coming.

He looked away from the window. Rodney almost had the bag open. The spitting and hissing form inside was thrashing harder than before. Rodney stopped chanting long enough to grab the mouth of the bag.

"No."

Kenny heard the word but didn't realize he said it. Rodney only glanced at him as he continued to struggle with the bag's contents.

Myra glared at him. "What do you mean no? Can't you see…"

"Somebody just drove up," he said, getting to his feet, "and I'm getting out of here now. Come on." He started toward the kitchen, hoping to make it out the back door before anyone showed up.

"How do you know somebody's coming?" she said even as she got to her feet. "Nobody knows we're up here."

"I saw headlights reflected in the windows. Somebody turned in at the bottom of the hill." He grabbed Rodney's arm and pulled. "You've got to stop it now. We've got to get out of here."

"Get your hands off me." The older boy shoved him hard, then pulled against the mouth of the bag once more and the cloth ripped. Myra and Kenny saw what Rodney had been struggling to release. Kenny reached out and grabbed for him again despite the warning.

Rodney held the squirming form with one hand and pulled a curved dagger from the duffel bag at his feet. "I've got to finish this," he said. "It has to be now." His eyes gleamed and he drew the blade back.

The cat squirmed around and clawed his wrist. Rodney dropped the animal and jerked his hand back. Blood spattered the floor and the cat upended the bowls as it streaked out of the room.

"Come *on*," Myra said, as a headlight flashed through the glass door panes. Whoever had turned in at the bottom of the hill was now in the circular drive. "It's over Rodney...let's *go*."

Rodney stared at her, uncomprehending. "Go," he said, then looked over his shoulder at the bowls and the writhing bag..

Myra shook him and moved in closer. "Rodney, we have got to go now, or so help me, I will leave you here." She shoved him hard toward the door. "Move," she said.

Rodney paused another second, then shook his head as if to clear it. "OK," he said, and moved toward the kitchen and back door where Kenny was already fumbling with the lock.

Someone knocked on the front door.

"Get that thing open," Rodney hissed. He punched Kenny's shoulder. "Do it now." Kenny turned the knob again. The door was stuck. He turned the knob again and threw his weight against the door. It shuddered against the jamb, still stuck. Kenny half squatted and hit the door a second time. It resisted a second longer, then swung open. He fell through the opening as the second set of knocks reverberated through the house.

On the living room floor, scattered droplets of blood quivered, stretched into thin rivulets, and merged with the spilled contents from the bowl. The floor rippled like heat waves rising off hot tarmac, and the blood seeped into the wood until there was no trace.

DEPUTY STEVE Hughes eased the door open and waited. Silence. He called out, then paused a moment more before he went inside.

He sensed movement in the edges of dancing shadows. He eased the door open until he had an unobstructed view of the source.

Five candles surrounding a pentagram.

Something shuffled on the far side of the room. He pointed the beam from his flashlight in the direction of the noise. Twin red reflections glinted in the artificial light and a form came hurtling straight for him.

SOMETHING STIRS

The deputy leveled his Glock 22 at the approaching figure but it was moving too fast. A blur of brown and tan screeched as it careened off his leg and out the front door into the waiting night.

He watched the cat disappear in the dark, then made his way through the house, mindful of every creak and footstep echo. Satisfied that he was alone, he walked back to the living room to take a closer look at what he had seen on the floor.

He looked at the bowls, the dried material, and the knife half hidden in the tatters of a heavy cloth bag. He remembered the cat and his stomach clinched.

What happened in here?

The deputy swept his light around the inner skeleton of the house. It would be next to impossible for someone to hide in the maze of framed walls. There was no drywall up so it was possible to see from one end of the house to the other with few obstructions. He walked through the house and out the open back door, careful not to disturb the soft earth at the base of the steps. He walked the edge of the woods behind the house on the off chance he might spot some clue to the intruder's identity. He didn't hold out hope that he would find much with just his flashlight for illumination. It was too dark and there was no temporary lighting around the construction site.

After another quick look around the area, he went back out to the cruiser and grabbed the radio microphone.

"Dispatch, this is Hughes. I'm at the new house on Grant's Ridge. Get the sheriff out here quick."

"Roger that. What's the trouble out there?"

"I'll fill you in later. Just get her out here quick."

A crackle of static and the pounding of his heart broke the silence. The dispatcher responded, the concern in her voice evident. "Steve, the sheriff's on the way. Are you sure you're OK?"

"Yeah, I'm fine…" He looked back toward the house.

"But it's not me I'm worried about."

CHAPTER ONE

"**E**D, GO PULL that back door off and plane it. And make sure the door jamb isn't messed up." The carpenter nodded and loped toward the back of the house. Norman Scott turned toward the sheriff. She was waiting for him when he arrived at the site and had filled him in on as many of the details as she knew. He immediately sent the crew in to look over the interior.

"Norman, I don't have the slightest idea who was in here this weekend. But other than what Hank Turnage cleaned up after I called him, and the problem with the back door, I didn't see any other real damage."

The general contractor propped his foot on a nearby toolbox and scanned the interior of the house. "No, you're probably right. When the guys walked the house, they'd have seen anything major. But I'll have everybody keep an eye open just in case." He turned his full attention back to the sheriff.

ELIZABETH CANTRELL'S father had called her his Amazon princess since she was fourteen years old. She developed in the ways most girls her age did, but she also had a growth spurt that pushed her toward the five foot eleven mark. She was a natural for the girls' basketball team, but she also found that being the tallest girl in the class was not much of an issue since she had grown up in town and had known her classmates all her life.

Only when she arrived at the academy did people begin to treat her like something other than a colleague. Unfortunately for them, she excelled in marksmanship, combat tactics, and arrest techniques. Those who attempted to belittle her or tried to make an example of "the big girl" found out just how painful a joint lock could be, or had to explain to "the guys" why Amazon girl was outshooting them on the range without really trying.

After graduation she moved to Raleigh and worked as a Wake County deputy. That was ten years ago. When the previous Cherokee County sheriff retired, he asked the county council to consider allowing Elizabeth to finish his term. She was one of their own and had proved herself in the field a dozen times over. They agreed, and she had come back home and filled out the remainder of the sheriff's unexpired term admirably. Then she ran for election unopposed. Still, she was acutely aware that a home-town boy or girl who leaves, then comes back after a significant amount of time, carries the taint of being an outsider.

She would have to be careful in how she handled things with this particular case.

"Thank you, Norman," she said, "I really appreciate it. And if you do find anything, be sure and let me know. I want to make sure we didn't miss anything."

"Sure sheriff, no problem." She turned to leave. "Hey, before you go, what exactly was it they cleaned up yesterday?"

She turned and looked at him. "It was just some graffiti. Like I said, I called Hank and asked him if he would come out here and get it cleaned up before your crew got here this morning. The county uses his cleaning business when kids spray paint the school or something like that. I thought he'd bring out a crew, but since it meant coming out and cleaning it up on a

Sunday, he just came after church and cleaned it up himself. Said he didn't want to bother the folks on his crew since they all have families and most of them have family plans on Sundays." She closed her eyes and sighed. She didn't volunteer anything about the nature of the evidence they had bagged at the scene.

"I was out here with Steve Hughes from about quarter to one Saturday morning on. We gathered what evidence there was, then we walked the woods behind the house at first light. I called and left a message for Hank late Saturday morning to let him know what I needed, but he wasn't able to call back until that afternoon. And we still weren't finished when he called back. So he said he'd just come out and do it Sunday."

She motioned for Norman to follow and walked over to the living room area. The pentagram was only a faint blur. "This is where it was, but it looks like Hank got up most of it. Can you do anything with what's left?"

Norman squatted and ran a finger across a few random lines. "This won't be a problem. We'll be laying down a moisture barrier, and covering the whole thing with a hardwood floor in the next week or two. No, this is no problem at all. In fact, you could have just left it like it was if all they did was draw something on the floor."

The image of what she had seen flashed in her mind.

"No," she said, "if something ever happened and the owner had to take up the floor, you wouldn't want them to see somebody had done that and nobody made an effort to clean it up."

"True enough." He stood and walked with the sheriff to the front door. "Look, I'll tell you what. When Hank brings you his bill, just give it to me and I'll take care of it. After all, when you look at it like that, I guess he did me a favor. Besides, we can sand out what's left of that image and nobody will ever know the difference."

"Are you sure?"

"Yeah. I'll be glad to."

Sheriff Cantrell reached in her shirt pocket and pulled out a handwritten invoice from Turnage Janitorial Services. "Good thing Hank gave this to me before he left." She grinned. "And since I don't have to worry about dropping it off at the county clerk's office now, I think I'll head back in and see if I can get a little work done."

The contractor laughed. "Fair enough." He put the invoice on his clipboard, and walked her to the door. "Thanks again sheriff. And don't worry; I'll get a check to Hank right away."

She thanked him and got in the car.

ED WYATT yelled across the framed expanse of the house as the sheriff drove off. Norman turned to see the carpenter waving him over to the kitchen door.

"Hey, boss, the door wasn't a problem. I took a little off the bottom and she swings like a monkey in a tree. But look here." He pointed to a dozen light gouges in the wood. "This door was all swollen up because of the rain and when it was forced open, it gouged the door frame some. I can replace it, but if you got some wood putty, I think I can patch it and sand it off so you can't tell. Then the painters can just paint over it and she'll look good as new."

Norman studied the door frame a moment. The gouges were little more than deep scratches, and wood putty would probably do the trick. "Yeah, I think that'll be OK. If there's not any putty in the truck, run out to the hardware store and pick up a can."

"Hey, Norman, come take a look at this."

Now what? Norman closed the kitchen door and looked across the room. "Rev, don't tell me you've got a problem too."

Jim Perry gestured toward a framed section of the kitchen. "Not so much a problem as a puzzle. Come look at this and tell me what you think."

Norman studied the wood for a moment, then took a few measurements. "Man alive, some of these are a quarter to a half an inch off. What dunce out here can't nail a two-by-four straight?"

"I don't think it's a problem with them being nailed in straight. In fact, I think they probably were." The stocky cabinetmaker motioned toward another wall on the other side of the kitchen. "Come look at these. You can see it a little better over here." He pointed to a gap between the top of the wood and the supporting member it was nailed to.

"Look at the nails," Jim said.

Norman looked at the nails through the gap, then moved to the next stud and looked at the portion of nail visible through a second gap. "What in the world?" He looked at Jim. "What made the wood separate like that, and why are the nails twisted?"

"Good question. I thought at first they were concrete nails, but then I realized they were twisted and not grooved. And they're not quite big enough to be concrete nails anyway."

"Yeah, you're right. I'll tell you what. Let's look at the rest of them just to be on the safe side," Norman said. "I want to see something."

They moved in and out among the other workmen and checked the rest of the framing, then met back in the kitchen.

"Jim, every stud I found out of place had those same twisted nails. Surely to goodness if somebody had a box of nails that defective, they would have realized it." He shook his head. "But we've been using nail guns a lot, and if one of those was bad and somehow torqued the nails as they went in, the guys might not have known it." He scratched his head. "Maybe that's what did it."

"Could be. But that doesn't explain the gaps. If a nail torque, it would still hold everything together unless it snapped in the process. Then again, I've seen some pretty strange things happen on a work site."

"Amen, Rev. And speaking of sites, what are you doing out here? You're not supposed to put in the cabinets until long about next Thursday or so."

"I know. I just came out to check some measurements. I've got more oak than I'm going to need for the kitchen cabinets, so I thought if there were room, I would add sliding shelves to the bottom cabinets. Then I'll put in the runners for the bottom units and still have everything ready on time."

The contractor smiled. "Rev, were you as good at being a preacher as you are at being a cabinetmaker?"

Jim's smile froze. "I don't know."

Before Norman could respond, one of the workers screamed.

The two men ran toward the sounds coming from the far end of the house. Within seconds the sound changed from a wail of pain to a terrified, high, keening sound.

They saw the blood first. It was everywhere. Blood dripped from the support beams overhead and a large section of the wall. A dark puddle formed on the floor at the screaming man's feet. Winston Pucket looked at what was left of his left hand and gagged.

Winston's assistant pulled off his shirt and used it to cover the mangled hand. "Hey, man, hold this on it until we can get you to a doctor."

Winston made a series of *aah* sounds, like a child about to have his first tooth pulled. Tears streamed down his face, and blood from the mangled stump soaked the shirt. He repeated the pitiful sound with each fresh gush. His face was pale and gray, and his eyes rolled in their sockets, making him look like a frightened animal.

"Ah, ahh please, somebody, do something. Please…" The carpenter cradled the sodden shirt-wrapped hand against his chest. "I…I think I'm gonna be sick." He hugged the hand to himself tighter and gulped small breaths.

"Kevin, here!" Norman tossed his truck keys to Winston's helper, Kevin Neeley. "Pull my truck around and let's get him to the emergency room."

The younger carpenter grabbed the keys in midair and ran. "Come on Winston," he said as he wrapped an arm around the injured man's shoulders. "Let's get you to the hospital."

Tears streamed down the pale landscape of Winston's face. "I'm sorry boss. It just hurts so bad." He winced and hugged the mangled hand tighter to his chest. "I'm sorry."

"Shhh. You just hang on to me and let's get you out of here. There's nothing for you to be sorry about. I'd probably have soaked my pants by now."

The carpenter tried a small grin. "I guess it's a good thing I just got back from taking a break." The grin turned into a grimace.

Kevin was outside waiting with the doors on the passenger side of the big Silverado already open. "Come on," he said. "Get in the back and I'll drive." He bounced in place, unable to look away from the blood-soaked front of Winston's shirt.

Winston, now ghost white, stopped at the truck door. "Did anybody get my fingers? Maybe they can sew them back on."

"Please, just get in. Somebody will bring them to the hospital. Just come *on*," Kevin pleaded.

When the two men were in the back seat, he slammed the doors and ran to the driver's side.

"Hang on," he said at the same time he dropped the truck in gear and shot down the driveway. He glanced in the rearview mirror and saw the top of Winston's head.

The carpenter rocked back and forth on the seat, and a fresh wave of tears glistened against his pallid skin. He rocked and whimpered; Norman kept an arm around his shoulder and reassured him as best he could. The words didn't seem to connect.

Kevin hit the brakes at the bottom of the hill and slid toward the road. The truck lurched ahead when the big tires bit pavement. The tires screamed when he floored the accelerator.

Winston screamed when his ruined hand hit the door.

"Kevin, get us there in one piece," Norman said a little too sharp. He saw the driver's concerned glance in the mirror.

"Sorry." The truck leveled out and climbed past the speed limit. "I'm sorry."

"Yeah," Norman said. "Me too." He held on to the man beside him and prayed.

JIM WATCHED the truck slide onto the road and rocket down the asphalt. He stood there until the tail lights blinked out of sight.

"Man alive, have you ever seen anything like that in your life?"

Jim turned to see one of the carpenters looking back toward the site of the accident. Long rust-colored patches were already drying on his clothes, and a thin rivulet of blood divided the back of one hand into two hemispheres. Beyond the carpenter he could see others already working on cleaning up the area as best they could.

"No," Jim said. "I've seen some bad accidents, but never…"

"Hey," Ed yelled, "where are his fingers?"

Jim walked over to the accident site. "Where are the what?"

"The fingers." Jim looked around the room. Men worked with whatever makeshift cleaning supplies they had at hand: old rags, seat covers from their vehicles, tee shirts.

"What do you mean where are the fingers? Didn't they take them?"

Ed motioned toward the greatest concentration of blood. "I don't think so. And unless they stopped to pick them up off the floor before they left, the fingers he cut off are gone."

CHAPTER TWO

STACY CHALMERS BOUNCED on the back seat, and her doll Piggy Anne bounced along with her. "Are we there yet?"

"How did I know you were going to ask that?" Ben Chalmers glanced in the rearview mirror and grinned. "No ma'am, we're not there yet. We won't be there for another thirty-eleven hours, and if you keep asking me, I'm going to take the long way."

Brown eyes twinkled beneath her brown bangs. "Mama, are we there yet?"

Rachel Chalmers turned around in the passenger seat and sighed. "Nope, we're not there yet. And thanks to you little miss smarty pants, now we won't be there for forty-eleven hours."

"Make that forty-eleven and two," Ben said. "I'm going to take the really long way."

"If it's going to take forty-eleven and two hours to get there," Stacy said, "then let's stop somewhere and get some ice cream."

Ben looked over his shoulder and grinned. "Ice cream? It's the middle of October. Nobody eats ice cream in the middle of October. It's too cold."

"Uh-huh they do. Piggy Anne eats ice cream in October all the time and so do I."

Ben turned his attention back to the road. "Piggy Anne really eats ice cream in October? I've never even seen her eat it in the middle of July when it's a hundred degrees."

"Well she usually gets me to ask for it and then doesn't want it, so I have to eat it for her."

"Oh, so that's how it works?"

Rachel nudged her husband. "You know; I think Piggy Anne might actually want two servings. In fact, she might even want sprinkles and a cherry on one of them."

"Not you too?" Ben shook his head. "Why do I get the feeling I'm about to be outnumbered three to one?"

"Because you are a smart husband and a good father who knows when he is outnumbered."

"You're probably right," he said, "and if you really want some ice cream, I guess we could stop somewhere. But with all this talking I forgot to go the long way, so now we'll be there in about half an hour." He flipped the turn signal lever and nudged the Jeep Cherokee toward the upcoming exit. "So, how about if we go see the new house first and find some ice cream after that?"

"OK," Stacy said. She settled back in the seat and pushed Piggy Anne's face onto the window. "We'll start looking for the new house." She pressed her nose against the window and scanned the passing scenery.

Rachel smiled and propped her arm on the passenger seat armrest.

Home.

The word sounded nice.

She settled back on the headrest and watched Ben from the corner of her eye. They had struggled for so long, or at least it had seemed that way, until his third book sold. The first two books were good. In fact, they were better than good. The writing was some of his best and both should have been on various bestseller lists.

And in better hands they probably would have been.

But the publisher had made more promises than efforts on his behalf, and the novels had died a quick death. Two weeks on the shelves and then off to that big remainder bin in the sky.

By the time Ben completed his third novel, he had fired his agent—an industry dinosaur who pushed his few remaining stars' work and let his other clients' work die on the vine—and signed with a relatively new agent who had only a few clients. What he lacked in experience he made up for with a desire to work hard on behalf of the writers in his stable. In Ben's case the result had been a bidding war between three publishers for the novel and a contract for two more.

The initial check for the novel had been enough for him to leave his job and write full time. The subsequent contract made it possible for them to buy the house in Pike's Crossing and start a new life.

Rachel closed her eyes and listened to the steady thrum of tires on asphalt. She could see the house in her mind. All stone and glass sitting on the top of a small ridge. It looked like one of those houses she sometimes saw on Mansion Makeover on HGTV. Though she had dreamed of this day, she had actually pinched herself at one point to make sure it was real. When Ben's career took off, things started happening so fast it was unreal.

Almost like it was meant to be.

She had prayed that Ben's writing career would flourish, then when the prayer had been answered, the sheer power of the response left her reeling. Her husband was a successful writer, she finally had a real studio where she could paint as much as she wanted, and Stacy would grow up in a small town away from many of the dangers that were too often a part of life in a big city.

Ben showed her pictures of the house when he returned from his trip to finalize the book deal. He had picked up a real estate magazine to read on the plane trip back from his agent's office. The cover of the magazine showed Charles Monroe standing at the base of a long driveway, with the house providing an elegant backdrop. The inside ad showed a close-up shot of the house itself. The stone walls, long expanses of glass, glittering brass fixtures and exposed oak beams visible through the windows, merged to form the most beautiful house she had ever seen.

She couldn't believe it when Ben had suggested they go look at it. She was even more astonished when they walked out of the closing thirty days later as the first owners of a true showplace. It was the sort of place where other people lived, not ordinary people like them.

The memory of her first moments in the empty house receded when she felt a hand on her shoulder, then heard a voice calling her from a very long distance.

"Hmmmmm…"

"Honey, are you awake?"

Rachel opened her eyes and smiled. "I'm awake." Ben cocked one eyebrow. "OK, I'm about eighty percent awake. I was in the middle of a happy dream."

"If that's the case," he said, "what's coming up over the next rise should really make you smile."

Rachel knew what was coming, but she felt the same butterflies she experienced the first time they saw the house together.

As soon as the Jeep crested the hill, she saw it. Just a glimpse through the trees, but that was enough. "Hey, doodlebug, you better wake Piggy Anne up and look out the window."

BEN GLANCED in the mirror in time to catch Stacy stretching and rubbing her eyes. "I don't believe it. I'm doing all the work while the women snooze." He grinned at Rachel. "Oh well…at least you weren't all snoring at the same time."

Stacy positioned the doll against the window. "Daddy, I don't snore, and Piggy Anne doesn't know how." She turned her attention to the passing landscape and watched for the new house to come into view. Oaks, birches, and maples blended into a curtain of rust and gold. "Will we see the house again before we get to town?"

Rachel pointed to a curve in the road. "As soon as we start around that curve, look way up in the trees and tell me what you see."

Ben checked to make sure there was no one behind them, slowed the Jeep, and eased into the curve. This would be the first time his daughter had seen it and he wanted to make sure she got a good look. The other part of him wanted to make sure he didn't miss it either.

"Look, daddy, look. There it is, way up in the trees." Piggy Anne, forgotten for the moment, slumped over in the seat. "Mama, look. It looks like a castle up in the sky." A few seconds later the castle was hidden behind a wall of trees again and Ben pushed the Jeep closer to the speed limit.

"Daddy, is that ours? Is it really ours to live in?"

"It really is doodlebug. It's a castle for the two lovely princesses and the ugly old troll to live in forever and ever."

"What about Piggy Anne?"

"Oh yes," he said. "I almost forgot. It's a castle for the two lovely princesses, the ugly old troll, and the reject from a sock factory to live in forever and ever."

"She's not a reject from the sock factory. She came from that big store where we used to live."

"Excuse me, I stand corrected," Ben said. "The overgrown sock came from Macy's in Atlanta, not the sock factory."

"Oh Daddy…"

"HEY, YOU two. Before you get too wrapped up in Piggy Anne's heritage, who wants pizza for lunch?" While Ben and Stacy loved making jokes and picking on one another, Stacy never crossed the line between good-natured fun and insolence, and Ben encouraged her, but never to the level of taunting or teasing. The three of them had a loving relationship, and laughter had always been a welcome guest in their home, even after the accident.

Rachel didn't like to think of those days. But on those occasions when the memories would not be denied, the scenes played out in excruciating slowness. Ben never talked about the accident any more. But he still had nightmares and still called out in the night. Not as often, but just as forcefully as he had in the beginning. And every time she tried to reach out to him, he avoided the topic. He was "fine."

Even so, it seemed that everything was back to normal despite the fact that Piggy Anne was Stacy's constant companion. She thought her daughter should have relegated the doll to the back of the closet with the other forgotten toys and moved on to other things by now, but the doctor said it may be a while before she felt she could give up the doll, and under the circumstances, he didn't think it would be too much longer. She had made a good recovery.

Stacy interrupted Rachel's thoughts. "Pizza? Can we really have pizza for lunch?"

"Sure we can. There's a little Italian place not too far from the house, and as much as your daddy likes pizza, I'm pretty sure we can talk him into stopping." She looked to her left. "What do you think, Dad? Pizza for lunch at our soon-to-be favorite Italian restaurant?"

Ben glanced at the clock in the dashboard and nodded. "Looks like we've got plenty of time. The movers aren't supposed to be here for another hour and a half." He slowed to make the turn onto the main road into town. "So let's go get some pizza."

Stacy clapped her hands and went back to watching the scenery pass by.

Just beyond the tree line, the house waited.

CHAPTER THREE

"I COULDN'T EAT ANOTHER bite if you paid me," Ben said. He leaned back in the booth and closed his eyes. "But I'll tell you something, I believe that was the best pizza I have ever had."

"We would have never guessed," Rachel said. She winked at Stacy. "You only had five pieces, plus half of my salad."

"I didn't have half of your salad. It was more like two or three bites." He picked the last bit of cheese off the pizza pan and ate it. "If I had eaten half of your salad, it would have spoiled my appetite. Then I would have only been able to eat three or four pieces."

"I've got some crust left over if you want it," Stacy said. "I can't eat another bite either."

Ben leaned across the table and spoke in a low, conspiratorial voice. "Thanks, doodlebug, but I'd better not. Your mama might think I'm a pig."

"I wouldn't call your daddy a pig. That would be rude." Rachel grinned. "He's more like a human garbage disposal." She nudged a piece of crust on the child-sized plate beside hers. "As a matter of fact, you look like you did a pretty good number on that big piece you had, too. So what do you think? Should we come back sometime and do this again, or was one trip enough?"

"Mama, I could come here every day."

"Well that's what I like to hear. Another satisfied customer." The round man standing beside their table had a large handlebar mustache, wiry gray tufts of hair that framed his bald head, and a big smile.

"Excuse me for intruding," he said. "I am Mario Binelli, owner and chief pizza chef here at Casa Binelli, and I am so happy you enjoyed your pizza."

"Enjoyed is an understatement. That was great." Ben extended his hand. "Hi, my name's—"

"Mr. Chalmers, I certainly know who you are. Your arrival has been the source of much conversation over the past few weeks." He shook Ben's hand.

"Wow, we've already started the town gossip mill. That must be some kind of record."

"Oh no," the round Italian chef laughed. "Nothing like that. It is more speculation than gossip. After all, it is not every day a celebrity and his charming family move into our town." He gave a slight bow and continued. "And speaking of charming family, who are these lovely ladies?"

"Pardon my lack of manners." Ben gestured across the table. "This is my wife, Rachel, and the little ragamuffin sitting next to her is our daughter Stacy."

"It is a pleasure to meet you both," he said as he spied the large doll in the corner of the booth. "And who is your red-haired friend?"

"This is Piggy Anne." Stacy straightened the doll and turned back to Mario. "She didn't eat much, but she thinks it smelled good."

"Tell her that is quite a compliment coming from a doll. Usually they don't say very much; they just sit in the booth and look bored. So I am especially glad she has had a pleasant afternoon in my little restaurant. But if I may be so bold, how did she happen to acquire such an unusual name?"

Rachel smiled. "It was a gift from my sister a few years ago. Stacy liked it so much, she wanted to name the doll after her, but back then she couldn't pronounce Peggy Anne, so it came out Piggy Anne, and the name stuck."

"Well, Miss Piggy Anne, I hope you and your family will come back again. You are always welcome. In fact, in honor of your first visit to Casa Binelli, your meal is my treat."

"Mr. Binelli, that's very kind of you, but it's really not necessary. The way my husband packed away the pizza, I think you have made a friend for life already."

Mario beamed. "In that case, call me Mario, and allow me the pleasure of providing lunch for my newfound friends, including Stacy and Miss Piggy Anne. I would consider it a great pleasure."

"Thank you very much for your kindness," Ben said. "I have a feeling you will be seeing a lot more of us here from now on. This has been just great."

The handlebar mustache framed the growing smile. "Then this is indeed a good day for Casa Binelli. We love loyal customers. Thank you precious Jesus for sending such wonderful people my way." Binelli extended his hand to Ben. They shook again and the restaurant owner took a step back. "Mr. Chalmers, if it is not too much of an imposition, may I ask a personal question?"

"Please do."

"Is there an assistant or some other person I can send one of your books to for your signature? I hesitate to ask, but I have enjoyed your books so much and I would be honored to have one signed."

"Are you kidding?" Ben rubbed his stomach. "No man who makes a pizza like that is ever going to have to go through my assistant to get a book signed. Not even if I had an assistant to go through." He leaned forward and put his elbows on the table. "And yes, I will be more than happy to sign your book. As a matter of fact, I have some contributor copies of my new book in a box somewhere on the truck and I will bring you a copy of that one too if you'd like one. It's not due out in stores for another few weeks, so you will be the first on the block to have a copy."

"Mr. Chalmers, I have already asked too much. I certainly didn't expect anything like this."

"Please, it's Ben, not Mr. Chalmers. And it would be my pleasure. In fact, I will probably come by here again Friday night to pick up some supper for us. So if you will bring any books you want me to sign, I'll bring along a copy of *Portent* for you."

Mario stepped up to the booth and shook Ben's hand again. "Mr. Chalmers…Ben…thank you very much. I will look forward to Friday." He extended his hand to Rachel. "And Mrs. Chalmers, I hope to see more of you and your charming daughter."

"It's Rachel. And I have a feeling Stacy and I may have to have a girl's afternoon out and come by for a little dessert before long."

"I will look forward to it, my new friends."

"WELL, MR. Celebrity, shall we head to the house and wait for the movers?" Rachel nudged her husband in the ribs as he buckled his seatbelt. Though she knew he would never admit it, Ben was becoming something of a celebrity. And his agent said it was only going to get better…or worse… depending how you looked at it. But so far he was handling it well.

The growing fame hadn't gone to his head, and she felt sure it wouldn't. He had told her horror stories about some of the authors he had met at writers' conferences around the country. Most were down-to-earth folks who seemed to enjoy encounters with both their fans and their colleagues. But there were also the stories about writers whose books he would not read anymore because they were phony, condescending, just plain rude, or worse.

"Come on Rachel, don't start that again." His face was going from a pink blush to crimson. "He was just a very nice man who wanted an autograph. Don't make more out of it than it really is." He turned the ignition and reached for the gearshift. Rachel put her hand on his.

"Ben, that kind of thing is starting to happen on a regular basis. Remember the folks that mobbed you at the Christian book store last month?"

"Honey, five folks is not a mob." The red was coming back.

"OK, maybe not. But they all recognized you from the book jacket and they all bought extra copies of your books so they could give signed copies to their friends. And that kind of thing is happening more and more often."

"I know, but I don't know what to do about it. I didn't expect things to take off quite like this."

She took his face in her hands. "Ben, I don't want you to do anything about it. I think it's great. I can't tell you how happy I am for you. And when I saw how you reacted when Mr. Binelli asked you to sign his book, I was so proud of you. You didn't have to offer him one of your new books. To you it was a small thing, but it came from your heart." She kissed him lightly. "No sir, I don't want you to change a thing. I just want you to realize, you are a pretty big deal. Especially to us."

"Piggy Anne, don't look. They're about to get mushy."

Ben and Rachel turned around and looked in the back seat. Stacy's eyes were closed, and she had her hands over Piggy Anne's eyes. Ben laughed.

"OK, we get the message." He put the Jeep in gear. "You and Piggy Anne get ready, because our next stop is home sweet home."

The afternoon sun moved behind a passing cloud as the Jeep and its passengers headed toward Grant's Ridge…and the house.

CHAPTER FOUR

PINES WHISPER IN the passing of a slow wind; an oak leaf, brittle and brown, pinwheels across the ground into waiting shadows; a dog barks hard and sharp, then falls silent.

A shadow forms, takes shape.

A chipmunk emerges from the shadows, dragging its injured leg behind. A close encounter with a fox left it more the worse for wear, but still alive. The chipmunk pulls itself toward the massive wood and stone structure. It smells the people-scent, but they are inside and it wants only a place to lie down for the night. The people-scent may keep the predators at bay.

The rodent pulls itself under the deck and makes its way toward a few leaves scattered next to the foundation. It is a good place. The chipmunk drops onto the leaves and lies still, its heart pounding in its chest.

A sliver of cloud touches the moon; the chipmunk shifts and settles in next to the foundation of the house.

IT SENSES blood. The draw is almost imperceptible. Almost nonexistent.

Almost.

The pull comes from outside, and a weak ripple moves across the face of the house, around the side, and across the back.

There it is.

A tiny heartbeat.

Almost imperceptible.

Almost.

It clutches the tiny rodent holding it by the sheer force of Its will.

The chipmunk stops in its tracks, the tiny heart beating at almost twice its normal rhythm. It's lungs struggle to take in oxygen. It has gone beyond terror. Its bladder releases as does its sphincter. The tiny body begins to whip back and forth, though it is rooted in place. Like it's connected to the wood of the house. The tiny legs snap with the force of its struggle to break free. The legs spasm and twitch as the chipmunk's back arches with enough force to crack the minute vertebrae.

A tiny squeal is cut short as its lungs collapse.

It feeds. Not nearly enough to force its way through the barrier, but every drop of blood brings *It* closer to the manifestation.

The section of foundation against which the rodent thrashes moves almost imperceptibly.

Almost.

It reaches out and drains the life from the rodent; sucking it down to a husk, then retreats to conserve Its strength.

There will be more.

CHAPTER FIVE

EN PLACED THE last box of books on the floor and rubbed the small of his back. The movers offered to take his computer and the boxes of books up the stairs to his new office, but that was a job he relegated to himself. He looked around the room and found it hard to believe that he was standing in the middle of the office of his dreams.

One entire wall consisted of built-in bookcases. His combination writing desk and work area took up a second wall. The desk was actually a three-foot-wide oak shelf that stretched along the entire wall. Two custom-made units, one containing a series of drawers and a second, which was a filing cabinet, sat in the center of the room. Both were built of the same blonde wood as the work area and would blend in with the work surface, once rolled into place. The only window in the room was situated at the midpoint of the wall and looked out over the town.

"Looks like a postcard doesn't it?" He sensed Rachel's light touch before he felt her hand on his shoulder. He placed his hand on top of hers and continued to look at the view.

"It looks like God worked overtime painting the fall colors," Ben said. He turned and took her in his arms. "Is this really happening?"

She hugged him hard. "Yes, this is happening. God has smiled on us, and you're just going to have to get used to the fact that not only does He smile, but He answers prayers."

"I know He does, but I never expected an answer like this. Think about it. There are a lot of good writers out there, a lot of them better than me." He glanced out the window again. "So why did God pick me? That's the thing I don't understand."

She laughed and took a step back. "Honey, you're not the only one whose writing career ever took off. Think about it. You haven't seen Frank Peretti digging through trash cans looking for his next meal have you? I'm pretty sure Dean Koontz hasn't had to pick up a second job at Walmart. And when was the last time you saw Joe Hill standing on the sidewalk selling pencils for a nickel so he could buy printer cartridges?"

She sat on the edge of the desk and continued. "Ben, every day you pray for God to use your talents for His glory and that's just what He's doing. But if it will make you feel any better, just remember this. Jonathan Maberry is blowing your numbers right out the door. So far, he has sold more books than you'll ever see in your whole life." She grinned and motioned for him to move closer.

Ben stepped toward her but his attention drifted back to the scene outside the window again. She let him drift for another moment, then put her arms around him.

"That's not all is it?"

Ben closed his eyes, sighed, then looked at his wife.

"No. Not all. I was just thinking about how fortunate we've been. About how I really don't deserve all this," he pulled her close. "Then I started thinking about…" his voice faltered. His chest hitched. "…started thinking about…"

Rachel stepped back and took her husband's face between her hands. "Honey, I miss our son too, but there is nothing you could have done to save him."

"I know, but—"

"No buts. I know it still hurts. It still hurts plenty. But nobody blames you." She squeezed his face gently. "Nobody."

Ben looked into her eyes and saw nothing but love.

"Do you want to pray together?"

"I'd like that," he said.

She bowed her head and said, "You start."

He took her hands and bowed his head. "Heavenly Father, your faithfulness still amazes me. And while I do thank you for every blessing, I still have a hard time comprehending the magnitude of your love." Rachel squeezed his hand. "Sometimes I feel I don't deserve all you've given me, but I guess none of us really..."

The scream came from everywhere at once.

"What the...?" Rachel looked around the room.

A second scream, this one more frantic.

Rachel's grip became a vice. "That's Stacy."

They ran from the office and down the hall, calling their daughter. Ben saw her first. She was standing at the bottom of the steps with her eyes closed, rocking back and forth.

Rachel broke away and ran down the steps two at a time. Ben followed close behind. "Stacy honey, what's wrong?" There was no response. Rachel wrapped her arms around Stacy and stroked her hair. "Are you OK?" A spatter of blood was on the shoulder of Stacy's blouse. "Baby, are you cut somewhere?" She looked her over for an injury of some kind and found none. Ben knelt beside Stacy and rubbed her shoulders.

"Stacy, you're OK now. You're OK. Can you tell us what happened?"

Stacy sniffed and looked across the room. One of the movers came into the room. According to the tag on his shirt pocket, his name was Ray. "Ma'am, I'm sorry. I'm afraid we scared your little girl."

Rachel wheeled around, her face a combination of surprise and anger, but at the sight of the speaker, the anger vanished. The man was compact, his thick arms a testament to the thousands of pounds of memories and heirlooms he had carried over the years. And he was as pale as moonlight.

The second mover stood at the far end of the room, his arm wrapped in a towel. He grimaced and held his injured arm close to his body. A dark stain had formed in the center of the towel, and it was spreading.

"I don't know how it happened ma'am," Ray said. "We had just put the china cabinet down in the dining room and it's like the door just flew open. It hit Marv's arm and the glass shattered." He looked back at Marv and held up one finger. "I'm sorry about all this, especially about scaring your little girl, and I'll send a crew back out with the truck to finish unloading your stuff, but I need to get him to a doctor right now."

Ben and Ray walked toward the injured mover. "Look," Ben said, "don't you worry about that. You just get your friend here to the doctor. The moving can wait until tomorrow." The movers started toward the front door, but stopped when they saw Stacy and Rachel still standing at the bottom of the steps.

"Come on Marv. Let's go out the back way."

"No, come on this way. It's quicker. We'll go upstairs and get cleaned up." Rachel guided Stacy toward the stairs.

Shards of shattered glass covered the floor in the dining room. Some of it was already tacky with the mover's blood. There was blood on the floor and a large spatter of blood on the china cabinet.

Marv apologized again while Ben opened the door and stood aside. "Please, don't worry about that china cabinet. You just get that arm looked after, and let me know if there is anything I can do." The men thanked him as he followed them to the truck. Ben motioned for them to get in while he closed the back doors and slid the ramp in place under the truck bed for them.

Ray ground into first gear and the truck bounced down the winding driveway.

Ben watched until the movers were out of sight. He hoped Marv would be OK. He hadn't seen the cut, but the amount of blood everywhere told him it must have been bad. He hoped the mover just needed some stitches and a little time off to heal.

But there was so much blood.

Ben sighed and walked back toward the house. To have started out so well, things sure weren't turning out that way. Over half of their belongings were still on the truck and that half included all of the bedroom furniture. At least Stacy would see it as an adventure. They could stay at a motel in town, get a burger at the local diner, and watch a little baseball on TV. Maybe by tomorrow things would be back on track.

He walked into the kitchen and looked through a box of cleaning supplies for a rag and some kind of cleanser. He settled for a roll of paper towels, and went in the dining room. There was still a lot of glass on the floor but no blood. He looked around to be sure, but this had to be the spot. Not ten minutes ago there had been a wide ribbon of blood running down the front of the china cabinet from the top drawer to the floor. Now there was no sign.

The floor was clean, the cabinet spotless.

When had Rachel had a chance to come down and clean it up? He put the paper towels back in the box in the kitchen and walked into the living room. No bloody footprints.

He went upstairs to look for Stacy and Rachel. He found them in Rachel's room unpacking games. Piggy Anne reclined on a stack of boxes and watched. Ben thought about the blood, or lack of blood now.

"Thanks honey, but you didn't have to do that. I was coming back in to help as soon as the movers were gone."

She straightened the stack of game boxes on the bottom shelf and turned back to take the next stack from Stacy. "Oh it wasn't all that bad. It actually looked worse than it was." She put the next stack in place. "But we're OK now aren't we, little bit?"

Stacy pulled more games from the box and stacked them in a small pile. "Yes ma'am. We're OK now. Daddy, how is the man who got cut? Is he OK too?"

Ben knelt in front of her. "He will be. His friend took him to the hospital to get some stitches." He hugged her, then held her at arm's length. "Now are you sure you're OK? That was kind of scary down there."

"I know," she said, "but I'm OK. It's a good thing Piggy Anne was up here. She would have really been scared."

Ben glanced at Rachel, then back at Stacy. "Yeah, that's probably a good thing. We wouldn't want her yelling her head off." Ben opened the last box of games and put it down in front of Stacy. "Hey, I've got an idea. How about if we head over to that motel we passed on the way into town and stay there tonight? We can get some burgers for supper and watch a little baseball in the room."

"What's wrong with staying here?" Rachel asked. "We did buy it, so we can stay in it any time we want to can't we?"

"Usually," Ben said. "But remember that big truck the two men drove off in? All of the bedroom furniture is still on it. And I'm not crazy about the idea of sleeping on the floor."

Rachel looked at him for a minute, then turned to Stacy. "So how about it, doodlebug? Are you up for burgers and baseball? We can watch the Braves stomp all over your daddy's piddly little team."

Ben grinned and headed toward the stairs.

CHAPTER SIX

_T_AP
   Tap
   taptaptap
Tap tap tap tap
Taptap
Tap

A withered branch scratched against Myra Webb's window, adding to the confusion around her. The old poplar tree flicked its wooden fingers against the outer wall as shadows painted the inner one with ebony and mottled gray streaks of night. She watched the shadows swirl and glide like patterns in a haunted kaleidoscope, then closed her eyes and willed the wind to stop.

The wind didn't obey, and outside, the wispy branches whispered against the side of the house.

Inside, there were whisperings of another kind.

TONIGHT THE wind had a voice all its own. And the voice told Rodney things. Dark things. Things that moved him on a level he had never experienced before. And he was a willing student, greedy for the secrets whispered by the wind.

He watched the faces grinning back at him from the death metal posters that covered his walls. They were his heroes. Their music spoke to him when his parents didn't understand him. Their words were true, words that told of the chaos and utter futility of living life by some artificial standards, created by a generation that didn't want to deal with the real truth.

The truth was, the old ways were dead. Anarchy was on the way and it was riding in on a black chariot pulled by four midnight black horses.

He listened to the voice in the wind again.

Put in his earbuds.

Cranked up the truth.

KENNY RANDALL sat, finger poised above the telephone touch pad. The same way he had done twice before. He wanted to call Myra. Wanted to see if she was OK.

He had even started to call Robin. Maybe she had been the one with good sense that night—it had been a couple of months, but it seemed like yesterday. Maybe he should have left when she did. Just told Rodney to get his own bag off the porch, then run toward town as fast as he could go.

What had they done?

Maybe he should have made a stand with Robin and stopped everything before it went too far.

He picked up the receiver again. It was late, but this was important. He wanted to talk to Myra. Wanted to see if she was OK.

He wanted to see if she was hearing voices.

SOMETHING STIRS

SHERIFF CANTRELL pulled the report from the file cabinet one more time. The deputy's investigation had been thorough. And everything in the report was outlined just the way she had seen it when she arrived at the house that Friday evening two months ago.

She put the report in its folder and dropped it on her desk.

Most of the vandalism they saw came to little more than graffiti on the high school gym or somebody's sister's virtue being questioned on the water tower. Pretty harmless all in all. Just typical small town boredom writ large.

Even when the pranks resulted in destruction, it was generally minor. Most often a carload of high school kids played a game of dirt road baseball with some farmer's mailbox, or the ever popular eggs and toilet paper artwork on the principal's aluminum siding.

But this was different. This was mean.

Violent.

This wasn't somebody's idea of a prank or school kid's attempt at revenge for a bad grade. This was ugly.

She sighed, propped her feet on the corner of the desk, and closed her eyes. The house had been completed and sold, and normally that would have been the end of it. But not this time. She was going to have to tell the new owners what had happened. But it could wait another day or two. Let them get settled in first. They didn't need this kind of news their first few days in a new house.

Another day or so shouldn't matter. It would keep.

CHAPTER SEVEN

T HE MOVING TRUCK pulled up to the front of the house as Ben turned the Jeep onto the driveway.

"How is that for timing?" he said. "I guess God smiles down on those of us who are pure in heart." He grinned at Rachel.

"Could be." She nudged his arm and grinned back. "Or maybe He just wants to make sure you don't miss any of the fun."

"That's probably it," Ben agreed. "And talking about fun, last night was really great wasn't it? It's not every night you get burgers, a hot fudge sundae, and a chance to watch your favorite team win by a grand slam home run in the bottom of the twelfth inning."

"Daddy, we didn't have a hot fudge sundae last night," Stacy said. "We just had a little vanilla ice cream with sprinkles. You had the hot fudge sundae. Remember?"

They got out of the Jeep and walked toward the moving truck. "That's right," he said. "I had a small sundae and you had a gallon of ice cream with two pounds of sprinkles."

Stacy looked up at him. "You had a big sundae and the part of my ice cream I was too stuffed to eat." She tossed Piggy Anne over her shoulder and carried her by the feet. "You said if you didn't eat the leftovers little children on Mars would starve."

"You must be thinking about somebody else. I don't remember eating that much ice cream. Maybe your mama ate it?" He grinned and Stacy giggled.

"Oink."

Ben turned his head to look at Rachel. She pretended to search the sky for some far off something.

"What was that, Rachel?"

"Probably a flying pig."

"Good morning folks."

The short, barrel-chested man making his way toward them was no more than five and a half feet tall, and looked to be just about as round. Because of his frame he moved like a small ape, but his simian-like appearance belied the powerful upper-body, forged by years of hard work.

His grip took Ben by surprise.

"I'm Sam, but my friends call me Monk. The company sent us out to finish delivering your furniture." He shook Rachel's hand, his grip as gentle as a child's.

"It's nice to meet you, Sam."

"Please ma'am, you folks just call me Monk."

"OK," she said, smiling, "Monk it is."

"Mister Monk," Stacy said, "Why do folks call you that?"

The mover laughed and scratched the top of his head with a thick hand. "I'll tell you the truth little lady, I'm not sure why they call me that. They just do."

The stocky mover wheeled around and loped off toward the moving truck scratching his head, swinging the other arm by his side and making monkey sounds.

Ben and Rachel stifled a laugh as they made their way to the porch. Stacy walked between them, Piggy Anne's head lolling against her back. Rachel unlocked the door and left it open so the movers would have a constant access to the house. Ben stayed outside while Monk's assistant pulled the truck into a better position. Ben and Monk extended the ramp from beneath the truck to the porch.

"Thanks for the help Mr. Chalmers," Monk said. "That ramp can be a little stubborn sometimes."

"Glad to do it," he answered, "and call me Ben."

"OK, Ben. Thanks for the help."

The driver set the parking brake and got out of the truck. He walked to the back, opened the double doors. He locked one into place against the side of the truck and Monk secured the other. The driver glanced at Ben, then at Monk. After a few seconds, he began studying the tops of his ancient canvas high top tennis shoes.

"Bobby," Monk said, and the younger man looked up. He was mostly red hair, freckles, and odd angles of elbows and knees. A cross between Ichabod Crane and Howdy Doody. "I'm sorry, I almost forgot." He looked at Ben. "Mr. Chalmers...I mean Ben...this is Bobby Pickett. He was saying all the way down here that he'd never seen a celebrity before and was wondering if he'd actually get the chance to meet you."

The boy flushed a deep red. He looked back at the tops of his high tops.

"Well, Bobby, I'm not sure about the celebrity part, but I am very happy to meet you." He put out his hand and the boy shook it tentatively. "Are you from Pike's Crossing, or are you a transplant like me?"

The boy looked up. "No sir, I'm from here. I live just about three miles down the road, not too far from the Methodist church."

Monk motioned with his head. "He's also going to be a little competition for you one of these days. He's studying English at the community college at night. He wants to be a writer."

The boy blushed again, but not as deep.

"That's great," Ben said. "Now I've met my first neighbor and it turns out he's a colleague. Come by sometime after we get settled and we'll talk shop." The redhead's freckles made way for a wide grin.

"Thank you." The grin spread.

"You're welcome. Tell me, Bobby, have you heard how the fellow who got cut out here yesterday is doing? His name was Marv, wasn't it?"

"Yes sir. Marv. I think he just had to have a few stitches."

Monk nodded. "I talked to his wife last night when they got back from the hospital. He got about sixteen stitches and two days off. Eileen—that's his wife—anyway, Eileen said the cut wasn't too bad once they got it all cleaned up. It was sort of deep, but not very long. He just has to rest a day or two, then he can come back on and do light duty for a few days. Then he'll be good as new."

Rachel called from the doorway. "Ben, ask them if they'd like a cup of coffee before they get started. I just found the coffee maker and the first pot's already brewing."

"How about it guys? She makes a pretty mean cup of coffee."

"I guess we had better start moving your stuff out of here. But a cup sure would be good about the time we get everything off the truck if that's OK."

Ben stepped up on the porch. "Just say the word and you've got it. I think I'll go on in, get a head start on the coffee and start unpacking my office. If you need anything, just let one of us know."

"Will do," Monk said. "Come on carrot top," he said to his lanky helper. "Let's see if you've got any muscles on those little sticks you call arms."

"Cut it out Monk." HHhhe glanced at Ben's retreating form.

The older mover gripped the boy's arm and squeezed. "Don't worry, you two are colleagues now. So let's get your colleague's stuff off the truck before we have to charge him a storage fee."

"IF EVERYBODY in town is like the folks we've met so far, this is going to be a great place to live," Rachel said. Ben sipped his coffee and nodded. He had never really felt at home anywhere before. Growing up his family never showed much affection. His father drifted from one job to another ever in search of the one that would bring him some sense of importance, and those tensions added to the sense of his always being held at arm's length.

Every house Ben had lived in had been just that. A house. Never a home. Mealtime was just the time everybody ate and conversation had usually been held to a minimum because his father was tired or his mother had one of her headaches. Those were usually brought on by a baby born late in life and worry brought on by too much month and not enough money.

"Earth to Ben."

He looked up from the cup and smiled. "I'm here."

She walked over and put her head on his shoulder. "Old phantoms?" When he nodded she put her arm around him. "Which ones? Dysfunctional family or dysfunctional family laying on a guilt trip?"

He looked into his coffee cup. His reflection stared back beneath a slight wisp of mocha steam. "I was just thinking about some of the places I've lived. You know, I never referred to any of them as home. It was always, 'I've got to go to the house,' or 'Come on, let's go to the house.' It was never home."

He slipped his arm around her. "But you're right. They are old phantoms living in their own haunted houses." He saw his reflection in her eyes. "And we're finally home."

They stood there a moment longer, then she took his face in her hands and smiled. "You're right. We're home. And right now we'd better get busy unpacking some of this stuff so we can make room for the next wave of boxes."

"I suppose so. I'll head up to the office and see how much I can get done up there unless you need me to do something down here."

"No, I can handle the kitchen. You go on and get back to work in the office." He started toward the counter. "Hey, on your way up, how about looking in and seeing what Stacy's up to. She's been mighty quiet since we got back."

He added some coffee to his cup and took a sip. "OK. And if you need any help down here, let me know."

He headed upstairs to his office. On the way, he stopped and looked in Stacy's room. Boxes lined the walls, and she was busy unpacking stuffed animals. She took each one out, fluffed its nylon fur, and placed it on the windowsill. Piggy Anne supervised from atop a small vanity, the only piece of furniture in the room.

Ben smiled and headed toward his office.

Home, he thought.

It had a nice ring to it.

He glanced at the computer components scattered around his workspace. It wouldn't take five minutes to connect the monitor, printer, keyboard, mouse, and speakers to the processing unit. He picked up a power cord and plugged it into the printer. Next, the printer cable.

"That may not be such a good idea," he said, his hand inches from the keyboard. "Lead me not into temptation and all that." He snickered and walked over to a stack of boxes in front of the bookcases. "I'd better stick with something safe like unpacking these books."

"Who are you talking to?"

"Huh…?" He turned around to see who had caught him off guard.

Stacy walked over and sat in his desk chair. "Who were you talking to Daddy?"

Ben grinned and spun her around in the chair. "Nobody honey. I was just talking to myself."

Stacy giggled and pushed off on the desktop to gain momentum. "Why? Won't Mama come up and talk to you?"

Ben spun the chair again. "She can't. She's downstairs unpacking stuff in the kitchen." He let the chair spin to a stop. "Sometimes people just talk to themselves. It's a way to pass the time."

"Sort of like when I talk to Piggy Anne?" she asked.

"Sort of like that. And I was about to hook up the computer but that can wait." He opened a box of books and put them on the floor. "Here, you want to help me get these put up? You take them out of the box and put them up on the counter and I'll put them on the shelves."

"Sure."

They worked together for about half an hour. The shelves were filling up with books. Reference books over the writing area, fiction and other assorted books on the shelves. The top two shelves were reserved for copies of his novels and a few anthologies that carried his stories.

"Mr. Chalmers, are you up here?" Bobby Pickett peeked around the doorframe. "Excuse me, Mr. Chalmers. I just wanted to check and see if it's OK for us to go ahead and start bringing the furniture up here."

"Sure. Bring it on up."

The head disappeared from view.

"Hey, Bobby." A second later the redhead reappeared in the doorway. "Before you head down, tell me. What do you think of the office?"

The boy looked around the room. Even with all the unopened boxes and flattened discards, the room's potential was obvious. "Man, this office is something else. You've even got room for a sofa and a couple of chairs in here."

Ben thought about that idea. "You know something Bobby, that's a great idea. I've been wondering how to use all the extra space." He paced off the far end of the room as best he could around the clutter. "I'll set up a little sitting area over here. And you'll be my first guest if you'll do something for me."

"Wow, anything. You want me to move the furniture over here when you get it?"

"No. Nothing like that." He clapped a hand on the boy's shoulder. "I want you to start calling me Ben. Either that or I'm going to have to start calling you Mr. Pickett."

Bobby took a deep breath. "OK...um...Ben. And I promise I won't go around bragging about how I met you and saw your office and all."

Ben smiled. He knew what the fledgling writer was feeling. The morning his agent introduced him to Dean Koontz, the veteran writer treated him like an old friend he hadn't seen in years and said, "Welcome to the writer's club."

"Bobby, I'm not worried about who you do or don't tell. I just want you to remember something. Some folks are doctors, some folks are accountants, and some are movers. Me? I make up stories for a living. I've just been very blessed, that's all."

"OK. I'll remember."

"Good man. Now there's just one other thing." He grinned. "Could we get a little furniture up here so Monk won't give you a hard time, and my wife won't catch me goofing off?"

"Oh man, yeah. I almost forgot." He turned and just barely missed crashing into the doorframe on his way out.

"Daddy?"

"What is it honey?" He gave Stacy another spin in the chair.

"Is being famous a pain?"

He glanced toward the doorframe and smiled. "No baby, not really."

CHAPTER EIGHT

JIM PERRY CHECKED his measurements a third time and cut the panels for a set of cabinet doors. The smell of sawdust and ozone from the circular saw permeated his shop. Originally the shop had been a two-car garage but after Gwen was killed, he eventually sold her car, parked his out in the driveway, and expanded the existing area until it suited his needs.

As a boy Jim discovered he had a talent for working with wood. Whittling, carving, making the obligatory bird feeder in Cub Scouts. He had a feel for wood and the tools used to shape it. Years later that talent had grown into true craftsmanship and his work was in demand. Some of the local shops carried his hand-carved boxes, puzzles, and figurines, and local builders kept him busy building custom cabinets and furniture.

His original woodworking shop had been housed in a prefabricated shed behind the house, but after the accident, he found himself spending more time with his wood and less time with his parishioners. When the church offered him a leave of absence to pull himself together, he spent the time moving his shop into the garage and working on his resignation letter.

At first he insisted moving the shop into the garage was a matter of convenience. He could go directly from the kitchen into the shop without having to walk outside in the cold or the rain to go to a separate building. In truth, the shop's new location meant he didn't have to leave the house at all for days on end. What started as a hobby had grown into a small business over the years, and before Gwen died three years earlier, it had been a pleasant distraction from the rigors of being the pastor of a small Episcopal church.

But things change.

It had been easier than he imagined tendering his resignation when the leave of absence was up. What had been hard was coming to grips with the fact that, in the process of building a new shop, he had built a fortress to house his memories and his anger. Memories of the life he had built with Gwen, and anger at the driver who ended her life because of a stupid choice.

The church members initially asked him to reconsider his decision to leave, but during a church board meeting he admitted he no longer had a heart for the pastorate. When his wife died, something inside him died as well. He thanked them for their caring and their prayers during his time of grief but asked that they respect his wishes to utilize the services of an interim priest until they found his replacement.

Since then he had kept mostly to himself and accepted few social invitations. Now the invitations had all but stopped and he spent his days working in wood and carving out a lid for his emotions.

The ringing phone pulled him back from his musing.

"Hello?"

"Hey Rev. How is my favorite cabinetmaker today?"

"Uh Oh. This sounds like trouble already," Jim said. "Norman, why do I get the feeling you're behind on a project and need a minor miracle from me to stay out of the doghouse?" He heard a chuckle on the other end of the line.

"Well, it could be because you're psychic, or a really good guesser. Either way, have you got a minute?"

Jim sat on a nearby stool and leaned back against the wall. "Sure. I'm just cutting the new kitchen cabinets panels for the Miles job, but I was ready for a break. What's on your mind?"

"Actually, that's the project I'm calling about. How far along are you on those cabinets?"

Jim thought for a moment. "All I've got to do is put in the last two panels and I'll be finished. Why?" The contractor's sigh told him what he already suspected.

"I was afraid of that. I just got a load of changes on the kitchen and they have decided on a completely different color scheme. All new hardware, all new stain colors, all new counter tops. All new everything. So now it looks like you'll have to strip everything down, get all new hardware, and start all over."

"Yeah," Jim said, "That could set things back a bit. Plus, it would cost you a pretty penny if I had to go back and redo what I've already done."

"Don't remind me. But be that as it may, how long will this take and how much will it hurt?"

"If I have to strip everything and restain it, plus take off all the old hardware and put on the new stuff, it could set me back a week and set you back another five hundred or so." He could imagine the contractor grimacing at the news. "On the other hand, I could take back the stain and hardware I have now and just use the new stuff when I assemble the cabinets tomorrow."

"Huh? I thought you said you were almost finished."

"I was just yanking your chain. You've got to remember, I knew Hank and Vera Miles from the church and they never made a solid decision on anything the whole time I knew them. I hated to put them on a committee because they would have to decide something three or four times before they made a final decision. That being the case, I figured they would probably be making changes up until the last minute. So just call the hardware store, tell them what hardware we need, and give them the new stain color. I'll swap out what you gave me last time and use the new stuff instead."

"Man, you really had me going there for a minute," Norman said. "If you weren't a former preacher I'd be tempted to cuss you out."

"You wouldn't be the first," Jim said. "Are there any more changes I need to know about?"

"No, nothing about the Miles job. This morning the sheriff called to follow up on some things we had talked about after everything happened up at the new house on Grant's Ridge. She mentioned that she wanted to talk to you too since you went over all that framing where the nails had been twisted out. So, I told her I had to call you this morning and said I'd ask you to give her a call."

"Sure, I'll be glad to, though I don't know how much I can add to what you probably already told her."

"Who knows? I guess that's just part of the job." The contractor paused a moment. "Hey, look. Speaking of the house, the folks that just bought the place wanted me to look at the office upstairs and see about adding another bookcase or two, but if you've got time to do it, why don't you just go by there, take a look, and see if you're interested? I'd probably sub it out to you anyway, and this way it would save us both a lot of time and effort."

Jim checked his watch. It was eleven thirty. "OK, I'll tell you what. You call the hardware store and I'll call the sheriff. Then I'll head over to the new house later this afternoon and see about the bookcases. On the way home I'll swing by the hardware store in case they have the order ready early. If not, I'll check back tomorrow. Either way, I should still be able to get those cabinets finished by the end of the week. How's that?"

"That's perfect Rev. Look, I really appreciate it, even if you did almost give me heart failure. I'll call in the order as soon as we hang up."

"OK, that'll work. Oh yeah, do you have the number for those folks on the ridge?"

"Yeah, I've got it somewhere, but if you're going out that way today you won't need it. They told me to just come by anytime today because they are still unpacking and not planning to go anywhere. Just tell them I asked you to go by. It should be OK."

"OK, I'll do that. And thanks."

"No problem. I'll talk to you later."

Jim ended the call and turned back to the panels. He moved them to the router table, selected a bit, and ran each panel through until he was satisfied with the edges, then set them aside for sanding later.

He checked his watch again and headed toward the kitchen door. "I guess I'd better get cleaned up a little before I go out in public," he said. The echo of his footsteps was the shop's only reply.

JIM SAT in the outer office and waited for Sheriff Cantrell to return. He hadn't realized until he sat down just how much he still hated the place. The last time he had been in the waiting area was the night Gwen died. That night was the first time he dealt with the sheriff, and while it didn't register until days later, behind her professional manner there seemed to be a layer of genuine concern.

He had been away preaching a revival when it happened. Sometime around midnight of the second day of the services, Gene Eddins woke him from a sound sleep and said there was an urgent phone call for him. Gene was the pastor of Resurrection Episcopal Church, and his host for the series of revival services. He'd packed, made his apologies, and sped off into the night toward a future he didn't want to contemplate.

He arrived at the sheriff's office just in time to see a deputy bring in the man who had killed his wife. His name was Willis Horton, and he was drunk. He had been drinking all night, and even after the bartender took his keys and told him to call a cab, he went outside, fished a spare key out of his wallet, and started toward home. Five minutes later he rounded the curve just below Grant's Ridge at eighty miles per hour. He banked the old Ford truck hard to the left and came out of the curve on the wrong side of the road.

He never saw the blue Cavalier. Never saw the terrified redhead behind the wheel. Never felt his ancient farm truck ride up the hood and land on the roof of the car.

Jim closed his eyes, willing the memory to go back to the place where it normally hid. He didn't want to deal with it now. Couldn't deal with it now.

He felt a hand on his shoulder.

"Reverend Perry, are you OK?"

Jim opened his eyes. Elizabeth Cantrell was standing next to him. She looked concerned.

"Oh, hello." He stood and smoothed his pants. "Yes, I'm fine. Just daydreaming a little." He looked into her eyes. He had forgotten how tall she was. Under the right circumstances she could probably be a little imposing, but now was not one of those times, and he felt a little more at ease than he had moments earlier. "And please, just call me Jim."

"OK, Jim," she motioned toward her office and they moved in that direction, "come on in and have a seat. I just want to go over a few things about the incident while the house over on Grant's Ridge was under construction. It shouldn't take too long."

The office was standard Government Issue. Nondescript desk, pictures of the governor and lieutenant governor, ugly gray filing cabinets, a second desk with a computer, scanner, fax machine, and copier. Degrees and citations dotted the wall behind the main desk, and the one concession to any sort of real comfort was a pair of moderately padded office chairs. She motioned for him to take one of them and she moved around the desk and sat in the wooden desk chair.

"Thanks again for coming in on such short notice. Oh, and I apologize for calling you reverend out there. I know you've been away from that end of things for a while, but Norman referred to you as The Rev earlier today and—"

Jim shook his head and laughed. "Sheriff, there's nothing to apologize for. Norman and some of the guys on the construction sites started calling me Rev a couple of years ago, and it just stuck. But I don't really use the title anymore." He studied a spot on the desktop. "It just doesn't seem right." He looked out of the only window in the room and watched a squirrel run along the cracked parking lot. "I'm still ordained, but I figure if I'm not willing to take on the responsibilities that go along with it, I shouldn't use the title in any official capacity." He looked at her and smiled.

"So now I'm just Jim. Cabinetmaker, woodworker, and supporter of law enforcement professionals everywhere."

"That's encouraging," she smiled back. "We law enforcement professionals can use all the support we can get." She pulled a folder from the rack on her desk and leafed through it. "And with that in mind, I just wanted to ask you about something Norman said earlier." She read through a page of notes then turned her attention back to Jim.

"He said there was some sort of problem with some of the framing in the house; something that he thinks happened after his crew left for the weekend. Do you know what he was talking about?"

Jim sat back in the chair, folded his hands in his lap, and thought for a moment. "I know the problem he's talking about, and as I think about it, he's probably right. It almost had to have happened after his guys quit for the weekend."

"What makes you say that?" The sheriff picked up a pencil without looking away from Jim and waited.

"The fact is just about every construction crew takes a shortcut at some time or another, and most of them are pretty harmless. But something like this would have been hard to hide, and it is sure to have gotten somebody fired if it had been intentional. Norman may put up with a little good-natured foolishness on the site, but he's all business when it comes to the actual workmanship.

"If someone had done what we saw in the kitchen on purpose, they would have been filling out an unemployment claim form that Monday. And they would most likely have had Norman's boot print on their backside."

"That sounds like Norman," she said. The sheriff made a note, paused, then looked at Jim. "Tell me exactly what you saw up there."

"Well, the simplest way to describe it is that the studs were pulled away from the wall in the kitchen."

"You mean they had been removed?"

"No. It was more like they had been wrenched away from the wall. There was anywhere from a quarter to a half inch gap between the top of the studs and the framing above it."

"Aren't there sometimes gaps where two pieces of wood are nailed together?"

"Yes, sometimes," he said, "but not on every single piece. That was the odd part. It was like the wood had been knocked out of line. And there must have been some pretty significant force because the nails were all twisted."

"Twisted?" She put the pencil down and leaned forward slightly. "Why would they be twisted?"

"Well that's just it. At first we figured the guys may have gotten a bad nail or two, but there were so many, we realized nobody on the site would use a whole box of defective nails. That would be tantamount to asking for citations and delays from the city inspector.

"After we looked at the framing for a while we wondered if maybe the nail gun was torquing the nails when it shot them in, but even if that had been the case, the nails would still have held the wood in place. In fact, they might have held a little tighter than usual. But you could see the twists in the nails through the gaps. The crew had to redo the framing in the entire room before they could call in the electricians, and since the family wanted to move in just as soon as the house was finished, that was cutting things pretty close."

"Um-hum…" her voice trailed off. "Let me ask you this. Could somebody have taken a hammer or some other tool and knocked the framing out of line? If one of the workmen had left some tools behind, could somebody have taken one of them and caused the damage?"

He thought for a minute. "I guess they could, but to knock that much wood out of place the tools would have left a mark of some kind somewhere. A hammer would have left dents in the wood, or a crowbar would have left gouges. And I don't remember seeing anything like that while we were going over the framing." He paused again. "Still, I guess it's possible."

She flipped through the folder and found another note. "From what Norman said, that was the same day one of the carpenters almost lost a hand. So is it possible you might not have noticed that kind of damage in all the confusion?"

"I don't think so, because we found the problem with the wood well before Winston Puckett had the accident with the saw. That was when everything got so chaotic." Jim leaned forward. "Sheriff, have there been complaints of some kind? I mean, this all happened a good while ago, and from what I've heard so far, even though there was some vandalism, the framing was the worst of it. But I'm headed up to the house when I leave here, and I don't want to walk into any trouble if I can help it."

She closed the folder and sat back in the wooden swivel chair. The ancient springs groaned in protest. "No nothing like that. I'm just trying to cover all the bases. When I talked to Norman this morning, something he said started me thinking about the case again and I just wanted to check a few things out with you.

"If there was some physical explanation, like the foundation settling, that would be one thing. But if a person did the damage, then maybe there is still something I overlooked. Something that —" She tapped the desktop and stared at the wall behind Jim for a moment. "If it was a person, then maybe there is some evidence I missed, or some angle I haven't considered." She shook her head and looked at Jim.

"Sheriff, what I saw was a little unusual, but ultimately it wasn't that big a deal," Jim said. "You see some strange things on a work site, and while I've never seen anything like that framing before, it didn't take them that long to straighten it out. And if it was just some kids creating a little havoc, they're not likely to show up again with somebody living in the house."

She smiled. "Yes, you're probably right." She stood and extended her hand. "Well, look Jim, I know I'm keeping you. You have things to do and so do I. But I really do appreciate you taking the time to come by."

He stood and shook her hand. He looked at their clasped hands, then back at the sheriff. He noticed that her eyes were hazel. Deep hazel. "Oh... um...I was happy to do it, though I'm not sure I was much help."

She smiled at him and watched as he brushed a strand of hair back in place with his free hand. A stray that had worked loose from his ponytail. "Ah...no...you really did help quite a bit. Like I said, I'm just cleaning up a few loose ends. And I appreciate the help."

"Oh sure. Anytime. If I can be of service, don't hesitate to call on me," he said as he started to leave. He looked at their still clasped hands. She noticed at the same time. They broke the grip and she rubbed her hands together.

"Oh, of course," she said. "I won't hesitate to call on you if I need anything else."

He nodded and headed out of the office.

JIM STARTED the truck and rubbed his forehead. *Cabinetmaker, woodworker, and supporter of law enforcement professionals everywhere. Man, was that as lame as you could possibly sound?* He shook his head and pulled out of the parking lot, still wondering what caused the case of pre-puberty jitters in the sheriff's office.

ELIZABETH CANTRELL watched the truck pull out of the parking lot. As Jim pulled into traffic she closed her eyes and shook her head. *Oh, of course, I won't hesitate to call on you if I need anything else. Oh boy, all I needed to do was giggle and blush a little to make that little scene complete.* She sighed, then sat back down to look through the folder again.

JIM ARRIVED at the house and paused a moment to take it all in. He had liked the house from the first time he saw it. And as the framing was completed and the final form took shape, he liked it even more. It was a showplace by most standards, but not a showy house. The lines, the use of stone and wood, and the slightly tinted glass made the house seem like part of the landscape. It looked like it belonged there.

Jim got out of his truck and walked up to the door. He knocked and took a step back. Almost immediately the large oak door opened.

"Hello." The woman in the doorway was petite, her auburn hair pulled back, and she was in the process of pulling off a pair of pink rubber gloves. "Can I help you?"

Jim looked over her shoulder and saw a man coming toward them. He waited for the man to arrive. "Actually, I think I may be able to help you." He held out his hand. "My name is Jim Perry. Norman Scott sent me to look at your office and talk to you about building some new bookcases."

"Oh, right. That's great." The woman smiled and extended her hand. "It's nice to meet you. I'm Rachel Chalmers, and this fellow looming in the background is my husband, Ben." Ben stepped up and shook hands with Jim.

"Boy, that's some quick service," Ben said. "I just talked to Norman and he already has someone out here. Wow." He stood aside. "Come on in, just don't mind the mess. We're still trying to figure out where everything goes."

Jim stepped in the house and Rachel closed the door behind him.

"The real challenge isn't so much the actual move as it is trying to figure out where to put everything once the moving part is over." She led the way through the foyer and into the living room. "Come in and have a seat. We did at least figure out where to put the couch and a few chairs."

There were a few boxes scattered around the room but much of the furniture was already in place. A leather sofa, armchair, and love seat formed a conversation area in front of the large stone fireplace. A coffee table sat within reach of the couch.

There were a number of brass candleholders, a candlesnuffer, and two ornate cricket boxes on the mantle. Two wingback chairs flanked a picture window on the opposite end of the room, and a small table in front of the window held a display of colored glass birds.

Jim sat on the armchair while the Chalmerses sat on the couch. "Well it looks like you are making some real headway," Jim said. "What you've done so far looks very nice."

Rachel settled back a bit. "We've still got a pretty long way to go, but we're getting there. Little by little it's coming along." She looked toward the kitchen and started to stand. "Mr. Perry, please forgive my lack of manners. Can I get you something to drink? We've got a few soft drinks in the refrigerator and I can put on a pot of coffee real quick."

"No, please don't get up," Jim said. "I'm just fine." He motioned toward the sofa. "Besides, after all the work you two have put in the house just getting moved in, I imagine you would like a chance to be off your feet for at least a little while."

Rachel sat. "Too true. I appreciate the break, but to tell the truth, it really hasn't seemed that much like work. I don't mind telling you, I love this house."

Ben nodded. "Me too. I never thought I'd ever live in a place like this," he said. "And please don't get me wrong. I don't mean that in a prideful sense. We sure don't have enough furniture to fill it up, but we're not in any hurry to run out and buy things just yet. We just want to take what we have and make it feel like home.

"God has been very good to us, and I don't ever want to take that for granted. Right now we're concentrating on making this place our home. We can worry about what to put in the guest rooms and the extra bathrooms later."

Jim nodded. "I imagine that will take care of itself soon enough. Household projects tend to do that."

"That's the truth," Rachel said. "And speaking of household projects, let's talk about the new bookcases. What did you have in mind?"

Jim sat forward. "I don't know much about the office area. I worked mostly in the kitchen. I didn't get upstairs much at all, especially after they started the walls and that sort of thing."

"What exactly did you do in the kitchen?" Rachel asked.

"I built and installed the cabinets, the center island, and the built-in china cabinet."

Ben's mouth dropped open. "You did all that woodwork in the kitchen? It's absolutely beautiful."

"That's putting it mildly," Rachel said. I think the kitchen with the little breakfast nook is my favorite part of the house. It's so inviting. I can almost imagine how it will smell with bread baking or a pot of soup on the stove later this winter. I couldn't imagine a friendlier room."

Jim smiled. "I am happy that you like it. I'm really happy that I was able to build in some of the extras like the sliding shelves in the lower cabinets and the lazy Susans in the cabinets over the stove. I figured it would make life a little easier for whoever ultimately bought the house."

"I was wondering about those," Rachel said. "When I saw them I thought they were a great idea. And now I can thank you in person."

"You are very welcome," Jim said, "and if it's OK, I'd like to take a look at the office now and see what I can do for you up there."

Ben stood up. "OK, let's head upstairs and I'll give you the nickel tour around the rest of the boxes."

Rachel stood and motioned toward the kitchen. "Well, while you two are up there talking bookcases, I'm going to be down here trying to talk the last of the kitchen boxes into magically unpacking themselves and loading the pots and pans in those cabinets." She headed to the kitchen as the men headed upstairs.

"Jim, how long have you been a carpenter?"

They reached the landing at the top of the stairs. Jim waited for Ben to precede him down the hall. "I'm not really a carpenter per se. I'm more of a woodworker. A cabinetmaker. I know a little something about carpentry because I have to know how to install what I build, but believe me, you don't want to live in a house I built.

"But to answer your question, I have been working with wood since I was a little boy. I only took it up as a profession over…over the past few years."

Ben stopped in the hallway and waited for his guest. "Well you have certainly found your calling. The cabinet work you did downstairs is a real work of art."

Jim cocked an eyebrow slightly at the word "calling," but said nothing. Maybe Ben knew his background and was being kind. Or maybe it was just an odd turn of phrase. Either way…

"Oh, by the way Jim. There's someone else here I'd like you to meet." Ben was standing in front of an open door. "This little lady is our daughter, Stacy."

Jim walked in the room and stopped just inside the doorway. Stacy was busy arranging a group of stuffed animals on her bed. Piggy Anne sat on the window seat, her back against the window frame.

"Hello Stacy," Jim said. "That's sure some collection of animals you've got there."

"Stacy, this is Mr. Perry. He helped build part of the house, and he's going to build some bookcases in the office."

Stacy placed a pink baboon at the top of the headboard; its cartoonish feet dangled over the edge. "Hello Mr. Perry. This is a very nice house. Which part of it did you build?"

He squatted to talk with her on her level. "I built the kitchen cabinets and some other kitchen stuff. But it looks like I needed to build some shelves for this little zoo you have in here." He looked at the stuffed animals in various places around the room. Every spare surface housed ducks, bunnies, teddy bears, mice, horses, and a pink baboon. The large rag doll, Piggy Anne, rounded out the collection.

"You mean like a bookcase?"

"Not exactly." He stood up and looked around the room at the walls just below the ceiling. "But I could build some shelves that would go all the way around the room," he pointed to a spot on the wall, "just about this high. That way you would have a lot of room to put stuffed animals, and anything else you wanted to put up there."

Stacy looked around the room. "That's a little high." She pointed to a spot about shoulder height on the wall. "Could you do it about this high so I could reach it?"

"Hey, doodlebug," Ben said, "let's not be making extra work for Mr. Perry right off the bat." He looked at Jim and grinned. "We don't want to work him to death before he even gets to see the office."

At the word *death*, Piggy Anne's head turned ever so slightly in Jim's direction.

Ben moved toward the door and stopped. He turned and scanned the room. Jim looked around the room, not sure what he was looking for.

"Everything OK?"

"Yeah," Ben said. "I just thought...I just..." he shook his head. "Nothing. I'm not sure what I thought." He looked around the room once more. "Oh well," he shrugged, "I guess we'd better go down and see the office before Stacy has you building a house for Piggy Anne in the closet."

"Piggy Anne?" Jim looked puzzled. "Is that another one of your children?"

Ben laughed. "No, it just seems like it sometimes."

Stacy walked over and removed her doll from the window seat. One cloth hand lingered against the window frame for a second, then went limp at her side. "This is Piggy Anne. She's the doll my aunt gave me."

Jim nodded. "She's a fine looking doll. Do you think she'd like a house in the closet?"

Stacy held the doll close to her chest. "No. She likes to be wherever I am. She probably wouldn't like living in her own house."

"I see," Jim said. "In that case, I'll take doll house off of my list of things to build." Ben moved into the hall and Jim took one last look around. "Well, Stacy, it was nice to meet you. And you think about those shelves for your animals. I probably have enough wood left over from other projects to build you some if you want them." He looked at Jim. "No charge."

"That would be great. Thank you. I'll think about it some more." She returned to her animal arrangement. Piggy Anne lounged against the foot of the bed.

Jim followed Ben into the office. "She is a real sweetheart, Ben. A very nice little girl."

"Thank you. She's a real treasure. Sometimes I just watch her play or see the way she and Rachel are with each other and I just stop and thank God for all of it. You know what I mean?"

Jim nodded. "Do you have any other children?"

Ben folded his hands together as if holding a small object between his palms. He looked at the back of his right hand for a long moment.

"We had a son, but he was killed in an accident about three years ago." He looked up at the cabinetmaker. "We've handled things pretty well, all things considered. Between a little pastoral counseling and the support of our family and the church we attended, we've learned to cope." He looked toward the hallway. "And then there is Stacy. She is a constant reminder that life goes on, and life can be very good."

"I'm very sorry about your son, but you know, you're right about what you said. You're a lucky man."

"Yes, I am. And you didn't come here to hear all this. Let me show you what I have in mind for the bookcases." Ben moved toward an expanse of wall above the far left end of his wall-length work surface. "I was thinking it might be nice to have a bookcase that went from the top of the work table here to the ceiling. I like the floor-to-ceiling book cases on the other side of the room, but this is a place I could put copies of my books and books written by friends of mine."

The cabinetmaker took a few measurements, made a few notes, and looked under the work surface. "That won't be a problem at all, and it will give you some pretty good space for displaying your books. How many have you written?" He made another quick measurement under the tabletop and transferred the information to his notebook.

"Well, I've written four and am working on number five—that is if I ever finish getting the office in shape. In fact, the fourth one will be out in a few weeks.

"I'm not exactly churning them out like Nora Roberts, but with the various foreign language editions and the audio version of the new book, I should be able to at least fill up a shelf respectably."

"In that case," Jim said, "I'd better give you the good news now. The bookcase should take a day to build and stain. Then after it dries, I can bring the sections over and install them. The whole thing shouldn't cost more than three hundred and fifty dollars." He paused and looked at his notes again. "In fact, for that, I can also build a little storage cabinet under the work surface immediately below the bookcase." He pointed to the open space beneath the work area. "By doing that it would give you some additional storage space for paper, toner cartridges, and any other office supplies," he tapped the top of the work area, "and it would provide some added support for the bookcase itself.

"And I was serious about the shelves for your daughter's animal collection. I've got enough odds and ends pieces of wood in the shop to do it, and I would be happy to if you'd let me…that is, if you even want me to take on the project."

"And why wouldn't we?"

The voice startled both men. Rachel stood in the doorway with three mugs of coffee. "I thought you two might want to take a break from all this manly tool talk and fill me in on the plan so far." She handed the men their coffee and started sipping from a third mug of her own.

"Well, Jim suggested not only putting in the bookcase, but adding a cabinet below it to add some storage space and also provide additional support for the bookcase."

"That sounds great," she said. "And I like the idea of extra storage. That should come in handy for the packrat here." She nudged her husband and grinned. He shrugged his shoulders and took a sip of coffee.

"When could you start?" Rachel asked.

Jim thought for a moment. "I could start building the bookcase and the cabinet next Monday. Between that and staining them to match what you already have, I could probably come by to install them about next Thursday if that's OK."

Jim nodded. "I think Thursday should be fine. I'm probably going to have to sit over there and work most of the time you're here because I've got a nasty deadline to meet, but I could stop a while and give you a hand if you needed me to."

"Actually, I'll just bring the bookcase up in assembled sections, so I shouldn't have to bother you." He sipped his coffee. "I'll screw the sections into the wall, add some molding, and do something similar with the cabinet. I'll slide it in place, secure it, then put on the doors. It really shouldn't take very long once I bring the pieces up. Then I can take about a half an hour to put up the shelves in Stacy's room if you'd like."

"That sounds like a lot of work, but yes; we'd be very happy if you could do it next week," Ben said.

"Ben, what's that about shelves in Stacy's room?" Rachel asked.

"Jim met Stacy when we came up, and when he saw the menagerie in her room, he offered to build her some shelves to keep her animals on."

"That's a great idea," she said. "But just out of curiosity, how much is all this hammering and nailing going to run?"

"I told Ben I'd build the bookcase and the storage cabinet for three hundred and fifty dollars. The shelves for your daughter's room won't cost you anything."

"Wow," Rachel said, "the price is more than fair, but we certainly don't expect you to build the shelves for nothing. Go ahead and give us a price on those too."

He held up one hand, palm out. "No, no, it will be my pleasure. Just my way of welcoming you to the community. Besides," he said, handing her the empty mug when she motioned for it, "the shelves for her room won't take much time at all, and I've got enough extra lumber in my shop that I won't have to buy any materials. So I'd be pleased if you would allow me to do it for you."

"Well…" Rachel watched him for a moment. "Only if you agree to have supper with us Thursday night."

Jim grinned. "That kind of incentive I'll be happy to accept. Thank you."

"You're welcome. And please, if there is a Mrs. Perry, she is invited too," Rachel said.

The grin faltered.

"Thank you…I really appreciate that but…there is no Mrs. Perry now."

"Oh," Rachel said, "I'm sorry. Are you divorced?"

"No. My wife, Gwen, died three years ago."

"We didn't know," Ben said. "Had she been ill?"

"No." The feeling he experienced in the Sheriff's office resurfaced and flooded over him. Then, just as quickly, it receded. "She was killed by a drunk driver. There was a head-on collision." He sighed and turned to face Rachel.

"She was coming home from a friend's house after having a girls' night out. They had ordered pizza and watched an old movie on TV. On her way home about eleven that night, a drunk crossed the center line, came around the curve at the bottom of Grant's Ridge on the wrong side of the road, and…"

"Oh Jim, I'm so sorry. We didn't know."

He nodded. "Like Ben said a little while ago, you learn to cope." They stood, each looking at a different part of the room, the uncomfortable silence stretching into awkwardness.

"Well," Jim said after a long moment, "I guess I need to head out and get back to work on the cabinets for Hank and Vera Miles's house so I can get your bookcase finished on time.

"And thank you for the supper invitation. I look forward to that."

"WHAT DID he mean about 'you learn to cope'?" Rachel looked at Ben, but he continued to look out the window.

"We were talking earlier and he asked if we had any other children, so I told him about Brandon."

Rachel walked over and stood beside her husband. They both looked straight ahead, looking at the scenery beyond the window but not really seeing it. "What did you tell him?"

Ben kept his gaze steady. "I told him the truth. I told him that we had a son who died in an accident about three years ago, but with a little help and a lot of prayer, we are learning to cope. I didn't go into the details." He took his wife's hand and turned to face her. "And we really are coping pretty well for the most part."

Rachel looked at Ben, then shifted her gaze in the direction of Stacy's room. "I guess so," she said, "for the most part."

CHAPTER NINE

RACHEL REMOVED A chicken from its plastic bag, drained it, and tossed the bag in the garbage can.

A thin ribbon of bloody water drooled down the drain.

As she made the first cut through the carcass on the cutting board, a cabinet door swung open a few inches.

Rachel glanced up, closed the cabinet door, and returned to the job of cutting up chickens. She was halfway through the second one when Stacy came in the kitchen with Piggy Anne in tow.

"Hey, doodlebug. What have you been up to this morning?"

"Nothing much," Stacy said as she climbed up on a stool to watch her mother. "Piggy Anne and I have just been putting the rest of my stuff up."

"Well you two should just about have everything finished by now."

"We do. And I put the boxes in the hall like you said so Daddy can take them to the recycling place later."

Rachel took another chicken from its bag and drained it in the sink as she had done with the two previous birds. Before she made the first cut, the cabinet door opened, this time a little wider than before.

"When Mr. Perry comes to put in the bookcase, I'm going to have to get him to look at the cabinets," Rachel said. "That's the third time that one has come open this morning." She reached up and closed it again. "It's probably just a hinge that needs tightening or something." She gave the door handle a tug to see if it was closed properly.

It was.

Rachel returned to the cutting board.

"What are you doing with all those chickens?" Stacy propped Piggy Anne on the counter and watched her mother.

"I went out to the grocery store this morning and they had chicken on sale, so I bought four of them for later." She cut off the leg quarters and the wings. "As soon as I get them cut up, I'm going to put them in the freezer. That way we can have fried chicken one night next week, and I'll have some extra for chicken and rice and chicken stew when it gets cold." She pulled the last of the chickens out of its bag, put the butcher knife on the cutting board, then turned to face Stacy.

"I've got an idea. How about if you go upstairs and get a jacket, I'll finish cutting up this chicken, and then we'll go to Casa Binelli for lunch. We can split a meatball sandwich and have something absolutely yummy for dessert."

Stacy took Piggy Anne from the counter and climbed off the stool. "What about Daddy?" she asked.

"I'll fix him a sandwich and leave it in the fridge," she said. "He wants to finish the new book, so he'll probably write all afternoon."

Rachel put the chicken in the freezer side of the refrigerator and went back to the sink. "So you head on upstairs and get ready. As soon as I get this all cleaned up, we'll head downtown and have a girls only afternoon. OK?"

"OK!" Stacy headed for the door.

Rachel smiled and turned back to the work at hand. She washed the cutting board, dried it, and put it in its place. Then she picked up the butcher knife and ran it under the hot water. She scrubbed the handle and blade with a soapy washcloth, rinsed it in hot water, and picked up a drying towel.

On the third pass with the towel, the blade cut through the towel and into the fingers of her left hand.

Rachel grabbed her hand through the towel. The knife clattered in the sink.

"Oh man, that hurts."

Rachel squeezed her hand, waiting for the initial pain and shock to subside. After about half a minute, she unclenched her hand and the bloody towel fell in the sink. She ran some warm water over the cuts and looked at the damage.

The cuts weren't too deep, nothing that would require stitches, but they stung like a hundred little wasp stings. Blood welled up in the cuts and she washed it off again. She glanced at the knife in the sink. It was part of a new set. All professional quality and each one very sharp.

She washed the cuts one more time, this time with soap and warm water. She grimaced as she finished cleaning the wounds. That was going to smart the rest of the day. She flexed her fingers and inhaled sharply.

"Aaah...that was just plain stupid," she said to the surrounding walls as she rinsed out the towel. The drain eagerly accepted the bloody water. Something in the walls made a popping sound, like a joint being dislodged. Rachel paused and listened. A few seconds later, it popped again.

Rachel washed the knife and returned it to the knife holder on the counter. Then she went upstairs toward the master bathroom to find a bandage for her fingers. They were already starting to throb.

Stacy looked up as Rachel passed by. She seemed to be looking for something. She called to her daughter.

"Hey, doodlebug, I'll be ready in a minute. Then we'll start our official girls' afternoon out." Stacy nodded and looked around the room. "What are you looking for?"

Stacy stopped and looked up, her eyes wide. "I can't find Piggy Anne. I put her on the floor beside my bed when I went to the bathroom. Then when I got back, she wasn't there."

Rachel's hand throbbed again. "I'll tell you what. Go put on your coat, and as soon as I finish up in the bathroom, I'll help you look. OK?"

"OK." Stacy headed down the hall and Rachel turned her attention to the medicine cabinet. She found a box of adhesive bandages and put a small one on each finger. Then she touched up her hair a bit and went down the hall to Ben's office.

Ben's fingers tapped steadily at the keyboard. He had an unorthodox three-fingered typing style but it got the job done. He reminded her of Carl Kolchak, the title character on the old seventies TV show about the investigative reporter with the out-of-date suits and the beat up hat.

"How is it coming so far?"

Ben jumped. "It must be going OK," he said through his grin, "I was so involved in the scene I didn't hear you come in." He saw the bandaged fingers. "What happened to you?" He took her hand gently and looked at the bandages.

"I had a run in with the butcher knife while I was cutting up some chickens, and I lost. But it's not as bad as it looks. I was washing up and the knife cut through the towel I was drying it off with. If I hadn't had the towel, it would probably have been worse." She wiggled her fingers.

"No real damage. It's just aggravating and a little painful." She hugged him. "I think a little finger smooching will make them all better."

Ben kissed each finger and patted her hand. "How is that?"

She kissed the top of his head. "Practically cured already." She wiggled them at him. "See, they feel so good they're going out to lunch with Stacy and me."

"Where are you going?"

"Oh, you wouldn't be interested. It's just some little Italian place in town. We're having girls' afternoon out."

"You rat. You're going to Casa Binelli's. And I bet all you left me was a pan of gruel for lunch."

She laughed. "Worse than that…a ham and Swiss on rye with that disgusting stinky German mustard you like. I told Stacy you would probably want to stay here and get as much work done on the book as you could since you have that deadline, but you can go with us if you want to."

Ben shook his head. "No, you're right. I'll probably just head down in a little while and bring my stinky mustard sandwich up here so I can eat it while I work."

"OK. Well, we'll be back in a couple of hours or so."

"Take your time. I have a feeling I'll be writing straight through until I go pick up supper tonight." He paused and looked around the room. "Hey, since you're going to be out there anyway, would you mind taking this to Mario?" He rolled his chair over to a stack of boxes near the area that would soon become the new bookcase and supply storage area. He removed a contributor copy of his upcoming novel and rolled back to his desk.

Rachel shook her head. "A normal person would have walked over there."

Ben grinned. "Probably so." He took a pen from the holder on his desk, and inscribed and signed the book. "I told him I'd bring it by when I went to pick up supper, but since you're going there for lunch, I'll pick up supper somewhere else."

"Sure, I'll take it to him, but you can still go by and pick up supper. We're having pizza aren't we?"

"I thought so, but if you and Stacy are having lunch there…"

"Don't worry about that. We will probably just split a salad and load up on dessert. And you know Stacy," she reached out to take the book. "She could eat pizza three times a day and have a slice for dessert."

"OK, tell him I'll be by later to pick up the pizza. Order whatever you want as long as it has extra cheese."

She hugged him hard. "Now you get back to whatever it is you're doing to those poor people in your book. We girls have some serious girl stuff to do."

He sat down. "OK. Tell Mario I said hello, and remind him that I'll sign his other books when I come by tonight."

She opened the book, read the inscription he had written, and closed it. "You are a sweet man. Do you know that?"

"I've heard the rumor somewhere, but I'm not sure I believe it." He grinned and swiveled the chair back toward his desk. "You two have fun."

"We always do," she said as she headed down the hall to Stacy's room. Stacy was sitting on her bed with Piggy Anne in her lap. "OK, Miss Stacy. I see you found your traveling companion. Are you ready to go?"

Stacy nodded and stood up. "Yes ma'am,"

"Let's go, then. We've got some serious girl stuff to do."

"OK. But I ought to leave Piggy Anne here after what she did."

"Really? What did she do?"

"She didn't stay where I put her."

Rachel stopped and looked at her daughter. "Didn't stay where you put her?"

They walked down the stairs and into the foyer. "No ma'am. Remember, I told you I put her beside the bed before I went to the bathroom. Then when I came back, she was gone?"

"That's what you said."

"When I opened the closet to get my coat, she was sitting on the floor in the back."

"Maybe the dog took her in the closet," Rachel said.

Stacy giggled. "We don't have a dog."

"Then that probably isn't it," Rachel said. She crouched down and looked at her daughter. Stacy had the only really pretty brown eyes she had ever seen. Brown with little flecks of gold.

She put her hands on her daughter's shoulders and took a deep breath. "Stacy, if you want to leave Piggy Anne here while we're gone, it will be OK." Maybe this would be the day she finally started letting go. The day she started dealing with the loss of her brother.

Stacy looked at Piggy Anne, then her mother. "No, that's OK. She can come too."

Rachel squeezed her daughter's shoulders gently. "You know, doodle-bug, you're going to have to…" Her voice trailed off.

"Have to what?" Stacy asked.

Rachel looked at her daughter for another moment, gave her shoulders another squeeze, then stood.

"Nothing, honey." She opened the door. "It can wait."

Stacy walked outside. Rachel watched as the doll's head lolled over her daughter's shoulder. *It can wait,* she thought, as she closed the door behind herself, *but not too much longer.*

CHAPTER TEN

Lightning split the sky and Richard Lassiter saw the face of the hooded figure. He closed his eyes as the white aura created by the lightning passed behind his eyelids. But the white after-flash couldn't blot out what he had seen under the hood. Richard fell to his knees as much out of fear as out of obedience.

The robed figure held out its left hand, palm up. Long, chipped fingernails curled up over the fingertips. Thunder grumbled as light pulsed behind the darkening clouds.

BEN LOOKED AT the passage he had just written. This book was something of a departure from his previous books. It was edgier. Instead of an absent-minded church history professor and his Mensa-oriented graduate student solving local crimes, this one dealt with a burned-out minister who comes to the realization that there is a New Age cult at work in the town he calls home, and its leader is tied to a series of murders across the country. The problem is the group seems so community oriented on the surface, and its leader is a charismatic character who preaches self-actualization and New Age philosophy coated in a thin veil of religious terminology.

He is a ruthless character with a national television following. The perfect cover for what he has in mind.

Ben was excited about the book at first, but one hundred pages into the manuscript he started wondering if the plot sounded too much like something that had already been done.

"Ben," Paul Michaels had said during their meeting, "the book is good. Really good. And you're right. There are a few other books about New Age infiltration in a small town, but not like this. It's like comparing *Gone with the Wind* and *Cold Mountain*. Sure, they both have a Civil War backdrop, but they aren't the same story."

With that reassurance, the excitement returned, and he wrote the next hundred pages in a flurry of clattering keys. At times he was so engrossed in the process of writing that hours passed in what seemed like no time at all.

Ben looked at the passage once more, made a few corrections, and started the next paragraph.

A page later, he heard something.

It came from overhead. Some sort of odd scratching sound.

Ben stopped and listened. There was no sound.

He scratched his head, listened a little longer, then went back to his book.

Scritch scritch…scritch

The sound again. This time it was closer.

Scritch scritch

Ben got out of his chair, stood in the center of the room, and listened.

The sound was coming from the ceiling.

"What is going on up there?" Ben said to the empty room. He moved around the room, listening every few feet.

Scritch

"I guess it's time to take a look in the attic," he said to the phantom sounds.

Ben walked to the end of the hall and reached for the ornate chain attached to the attic door. He pulled the door into position and unfolded the attached wooden steps. The springs sang in a discordant voice, but the new hinges whispered into place.

Ben mounted the steps until his head was above the attic floor. He listened. Warm air whispered through the heating ducts and the wood beneath his feet creaked slightly as he shifted his weight. Otherwise, the attic was as silent as the diffused light coming in through the vent at the peak of the roof.

He looked for a light switch or a pull cord, found none, and waited a bit longer in the semi-darkness. He scanned the dark attic once more, looking for any sign of what may have caused the noise. Dust motes rode the dimming shafts of light to the floor. Outside, a cloud passed in front of the sun, and the wind murmured secrets through the few remaining leaves on the oaks and maples.

"So much for that," Ben said to the gloom. "Whatever you were, you must be gone now."

He climbed down the steps and folded them back into place. Just before he pushed the door back up into the ceiling, he saw a single light switch on the wall at the end of the hall. He reached over and flicked it on.

Light blazed above his head through the attic opening.

"So that's where you are." He considered going back up in the attic, but thought better of it. He still had a deadline, and whatever he heard obviously wasn't up there anymore. "Next time I'll know," he said as he flipped the light off.

He closed the attic door and walked back to his office.

OVERHEAD, IN the farthest corner of the attic, the husk of a squirrel slumped against the wall, the last of its vital fluids drained from its body. Its eyes were wide and staring, its front paws held out in front of its body as if trying to keep something at bay.

A dozen more dessicated squirrel bodies were scattered throughout the attic.

BEN STARTED a new paragraph.

Later this afternoon he would call Paul to give him an update on his progress. At the rate he was going he would probably finish the manuscript about a month early. And while he had never missed a deadline, he knew his agent would be happy with the news that things were running ahead of schedule.

One thing they would also need to talk about is the use of a pen name. The only concern Ben had with the new book was the fact that it was so different from his previous ones that it might be advantageous to write the new book under a pen name. That way he could continue to write the professor series under his own name. It would allow him to more or less double his output without having to explain to the readers that he was also writing the darker books at the same time. Oh well, that was for later.

He began to find his rhythm again. The trek to the attic, though not far, had interrupted his train of thought. Fortunately, he could pick up a story in mid-sentence after a month and know exactly where he was when he left the project. So far he had not been cursed with writer's block, and it didn't take him long to get back on track.

The words started to flow. The story seemed to write itself and he was little more than an interested spectator. The characters developed their own lives, followed their own paths, and often did things that took him by surprise.

An hour later he printed out what he had written. As the pages glided into the printer tray, Ben went down to the kitchen to get his sandwich. It was well past noon, but between the trip to the attic and his burst of creative steam, he had only now come to a good stopping point.

He took a bottle of apple juice from the refrigerator and picked up the little paper plate that held his sandwich. He got an extra napkin and headed back upstairs.

SOMETHING STIRS

The pages were waiting in the print tray. He put his lunch on the desk and picked up the pile of papers. Pencil in hand, he ate and edited. Between bites of his sandwich and swallows of the cold juice, he made notes, struck a few paragraphs, and circled a few suspicious words. Spell Check was a real blessing, but sometimes even a word spelled correctly was not the correct word.

In the middle of the fifth edited page, his cell phone rang. Normally he would have ignored the phone, but only a few people had his cell number, and none of them would have called during working hours unless it was for something important.

"Hello." He looked over the rest of the page as he settled back in his chair.

"Hello Ben." Paul Michaels's voice was a little loud as always. He wasn't one of those obnoxiously loud people that made others cringe. His voice was just a little soft and he tended to overcompensate sometimes. "How is my favorite writer this afternoon?"

Ben chuckled. "Paul, I bet you say that to all your writers."

"Sure I do," he said, the volume a little closer to normal. "I don't work with any writers who aren't my favorite."

"In that case, your favorite writer is doing OK." He took another swallow of juice. "In fact, I was going to call you a little later this afternoon. Things are going so well on the new book I figured you'd want to know."

"That is great news in more ways than one," Paul said. "How far ahead are you?"

Ben swallowed a mouthful of sandwich. "I am probably about a month ahead of schedule. Parts of this book seem to be writing themselves. Actually, this afternoon was one of those times. I get in something almost like a fugue state. Kind of like God is doing all the writing and I'm just sort of along for the ride. You know?"

"I do. And I'm especially glad to hear you say that about the book. I was afraid there for a while you were going to scrap it. And that would be a shame. I think you're really on to something here."

"I hope so," Ben said. "The more I get into it, the more I see what you were saying about having a similar backdrop but being different than the Peretti stuff, although I hope I can finish it soon. I bought Frank's new book and I don't dare read it until I finish this one." He laughed. "I don't need that kind of temptation."

"But tell me, what prompted this call from the ivory tower?"

Paul went from chatty and easy-going to all business within a few syllables. Ben heard paper rustling on the other end of the line. "Well, I'm hoping to get a little advance publicity for us. A magazine editor I know is hoping to send someone out to do a story on you, with an emphasis on the new book and the one you're working on. He could probably do it at your new house if that's OK. It could make for some interesting pictures."

Ben sat back in the chair. "That's fine, but I have been thinking about the possibility of using a pen name for the new book since it is so different from the others. What do you think?"

"Actually I don't think you'll need it."

"Really? Why is that?" Ben heard a chair squeak in the background. He could imagine Paul leaning back in the chair and looking toward the ceiling. He knew from previous meetings with his agent that that was the position he assumed when he was thinking and pitching an idea at the same time. Ben smiled at the image.

"I think the readers who like the series will stick with you if you can provide them at least one book a year. On the other hand, I think you can tap into a whole new readership with the new, edgier books. I looked over the proposal you sent for the second one, and it looks good. Really good." More chair squeaking.

"You may be right," Ben said, "but wouldn't one line alienate the readers who prefer the other?" He looked at the manuscript page on his computer screen. "How do we deal with that?"

"As long as you are able to come up with a book a year for each, I think it will be all right. Christian fiction readers are an interesting group. They are loyal to the authors they like, and many are willing to read whatever an author writes as long as the book is theologically sound. As for the ones who only like the books in one genre, then they will read those and not let the author's other work be an issue. Kind of like Bill Myers writing suspense for adults and young adult books.

"On the other hand, if you were writing, say, hard-edged supernatural thrillers and also writing the kind of things that Paul Evans or Nicholas Sparks writes, then you might have a rough time of it because they are such different styles and genres. But with similar genres, I think you can pull it off."

"Well," Ben said, "I'm not going to try to second guess you, because you've been right about everything else in my career so far. And I think I can come up with two books a year. That part shouldn't be a problem. The only thing I wonder about…"

BAM

Ben jumped. The noise reverberated through the room like the aftermath of a massive peal of thunder.

"Paul, can you hang on a second?" He was up, phone in hand, making his way down the hall.

"Sure. Hey, what was that noise?"

Ben was moving faster, checking each room in the hallway as he went. "I don't know." He looked in Rachel's new studio. She had most of her art supplies out and in place. A few boxes stood sentry duty in two corners of the room, but all seemed in place otherwise. "It sounded like something being slammed into a wall."

He looked in Stacy's room. All OK. No problem in the bathroom. Nothing amiss with the hall closet.

He headed downstairs. "I don't see anything yet, but it sounded like something hit the house or something."

"Ben," Paul said, "since you live up in the mountains now, could it be a boulder from a rock slide or something like that?"

"No, I don't think so. We are on top of a ridge and there aren't any rock faces anywhere close to us." He made his way downstairs and stopped. "What the…"

"What is it?" Paul asked, the concern evident in his voice.

"Paul, I'll call you right back." He put the phone in his pocket without waiting for a reply. The front door was fully open. He looked around the room quickly, then went back upstairs. If someone was in the house, he wanted some kind of protection.

He went to his office and took a baseball bat from the shelf. One of the few luxuries he had splurged on since his career took off (all new art supplies for Rachel had been the other) was a baseball bat signed by Ted Williams, and Ben eventually wanted to put it in a shadow box and mount it over his writing area. Today, however, he had another use for it.

"Come on, Ted," Ben said. "I may need a little back-up."

He went downstairs and started searching the house. He reasoned that if intruders had come upstairs, he would have heard them or would have seen them when he checked earlier.

There was no one in the foyer or the family room. He checked the kitchen, pantry, dining room, and living room, all with the same results. He moved cautiously—bat ready. He walked back through the rooms again, then walked out on the deck just off the family room. He looked across the property toward the tree line. He wasn't sure what he expected to see, but there was no sign of an intruder. Just a chipmunk running across the lot.

Ben lowered the bat, but kept a tight grip just in case. He reentered the house, walked across the family room, through the foyer, and back to the open front door. He pulled on the outer door handle to close the door, but the door held fast. "What the…" He tried again. After two more good tugs, the door pulled free.

The impact of the door slamming open had embedded the ornate brass handle in the solid wood. Ben fingered the resulting gouge and frowned. What kind of force did it take to throw a door open hard enough to gash solid oak, much less actually embed the door handle in the wall?

He gripped the bat and made another circuit through the house, this one slower than the first. He ended his search in the family room. The last of the morning sun streamed in through the skylight, but standing in the center of the room he felt a decided chill, as if the temperature in the room had dropped by ten degrees. Ben looked around the room and again noticed the handle on the front door. It was bent out of shape from the impact with the wall.

"Enough of this," Ben said. His voice sounded hollow in the large room. He went to the kitchen and picked up the phone. Rachel had put Jim Perry's business card on the little corkboard note center on the refrigerator. He dialed the number and waited. Jim answered on the fourth ring.

"Hello?"

"Jim, this is Ben Chalmers. You're working on a bookcase for me."

"Yeah, Ben, I should have everything done right on time. In fact, I was putting on the last coat of stain when you called."

Ben was pacing. "Thanks, but that's not what I was calling about." He looked at his watch. There was no telling what time Rachel and Stacy would be back. He probably had an hour at the most. "Jim, I know I don't know you well, but I need a favor if it is at all possible." His voice trailed off.

"Sure, if I can. What do you need?"

Ben explained the events of the past fifteen minutes. Had it only been fifteen minutes? It seemed like an hour.

"That wood in the panels, that's a blonde oak isn't it?" Jim asked.

"I think so." Ben walked into the family room. When he passed under the skylight, the cold touched him again, lingered, then dissipated. He threw off the remnants of a shiver while he checked the panel. "Yes, it looks sort of blonde to me."

"OK, I'll tell you what. I can't replace the panel, but I can mix up some wood putty that color and it will pretty much match the wall. Once it dries, you probably won't be able to tell the difference. Then if you want to replace it later, you can. But this will do for now."

"Jim, I can't thank you enough. About how long will it take?"

A subtle shade of desperation tinted his words.

"I can probably be over there in about twenty minutes. And the job shouldn't take much longer than that." There was a slight pause on the line. "Ben, have you called the sheriff?"

Ben sat on the arm of the sofa. "No...no I haven't. Do you really think I should? I mean, I can't find any sign of someone having actually been in the house."

"Even so," Jim said, "it couldn't hurt just to let her know. She may have some suggestions, or there may be something you missed."

"Good point."

"Look, I'll get to work mixing the wood putty and be right over. You just hang tight and don't worry."

"Jim, I really appreciate this. Thank you again."

"You're welcome. See you in a few minutes." The connection clicked off.

Ben returned the phone to the kitchen and headed back toward his office. He didn't want to call 911, and there was a phone book in his office, so he could look up the main number for the Sheriff's office.

He sat at his desk and removed the phone book from the desk drawer. He flipped through the pages until he found the number. He reached for the phone, glanced at the monitor, and dropped the phone book.

He stared at the words written across the screen.

I

Am

Coming

Ben dialed 911.

CHAPTER ELEVEN

SHERIFF ELIZABETH CANTRELL took the turn off Gardner Road a little too fast, and the cruiser tires moaned in protest. As the car picked up speed, she keyed the microphone in her right hand.

"Maggie, I'm headed out to Ben Chalmers's place over on Grant's Ridge. When Steve checks in, have him contact me."

Elizabeth liked Maggie Hayes. She had been the dispatcher in Cherokee County for over a decade. Through her radio, she had heard the citizens of the county at their best and their worst. Still, Elizabeth knew Maggie had a knack for separating her personal and professional life. If she saw Ken Campbell in church on Sunday after listening to him being hauled in for being drunk and disorderly the previous Friday night, she would never so much as hint that she knew him to be anything other than a regular churchgoing family man. Her discretion had long since earned her the respect of many county residents as it did with the sheriff.

"Roger that. Is there some kind of trouble up there? Anything he needs to know before he contacts you?"

"I don't know yet." She gunned the big car through another curve.

"Does it have to do with what happened just before the house was finished?" Maggie asked.

"Yeah…maybe. I don't know." She opened the car up a little more. "I'll know better when I get there. But I sure hope not. Cantrell out."

Elizabeth thought back to what she had seen in the house. The few people who knew anything had happened at all thought it was just the aftermath of kids having a party and making a mess. Even Hank Turnage had passed it off as graffiti.

Oh Lord, she prayed, both eyes on the road ahead, *please let this be some weird coincidence.* She didn't relish the idea of telling the Chalmerses that there had been what appeared to be satanic activity in their home before they moved in. *I know I should have said something to them before now, but I was hoping…hoping…Lord, I really don't know what I was hoping. I just wanted that to be the end of it so I wouldn't have to tell them.* She huffed a humorless laugh. *I guess that's pretty much out of the question now, isn't it?*

Grant's Ridge loomed ahead. She caught a glimpse of the house through a blazing autumn wall of reds, ambers, and pale yellows.

Lord, please let this be nothing.

Her throat was dry, and her ribs ached. An explosive breath escaped and she was surprised to find she had been holding her breath.

"Come on girl, get yourself together," she said to her reflection in the rear view mirror. "You won't be any good to them like this."

For all its speed, the cruiser seemed to be moving in slow motion. Elizabeth rounded the final curve and headed up the main road toward the Chalmers' house. Elizabeth thought it was one of the prettiest homes she had ever seen. There was an understated elegance in the flow of its lines and the way the house seemed to fit into its surroundings. It was not just a house stuck on the side of a hill as a showplace. Even when it was under construction, the house seemed to belong on the spot where it sat.

Today, however, for some inexplicable reason, the house seemed different. Ominous. For the first time the house seemed like an alien part of the landscape. She passed it off as a combination of the overcast day and her apprehension about what she was going to tell the Chalmers family.

She pulled into the driveway entrance and made her way up the hill to the house. *Even if I had told them everything right after they moved in,* she reasoned, *that doesn't mean this still wouldn't be happening. But my conscience wouldn't be nagging me as much.*

She pulled around the circular driveway and stopped the car behind a small pickup truck. It looked vaguely familiar, but her mind was racing and the owner's identity was lost in the mix of emotions. *Time to go,* she thought. The sheriff adjusted her hat and got out of the car.

BEN CHALMERS answered the door before the sound of the doorbell faded. "Sheriff Cantrell, thank you for coming so quick." He stepped aside and motioned for her to come in. "I almost didn't call you, but after what I found in the office I didn't think I had much choice."

The sheriff stepped around a toolbox just inside the foyer. "If you were concerned for your safety, you did the right thing." She glanced around the foyer for a few seconds, then turned her attention back to Ben. "So tell me, what happened here?"

"This happened." He closed the door and pointed to the gash in the wall. The sheriff studied the damaged wall, then pulled a notepad from her pocket. Ben continued. "I was upstairs working earlier when I heard something in the attic. I figured it was a mouse or a squirrel or something, so I went up and looked around, but didn't see anything, so I came back down. Two hours later, while I was on the phone, I heard a loud bang down here." He pointed to the wall. "That's what I found."

"Was the door open or closed when you came down, Mr. Chalmers?"

"I'm sorry; I'm a little more rattled than I thought I was." He ran a hand through his hair. "The door was wide open when I came down. When I saw that, I went back upstairs, got a baseball bat, and started looking around. After I checked the house I came back and closed the door."

The sheriff made a few notes and looked at the wall again. "Is that when you called the station?"

"No, like I said, I almost didn't call you at all. Not until I went back upstairs, that is."

"What did you find upstairs?"

Ben started toward the stairs. "Come with me. I left everything exactly as I found it."

They mounted the stairs together, Ben in the lead. He led the way down the hall and walked into his office. He pointed toward the computer.

"There."

Sheriff Cantrell walked over and read the computer screen. "I don't get it," she said. "Is there something on here I am supposed to see?"

Ben walked over and pointed at the last three words on the page.

I

Am

Coming

"I didn't write that."

She looked at the page again. The words were completely out of context with the rest of the page.

"Well where did it come from?"

"I don't have the slightest idea. It wasn't on there when I went to see what the noise was downstairs."

"Was it like that when you came to get the bat?"

Ben scratched his head. "I really couldn't say. I didn't look at the screen that time. I was too busy looking for the baseball bat. But I don't think it would have been because whoever wrote it would have had to come right by me to get there."

The sheriff started making notes again. "What makes you think someone else wrote it?"

"Because I didn't write it, and I was the only one here at the time, or so I thought." His voice took on a harder edge than he meant for it to.

"Could someone have accessed your computer somehow? Could it have been some kind of virus or a hacker trying to mess with the famous writer in town?"

"What's that supposed to mean?" The edge was back, and this time it was intentional.

"I'm sorry," Sheriff Cantrell said. "I didn't mean that the way it sounded. What I meant was that celebrities are often targets of hackers and other people with too much free time and not enough sense to put it to good use."

Ben's voice softened a little. "No apology necessary. I'm still not used to the word 'celebrity' because I don't think of myself that way. I'm just a writer who has been very blessed."

"Well, blessed or otherwise, that kind of recognition has put people in all kinds of unfortunate situations. So…could it be someone hacking into your computer to get a peek at what you're working on?"

"No, I don't have Internet access on this computer. It would be too much of a distraction when I'm working. My wife has a computer in her studio and that one will have access, but we haven't even unpacked hers yet."

"Speaking of your wife, where is she right now?"

"She and my daughter went into town to have a little lunch and do some shopping. It's their girls' afternoon out, so they probably won't be back for another hour or so."

"In that case, let me take another look around. If somebody did type that message on your computer, they are probably long gone by now, but I'll feel better about that after I check things out." She turned toward the door, then paused. "When I get back, we need to have a little talk," she said over her shoulder. "I think there are a few things you need to know." She went into the hall and waved him back in the office. "You stay here and I'll be back in a few minutes."

She walked through each room upstairs. Master bedroom and bath, Stacy's room, the bathroom, the studio at the end of the hall. Each was empty with no signs of anything other than the ordered chaos that comes with moving into a new home.

She proceeded down the stairs. She moved cautiously, not expecting to find anyone if there actually had been an intruder in the house, but not foolish enough to take chances. She moved to the landing and was about to make the turn and descend the final four steps when she heard a sound. She stopped and listened. Her hand went to the safety strap on her holster. Seconds ticked by. She heard it again.

Elizabeth Cantrell flicked the strap and removed the Glock 22 pistol. She touched the safety and...

Sheriff, this is Hughes checking in.

In spite of the involuntary flinch, Elizabeth Cantrell raised the Glock and grabbed the radio attached to her belt. "Not now," she hissed and moved down the landing and into the foyer.

Jim Perry stopped in his tracks. "Sheriff, it's me..."

Elizabeth took a step back. "Reverend Perry, I'm so sorry. I heard something down here and I had no idea..." She stopped. Jim was still riveted to the spot. Staring.

"Reverend, what is it?" She looked over her shoulder. Nothing behind her.

"It's nothing really," he said, motioning toward the gun. "I was just thinking that since you're not planning to put a big hole in me with that thing, it would make me feel a lot better if you put it away."

She holstered the gun and walked toward him. Elizabeth touched his shoulder. "I am so sorry. I was just checking the house for Mr. Chalmers and when I heard you down here," she paused, but did not remove her hand, "well, I didn't know it was you. I didn't know who it was, and I'm afraid I reacted."

"It's OK, really," he said and put his hand on hers. "Really." He hesitated. "No harm done, and I certainly can't fault you for doing your job. Truth be told, I don't know which was more disconcerting, the gun or the radio going off out of nowhere."

"Oh," she said, "I almost forgot. Excuse me just a moment." She keyed the radio. "Sheriff to Hughes. Sorry I had to drop you so quick, Steve. We just had a momentary situation."

"That's alright. Is everything OK?" The voice was professional, but the concern was there just below the surface.

"Fine. Come on out to the house on Grant's Ridge. I think we need to fill Mr. Chalmers in on what happened before they moved in."

"10-4. I'm on the way. Hughes out."

"What happened before we moved in?"

The sheriff turned toward the sound of the voice. Ben Chalmers stood at the bottom of the stairs, one hand gripping the banister.

"Mr. Chalmers, let's sit here in the family room. As soon as my deputy gets here, I'll fill you in on everything I know.

CHAPTER TWELVE

SATAN'S HENCHMEN SANG a song about chaos, revolution, and mass suicide while Rodney Hardwick read the liner notes from their new CD. The world was headed toward its ultimate doom in a long, winding spiral, and the lyrics blasting through the oversized speakers in his bedroom promised a fiery death when the world crashed and burned for anybody who didn't get on board the chaos train.

> Holy rollers scream in pain,
> Their cries fall hard on the world's deaf ears.
> We drink their suffering once again,
> As we have done for a thousand years,
> Children suffer, the dark one reigns,
> Get on board the chaos train.

Rodney brushed a thick strand of hair away from his face and continued reading. It was the first time he had been settled since the night, eight weeks ago, when the deputy walked in on the ceremony and ruined everything. And it didn't help that he'd had to leave everything behind when they made their escape. That was the worst part of all.

But things were looking up. Last night while he slept, the answer came to him. It was so simple he was surprised that he hadn't thought of it earlier. Once he called Myra and that wet blanket, Kenny, the plan would be set.

Rodney heard his name, followed by three loud knocks. The sound of distorted guitars and the thump of a heavy bass line all but obliterated the voice.

"Rodney...Rodney, we're going now."

His mother opened the door and put her hands over her ears. "Rodney, could you turn that down for a moment?" Her voice was all but lost in the unholy cacophony. "Please..."

Rodney walked across the room and hit the stop button on his stereo system. The instant absence of overpowering sound was like a vacuum.

"That's better," she said as she looked around the room. Bizarre-looking musicians leered from posters tacked to the walls. Most wore black, were adorned with outlandish symbols and tattoos, and some made obscene gestures while masks or grisly makeup obscured their faces.

"Your father and I are going to the Kelloggs' for supper." Rodney flopped back on his bed and continued reading the liner notes. "Are you sure you don't want to go? They have a son your age."

"They have a dillweed my age," Rodney said to the page in his hand. "He's so lame it's pathetic."

"Rodney! Peter Kellogg is a fine young man."

"Whatever."

Adelaide looked at the CD cover in her son's hand. It showed a figure dressed in black leather, pasty white flesh visible through the eyeholes of the black hood he wore. There were dozens of fish hooks imbedded in the pale flesh of his hands.

"Well..."

Rodney continued reading, knowing if he ignored her long enough, she would give up and go away.

Just like she always did.

"If you're OK then," she said.

"I'm fine."

He reached over on his bedside table, picked up his earbuds, and thumbed the play button on his MP3 player. The sounds throbbing in his ears drowned out the sound of his mother leaving. As he listened, the final portion of his plan fell into place, and he nodded in time to both the music pounding around him, and the voices in his head.

CHAPTER THIRTEEN

EN WALKED BACK into the family room. "Thank you for agreeing to wait, sheriff," he said. "Rachel and Stacy were on their way back already, so they should be here in a few minutes." He sat on the sofa. "I think Rachel should hear this too."

"What about your little girl?" Elizabeth asked. "I'm not so sure you want her hearing this. Even if it turns out to be just a prank, it could be pretty scary for a child."

"We'll send her up to her room to play, or maybe let her paint in Rachel's studio. She loves to rearrange the stuff in her new room, so I think she'll be more than happy to stay up there while we talk."

Jim Perry walked in and sat in a wing back chair just inside the doorway. "Actually, as long as I am here," he said, "I can go up and take the measurements for her shelves. It normally wouldn't take too long, but under the circumstances, I think I can stretch the process out. Especially if I ask for a lot of decorating input from your daughter." He motioned toward the front door. "The wall is patched, so all you have to do is wait for the wood putty to set. When I come back to put in the bookcase and the shelves,

I'll give it a final sanding and that should do it. The color is going to be a good match, so you won't have to be in a hurry to replace it unless you just want to."

"Jim, I appreciate it, and normally I wouldn't dream of imposing any more than I have, but…"

"When you start to impose, I'll let you know. As for keeping Stacy busy, the sheriff is right." He looked at Elizabeth for a long second. "Even if this is just the tail end of a bad prank, it can't do her any good to know about it."

"You're right," Ben said, "and I do appreciate you offering to stay up there with her. I know Rachel will appreciate it too."

Elizabeth Cantrell opened her mouth to speak, but fell silent. From the sound of it, two cars were pulling into the circular driveway. The room's occupants looked toward the front door. A moment later, Stacy walked in followed by Deputy Steve Hughes and Rachel.

"Well, are we in time for the party?" Rachel asked. She glanced at Stacy, then looked at Ben.

"Just barely," he answered. "Did you two have fun?"

"We sure did," Stacy said. "We had cannoli and hot chocolate at Mr. Mario's, and he is going to bring supper out here for us tonight." She hugged her father, then looked at the other people in the room.

"Daddy, what are all the police doing out here?"

Deputy Hughes spoke up. "I pulled in about the same time Mrs. Chalmers did, so I was telling her on the way in that we like to stop by and say hello to all the new residents. Kind of introduce ourselves and people put a face with the Sheriff's Department."

"That's…" Rachel nodded in his direction slightly, "that's right. Deputy Hughes was coming by to say hello." She looked in the sheriff's direction. "I just didn't think we'd be getting a double visit." She walked over and put her arm around Stacy, and smiled at the cabinetmaker. "All this and a visit from Jim too. I guess this is what it's like to be married to a celebrity."

Ben blushed, and Sheriff Cantrell picked up the conversation. "Like Deputy Hughes said, we like to come by and visit with the new residents when they first move in." She gestured toward her deputy. "Today we brought the whole force."

"Can I get the force something to drink?" Rachel took a step toward the kitchen. "It looks like Ben has already put on some coffee."

"No, I'm fine," the sheriff said, "but please, don't let me stop you."

"Hey, Stacy," Jim said, "if they are going to talk about boring grown-up stuff, how about if we go upstairs and take some measurements for your new shelves?"

"Mom, can we?" She had Piggy Anne by one ankle. The doll looked like an overly limber gymnast.

Rachel glanced at her husband. He nodded slightly and mouthed *it's OK.*

"If Mr. Jim really doesn't mind, then you two go up and measure to your heart's content."

"Good deal," Jim said. "Come on, Stacy. Let's go upstairs and let these grown-ups talk about boring old grown-up stuff. We've got some shelves to build."

Stacy led the way. Jim paused before heading up the stairs and turned toward the group. "This could take half an hour or so. Is that OK?"

Ben looked to the sheriff for some indication. She nodded. Ben flashed the cabinetmaker an OK sign. "Sure, that should be perfect."

Jim winked and disappeared upstairs.

"OK," Rachel said, the edge in her voice evident. "What's this all about?"

Sheriff Cantrell motioned toward the sofa. "Let's all sit down and I'll let Deputy Hughes start. He was the one who found the pentagram."

RACHEL LOOKED at a spot on the floor near the sofa. The spot where the pentagram had been drawn. Ben looked at his steepled index fingers. His hands were clasped tight and the sides of his fingers were turning red from the effort.

"That's the place?" Rachel was the first to speak after listening to Deputy Hughes and the sheriff tell what they witnessed that Friday night. "That's where they drew that symbol?"

"Yes." Deputy Hughes stood up and walked over to the place he had seen the pentagram and stood in what would have been the center. He drew an imaginary circle around himself to indicate the size of the pentagram. "It was about here. There was a candle at each point of the star, and the other items we told you about were scattered around in this area."

Ben rested his head against his fingers. "Sheriff, why didn't you tell us about this before now?" He looked up and waited for her answer.

Elizabeth Cantrell met his gaze and answered without hesitation. "Mr. Chalmers, the fact of the matter is I thought it was just a minor case of vandalism. Just some kids out having a party or pulling some prank on a dare. And for all I know, that is all it was."

"A minor case of vandalism?" Rachel was incredulous. "This is a satanic symbol we're talking about, not somebody spray painting John Loves Marsha on the schoolhouse wall."

"Yes ma'am, I know that. And the first thing I did when I got back to the office the night we found it was to check with other law enforcement agencies in the area to see if they have had any similar instances. There were none."

"Yes," Rachel said, "but satanic symbols? Why us?"

"Mrs. Chalmers, as sad as it is, some kids get caught up in Ouija boards and the occult. They think it's cool to play with occult items and treat the experience like just another way of getting a thrill. Like telling ghost stories or walking through an old, abandoned, 'haunted' house on a dare. The kids see it as a game. Just something else to make them cool." She looked around the room. "As for why here, that's pretty simple. Your house was still under construction, and it sits above town on the ridge. So it was vacant and remote."

"OK, that all sounds plausible, Sheriff, but if this is a case of vandalism, then how do you explain the open door and the message on my computer screen?"

"Explain *what?*" Rachel turned on the couch to face her husband.

Ben relayed the events leading up to his 911 call, including his call to Jim.

Rachel blanched. "Do you mean to tell me someone has been in this house today? Somebody could have been in here for no telling how long?" She gripped her husband's arm. "They could have been in here while Stacy and I were still home." She squeezed his arm, her fingers leaving white indentions in the skin.

"And Ben…" she moved closer. "You could have been killed."

"Rachel, don't get carried away." Ben leaned into her, his left arm still trapped in her grip, and pulled her head to his shoulder with his other hand. He hugged her and tried to reassure her. "Honey, it's all over now and I'm OK."

"That's easy to say, but somebody was in this house and we had no idea about it." She snapped around and pointed to the sheriff. "Now what do you plan to do from here? Have you checked the house to make sure there is nobody still here?"

Elizabeth walked over and sat in the chair on the other side of the coffee table from the couple. "Yes, Mrs. Chalmers, I have. And I went up and took a look at the message on the computer screen." She showed Rachel a printout of what had been on the screen.

Rachel put a hand to her mouth and reread the message.

"My guess is that whoever wrote the message on the computer is the same person who slammed the door open. It was most likely one of the kids who drew the pentagram and almost got caught goofing around up here that night." She took the page back from Rachel and continued. "They probably opened the door, waited until your husband came down to see what had happened, then ran upstairs and typed on the computer while he was looking around the house."

Rachel shook her head.

"Honey, that does make sense." Ben took her hands in his. "It was probably some kids out on a dare. By tonight they'll be strutting around telling their friends how they really put a scare in that new mystery writer fellow up on the hill."

"Mrs. Chalmers," Deputy Hughes said, "he's probably right. The kids around here are pretty harmless, but they're not angels by any means. And this sounds just like the kind of thing that some kids might do." He turned his hat over in his hands, fiddling with the brim. "It sounds like a bad prank is all." He looked at a panel near the front door. "Is that security system active yet?"

"We've been so busy getting unpacked that we haven't even thought about the security system. I had almost forgotten it was part of the house."

"Mrs. Chalmers, I don't want to alarm you," the sheriff said, "because the probability is that this was all just a prank. But it's never a good idea to rely on assumptions.

"Things are clear right now, but I think you really should call the security company as soon as possible and have them set everything up. My guess is that will bring you a lot more peace of mind. Any kid with thoughts of pulling another prank around here will jump out of their skin if you have one of those outdoor horns that sound when the system is tripped." She looked toward the inert panel. "And it will safeguard you against anything that could happen in the future."

Rachel nodded. "I appreciate that Sheriff, and you're probably right." She turned to look at her husband. "Ben, why don't we go ahead and call them now, even if we just have to leave a message?"

Ben walked over to inspect the wall unit. He flipped the outer cover down and looked closely at the inside of the lid until he found the telephone number. He went in the kitchen and made the call. The others held any further conversation until he came back to join them.

"The lady at the security company said they will send an installer the first of next week—possibly a little earlier if they have a cancellation."

Rachel reached over and squeezed his arm.

Sheriff Cantrell stood and her deputy followed suit. "Well, since things seem to be settled down now, I guess we can go." Ben and Rachel stood, then Rachel motioned for the sheriff to wait.

"Let me run upstairs and rescue Jim real quick." She glanced at her watch. "He's probably measured every square foot of the upstairs by now." Rachel went upstairs while the remaining occupants of the room exchanged small talk. A few minutes later she reappeared with Jim in tow.

"Rescued was the right word," Rachel said. "If I had gone up about three minutes later, he would have been the guest of honor at a stuffed animal tea party." She turned to the cabinetmaker and smiled. "Thank you again for keeping Stacy occupied. I really do appreciate it." She looked at her husband. "We both do."

Ben agreed. "Yes, you have been great. I don't know how we can repay you."

Jim grinned. "When you get my bill, you'll figure it out." Everybody laughed. The sheriff and Deputy Hughes walked to the front door. Jim went behind them. "I'll be by in a few days to start putting in the bookcase unit," he said. "I should have the shelves for Stacy's room ready then too."

"Thanks Jim," Ben said. "Thank you all."

Sheriff Cantrell stopped and let the two men go out ahead of her. "You're welcome. Now will you be OK until the security people get here?"

Rachel put her arm around her husband. "I think so. This afternoon has been something of a nasty shock, but the more I think about it, the more you are probably right." Ben pulled her in a little closer. "The little scene from before we moved in seems to point in that direction. But I have to admit, I was a little shaken up when I first got home this afternoon."

"I can certainly understand that." The sheriff shook hands with them both. "And listen, if you need anything, don't hesitate to call me. I'll have Deputy Hughes make an extra pass or two out this way the next few nights, just to be on the safe side. Once the security people get out here, I think you'll be ready to put this all behind you."

"You're probably right," Ben said. "Thanks again for everything."

ELIZABETH CANTRELL watched the door close then walked toward her cruiser. Jim was getting in his truck as she walked by.

"Reverend Perry...I mean, Jim, do you have a minute?"

"Sure. What can I do for you?"

"I wonder if I could ask you for a favor since you'll be coming back up here over the next few days." She looked him in the eyes. *Funny, I'd never noticed they were as deep brown as they are.*

"Sheriff, are you OK?"

She shook off the momentary lapse. "Sorry," she said. "I was daydreaming there for a minute." She looked down for a second to compose herself, then back at him. "It's been a rather eventful afternoon," she said. "And please, call me Liz. I figure if I'm going to start asking for favors, we ought to at least be on a first name basis."

"Fair enough, Liz, what can I do for you?"

She looked toward the house. "Would you just kind of keep your eyes open when you come back up here over the next few days?" She directed her attention back to Jim. "They seem OK now, and there is probably nothing for them to worry about, but sometimes an event like this can catch up with people a day or two later."

"Oh sure," he said. "I'll be glad to. Is there anything in particular I ought to be looking for?"

"Nothing specific. I just want to make sure they put all this behind them. It's a bad way to start life in a new house. Also, if anything else happens," she took a notepad and pen from her pocket, "let me know." She wrote down her phone number. "This is my cell phone number. It seems like I take my phone with me everywhere except the shower." She handed him the slip of paper. "I'd probably take it in there too except I wouldn't have anywhere to clip it."

Jim laughed. "Yeah, I can see where that could pose a problem. But sure, if I see or hear anything, I'll let you know."

"Thanks Jim. I really do appreciate it." She headed toward the cruiser. *I can't believe I said that. It seems like I take my phone with me everywhere except the shower. Hoo boy. He's probably staring at me right now wondering what kind of loon I am.*

She didn't glance back to see.

※

"HONEY, I'M OK. You heard what they said. It was probably some kid being stupid."

Ben held Rachel and watched the sheriff drive away. He couldn't blame her for being a little worried. He had been more than a little unnerved when the whole episode began, but the sheriff's explanation of what must have happened and the deputy's explanation of what he found at the scene seemed to point to the same conclusion. It was just a prank and nothing more.

"I know you're right," she said, "but just the thought of somebody sneaking into our house, even as a joke, just gives me the creeps. She hugged him tighter, then let go. "Show me what happened with the door."

"There." Ben pointed to the place where the gash had been. There was only a slight difference in the color of the patch job Jim had done and the original wood. "It was pretty deep. Whoever slammed the door open must have really given it a shove because the door handle was stuck in the wall. I had to give it two or three good pulls to get the door to close."

Rachel touched the place where Jim had patched the wall, then ran her hand along the decided twist in the curved top of the door handle. She exhaled through her teeth.

"Uh-oh," Ben said. "I know that sound. Somebody is in the doghouse."

Rachel straightened up and faced her husband. "Oh yeah, somebody is most definitely in the doghouse. Up until now I was frightened, but if this is some kids' idea of fun, they're going to be in for a rude awakening when their parents get the bill for repairing all this." She looked at the door again. "A prank is one thing," she said, still looking at the bent handle, "but there is no call for this."

"You're right," Ben said, "and if they find out who did it, we'll deal with that when the time comes. But for now, let's just be thankful it's over. The security people will come out next week, and that should put an end to foolishness like this."

She squeezed his hand.

"I'll tell you what, let's go up and check on Stacy. She's been mighty quiet up there. After that, I'll give Paul a call and fill him in on what's going on. I sort of left him hanging when everything started happening."

CHAPTER FOURTEEN

BEN WATCHED STACY arrange stuffed animals along the baseboards in her room. A small zoo of purple monkeys, brown and white bears, gray whales, pink rabbits, orange tigers, three sock monkeys, a savannah full of lions and elephants, and a large red kangaroo watched him from various vantage points around the floor.

Piggy Anne supervised from her perch on top of the headboard of the miniature four-poster bed in the corner.

"Hey, doodlebug, what are you doing?"

Stacy placed a buck-toothed cartoon chimp on the floor beside a goofy looking fuzzy purple thing—Ben had never figured out what the purple thing was, and neither had Stacy, but it was one of her favorites—then turned to face her father.

"I'm figuring out where I want to put my animals. That way when Mr. Jim brings my shelves, it won't take long to put them up." She went over to the bed, found a smaller version of the goofy looking purple thing and placed it on the other side of the chimp, then stood back to evaluate her various animal arrangements. Jim watched her work another moment, then went into his office.

He looked at the computer screen.

I

Am

Coming

At first, the words had filled him with a sense of panic. His family could have been in danger. Then, after the explanation offered by the sheriff and her deputy, he had been angry. Some punk kids had the nerve to use their house and his computer for their stupid pranks.

As he looked at the screen, the mood changed to a sort of adolescent bravado. Something to match that of their intruder.

I

Am

Coming

He sat down at the computer, flexed his fingers, and typed a message of his own.

Bring It On!

He leaned back in his chair and smiled. "You got this one for free," he said to no one in particular, his message aimed at the long-gone prankster, "but I wouldn't try it again if I were you." He highlighted the two rogue phrases and paused, his finger above the keyboard. "Next time, I'll be ready."

He hit the delete key and the words vanished.

"That's that."

Ben reached for his cell phone and dialed his agent's number. Paul answered on the second ring. "Ben, what happened to you earlier? One minute you were chatting away and the next minute it sounded like you were a third world country under attack."

"Well," Ben said, "you're not too far off." He recapped the events from earlier in the day and reiterated the fact that everyone now believed it to be a bad prank.

"Prank or not, somebody needs to look into this," Paul said. "This could turn out to be serious."

"Paul, I told you, the sheriff and her deputy spent the better part of the afternoon out here, and the alarm company is sending someone out in a few days to activate the alarm and give us a crash course in how not to set it off accidentally. I really don't know of anything else we can do short of fencing in the place and putting a pack of Dobermans out in the yard."

"Look, are you sure you don't need to call in somebody else? I mean, I can come down if you need me to."

Ben laughed and shook his head. "Paul, I'm sure." He leaned back in his chair and closed his eyes. He knew all he had to do was say yes and his agent would be on the first plane out of New York. The thought gave him the first real sense of peace he had felt since the whole episode began. "Listen. The sheriff here is very competent. She knows what she's doing. In fact, when they found the graffiti originally, she and her deputy were out here most of the night and all the next morning making sure they hadn't missed anything.

"She's good at what she does, Paul, and if she thinks all this was just a bunch of kids goofing around, then I believe her."

"OK, if you're that sure. But you might want to keep an eye on the want ads from time to time to see if anybody has a pack of Dobermans for sale."

"You've got a deal. Now tell me some more about this interview you've got lined up. Isn't it a bit early to be pushing a book I haven't even finished yet?"

"Ben, have you ever walked by a bakery and smelled the bread baking? You wouldn't very well pull out a loaf that isn't done yet and start eating it, but you'd probably be willing to wait a few minutes to get a slice of some fresh baked bread. Right?"

"Who wouldn't?"

"Exactly my point. It's time to create a little anticipation. It's time to bake a little bread."

"OK." Ben sighed. He knew Paul was right, and he knew he would most likely do whatever his agent suggested. He just wanted to egg him on a little more. "When exactly do you want me to do the interview and start baking bread, or whatever it is you have in mind?"

"The sooner the better. How soon could you be ready to do it?"

"Hang on just a minute." Ben called Rachel and took the phone with him to her studio.

"Honey, Paul wants to send a writer up here to interview me about the new book."

Rachel grinned and took the phone from him. "Paul, this is Rachel. How are you?" She listened for a moment. At one point, she glanced at Ben and chuckled. "You've got that right." She winked at him, then listened a while longer.

"Oh sure," she said. "We're ready for the most part. Just a few assorted boxes here and there but nothing that can't be pushed in a closet while the celebrity does his thing."

Ben made a face and Rachel started laughing.

"Yeah, he hates it when I say things like that. But the man needs to get used to the fact that he's not exactly an unknown anymore." She listened, then laughed again. "Exactly, Paul. I don't think he realizes how good he is. I'm so happy for him." She smiled at Ben and touched his hand. "But listen, I know you two have a lot to talk over, so I'm going back to my painting. You two set up whatever you want to. Do it Monday if you want to."

She paused, nodded, and told Paul goodbye.

"Here you go," she said to Ben and handed him the phone. "You two get back to plotting literary mayhem." She kissed his cheek and shooed him out the door.

"Hello Paul. It's me again," Ben said as he walked back to his office. "From the end of the conversation I heard, you two are up to no good."

"Of course we are," the agent said, "but it's for your own good."

"I'll bet. Anyway, when did you want to send the fellow from the magazine around?" He heard the chair squeak in the background again. Paul was planning.

"Well, if your lovely bride was serious about Monday…"

"She probably was," Ben said, "but what makes you think you could get someone up here that fast? That's pretty short notice."

"Not for these folks. And since the magazine comes out the same week your new book hits the shelf, they would put somebody on a plane. I'm pretty sure they could have someone there by sometime early Monday afternoon."

"Not that you've had a similar conversation with the magazine editor before we talked today." Ben grinned.

"As a matter of fact, I did. The timing of the call is just a coincidence." Paul paused. "Or maybe God set it all up. You never know."

Ben was still grinning. "What makes you think God necessarily wants to be an accomplice in your scheme?"

Paul laughed. "What makes you think I'm not *God's* accomplice in all this?"

"Touché. If you can pull it off, call me and let me know what time to expect him so I can start shuffling boxes." He looked around the room. Most of the boxes were either unpacked, or ready to be put in a storage area. "Rachel was right, there really aren't that many left, and the ones that are will be going into storage until later. You know, Christmas decorations and that kind of thing."

"Good enough. I'll call you back in half an hour or so and let you know what the plan is." There was a pause on the other end of the line. "And listen, you think about the dog idea."

"Paul, you're not serious."

"Well, not a pack of dogs really, but please, just be careful. It's a strange world out there sometimes."

"Well…" Ben closed his eyes and leaned back in his chair, "you may be right. And once the security system is active next week, I think deep down we'll all feel better." He opened his eyes. "But no dogs. I know who would have to be on shovel duty."

"Fair enough," Paul said. "I'll talk to you in a few minutes."

The connection clicked off and Ben moved the mouse beside his keyboard and the sleeping computer system blinked back into focus. He read over the previous manuscript page to get the feel of what he had written, and picked up where he left off.

The book was about two men on a collision course with each other. Both were seeking a holy relic. One wanted to return it to its original burial place while the other wanted to use it to unleash the equivalent of a supernatural Armageddon.

Ben liked the way the book was taking shape. The characters were believable and the storyline was opening itself up to a series of possibilities he had never considered. Some parts almost wrote themselves.

Two hours later he heard Rachel call him from downstairs. Except for a brief call from Paul almost exactly a half hour after their previous conversation, there had been no other distractions and Ben had turned out some really good pages.

"What is it?" he called back down. He looked out the window and saw afternoon had turned to dusk. It was approaching early evening and the time had passed while he was in his own fictional world.

"Supper's on the way," Rachel called back up. "Mario Binelli just pulled up, and it looks like he has a box full of goodies."

Ben saved the work he had completed and went downstairs. He opened the door and went out to offer his assistance. He was in the driveway when he saw a Border Collie walking beside the jovial restaurant owner.

"Hello Mario. Let me give you a hand with that." He reached for the box but Mario shook his head. "I have it. If you'll just get the door for me—that will be wonderful." As they approached the front steps, Mario glanced at the dog. "Tippy, go to the car."

The Border Collie turned immediately, ran toward the car, and jumped in through the open driver's window.

"Now that's impressive," Ben said as he opened the front door.

Mario glanced back toward the car. Tippy was sitting on the driver's side, his paws resting on the door. "Tippy is a good dog. He will sit there in the car until I give him another command. He is well trained, my Tippy is." He paused. "I've had him for six years. I bought him as a gift for my wife about a year before she died." He looked at Ben, his eyes solemn. "He was good company for her while I was at the restaurant. Now, he is good company for me."

He entered the house and Ben closed the door behind them. Rachel greeted them from just beyond the foyer.

"Ah, Mrs. Chalmers. I am indeed blessed to share your company twice in one day." Mario looked around the family room. "Where would you like me to put this?"

Rachel touched his arm. "Let's put it in here." She started toward the kitchen. "It smells absolutely wonderful, and judging from the size of the box, you must have invited a few neighbors to join us." She motioned toward the butcher block in the center of the kitchen. "You can just put it there."

Mario put the box of food on the island and turned back to address Rachel.

"It's not that much. Just a little pasta, some salad, fresh bread, a little bit of lasagna, a little ravioli, and some cannoli and tiramisu. Not too much."

Ben entered the kitchen. "Not too much? I just gained three pounds listening to the menu."

Rachel inhaled deeply over the box. "He's not kidding. I think I need to walk a mile or so just to walk off the aroma." She sniffed the Italian delicacies once more. "Yep, that's definitely a little touch of heaven on earth."

"Well that is the least I can do after the very kind gift Mr. Chalmers…I mean Ben, sent to me today. The book was quite a treat in itself, but your gracious inscription was a true blessing." He closed his eyes and looked like a schoolboy reciting Chaucer from memory.

"For my new friend Mario, pizza chef extraordinaire. The smile that adorns your face comes straight from your heart. You are one of God's true noblemen. With sincere gratitude for your friendship, Ben." He opened his eyes. "I am the one who is grateful."

"I meant every word. You have been very kind to us already, and I appreciate it. It can be hard moving into a new place, and from the first day I felt like we had a good friend here waiting for us."

"I agree," Rachel said. "Stacy and I had a delightful time today when we were at the restaurant. And I imagine there will be many more."

"That is certain," Mario said. "But for now I think I should go so you can have your supper."

"Hello Mr. Mario."

The three turned to see Stacy standing in the kitchen doorway. She held Piggy Anne by one rag doll arm.

"Hello Stacy. And hello to you too, Miss Piggy Anne."

Stacy walked to the island and leaned toward the box. "Mmmm. This smells great. What is it?"

Mario repeated the contents for her.

"Can you stay for supper Mr. Mario?" She looked at her parents. "Can he stay and eat with us?"

Ben and Rachel nodded. "I think that is a wonderful idea," Rachel said. "How about it?" she asked Mario. "Would you stay and have supper with us?"

"From the looks of things, there is more than enough, and you are certainly more than welcome," Ben said.

Mario placed both hands over his heart. "As much as I would love to stay and have supper with you and your lovely family, I have to get back to the restaurant. Our dinner crowd will be arriving soon and since my manager is out for a few days with a cold, I don't want to leave my staff to deal with that by themselves." A warm smile highlighted the laugh lines in his face. "But I do thank you for your kind invitation."

"In that case," Ben said, "you plan to come for supper sometime after your manager comes back to work."

"Yes," Rachel said, "please do. It won't be an Italian feast like this, but I think I can probably manage something."

Mario took Rachel's hands in his. "Mrs. Chalmers…Rachel…I will be delighted to join you and your family for dinner very soon, and I am certain whatever you make will be a feast." He released her hands and patted his generous stomach. "As you can tell, I like all kinds of food. A tummy like this is an international effort."

Their laughter warmed the kitchen. After a little more small talk, Mario made his way to the foyer.

"Oh Ben, I almost forgot. I have two of your books in my car. If you are still willing to sign them, I would be honored."

"I'll be happy to. Of course, Tippy is smart enough that he could probably bring them to you and save you a trip to the car."

"Who is Tippy?" Stacy asked.

Mario leaned down and put his hands on his knees to be closer to her level. "Tippy is my dog and my good friend, although he thinks he's a person. Would you like to meet him?"

Stacy looked at her parents. "Could I?"

"Sure," Rachel said. "In fact, let's all go out and meet Tippy."

Mario led the way. Ben was the last one out. He paused a moment to look at the place where the door handle smashed into the wall. Jim had done a good job of patching it. So good, it was hardly noticeable. The color was almost an exact match.

He ran a finger along the repaired surface, then went out to join the others.

Dusk settled along the landscape, merging its long shadows into evening.

"Tippy, come here boy."

They waited a moment and Mario called again. "Tippy, here boy. Come here Tippy."

There was no sound from the car. No movement.

"Tippy, come here you little rascal. Don't keep these people waiting." Mario stopped a few feet from the car. He looked at the Chalmers family over his shoulder. The smile was gone and worry lines had replaced the laugh lines that normally played around his mouth and eyes.

"He usually comes when I call." He took a tentative step toward the car, his eyes still on his new friends. "He usually..." Mario took the last three steps toward his car and looked inside.

The car was empty.

"Tippy?"

Panic colored his voice.

"I don't understand," Mario said, still looking in through the open driver's side window. "He should be right here on my side of the car." He looked around the immediate area, "Tippy, where are you?"

"Maybe he got out of the car once you went inside," Rachel offered.

"No, not Tippy," Mario said. "He is too well trained for that. He has never left the car without permission. Not even for a moment. No, something has happened to him.

"Tippy...Tippy..."

Rachel touched his arm. "Just to be on the safe side, let's walk around the house and out toward the woods. After all, if he's not in the car, he has to be somewhere close by. This may be the one time he slipped out for a bit of an adventure. There's a lot to explore up here, even for a well-behaved dog like your Tippy."

Mario looked at her. His eyes were moist and his breathing was ragged. Like a child holding back a sob.

"I suppose you are right." He looked to Ben. "He has never left the car on his own. Never. You saw how well behaved he was."

"Yes," Ben said. "I did. But Rachel's right. Dogs are like kids, and I suppose they will surprise you once in a while." He reached down and took Stacy's hand. "Let's all go look for Tippy."

The quartet walked around the house, down to the woods, and as far in the woods as the deepening shadows would allow. They called, listened, and called again. The only response was a light wind speaking through the dry clattering of a few remaining fall leaves. A rustling sound nearby gave them hope, but the large rabbit that emerged from the woods was not the animal they had hoped for.

A half hour later, when it was too dark to see without a light, they walked back to the house. Mario looked at his watch, then back towards his car. The glance was not lost on Ben.

"Mario, why don't you go back to the restaurant and Rachel and I will get a couple of flashlights and keep looking. We'll even ride around for a while in case he wandered in another direction. If we don't find him tonight, we'll look some more tomorrow.

A single tear spilled down Mario's ruddy cheek.

"You are so kind, but I can't ask you to do that."

"You didn't ask. We offered," Rachel said.

Stacy held Mario's hand. "Mr. Mario, we'll find him. Even Piggy Anne will help." She held up the doll for him to see.

Mario smiled at the little girl. "In that case, I guess I can go. I know he'll…" He couldn't stop the small sob that escaped. Stacy hugged him and the little pizza chef hugged her back. After a moment, he released her and stood.

"I can't thank you enough."

"No need," Ben said. "I'll call you at the restaurant the minute we find him."

"And we will find him," Rachel said. She hugged him, then took his hands in hers, and looked into his eyes. "We will."

He nodded, wiped away another tear. They watched as he walked to his car. Once inside, he looked around like a child looking for a lost treasure, his robust features now drawn and cheerless. They returned his wave as he navigated the circular driveway and drove away. The Chalmerses watched the tail lights blink out of sight. They stood for another moment, then as if they shared a telepathic link, they all turned and walked toward the house to get their flashlights.

The next hour of walking the property and the woods behind it proved as fruitless as their previous search.

Tippy.

Tippy.

Here boy. Good dog. Here Tippy.

Tiiiippyyyyy.

Ben didn't relish the call that felt inevitable by the moment. "OK everybody," he said. "Let's pile in the Jeep and see if maybe he headed toward the road."

As the family pulled out of the driveway to search for their new friend's lost companion, the trees watched, nodding in the evening breeze, but held their secrets. A half hour later when the Chambers returned, Ben made the call. Mario expressed his gratitude for their efforts, and Ben hoped his reassurance that the little Border Collie would most likely be found the next day did not sound as hollow as it felt.

CHAPTER FIFTEEN

1 A.M.

SOMEWHERE IN THE darkness, a night bird called. Its haunting cry rose and fell, a mournful note that hung in the air, then faded into nothingness. Brittle leaves rattled and chattered; dry, dead husks now little more than the ghosts of spring's green bounty.

Rachel listened to the night sounds, and strained against the late night gloom to listen for any unusual sounds from within the house.

The antique wooden clock tocked softly on her dresser. The heat pump hummed outside, its warmth whispering through the vents in the bedroom. Beneath her, the bed frame creaked as she shuffled to find a comfortable position, one that would exorcise the events of the day and calm her rushing thoughts.

Someone had been in the house. In their house. And while everything turned out OK this time, what if things had been different? What if it hadn't been some stupid kids? What if there had been a different outcome?

Hadn't Paul once told Ben about the deranged fan who broke into Stephen King's house? His wife actually caught the man inside the house and confronted him.

Rachel slipped out of bed and walked down the hall to Stacy's room. Her daughter lay in a tangle of sheets, blankets, and stuffed animals, while Piggy Anne looked down from her position sprawled across the headboard.

She watched her daughter sleep, then went back to her own room, the soft padding of bare feet against the hardwood floor her only companion. She settled between the thick covers and waited.

Ben snored softly beside her, his shoulders rising and falling with every breath.

She envied him.

At least he could sleep.

---

3 A.M.

A single cabinet door above the stove opened. The hushed click of the latch made a soft *snick* sound. Two minutes later, every cabinet door swung open as if on command.

The noise made by the movement of new well-oiled hinges sounded like a sigh.

CHAPTER SIXTEEN

OON...

Rodney seated the earbuds firmly in his ears.

Soon...it must be soon.

Rodney nodded in time to the voices. There was a new darkness in the lyrics. Hidden meanings he had never heard before. He rocked back and forth in his chair, the motion becoming more violent with each passing moment. The urgent pounding of the lyrics inside his head grew in intensity and the voices built to a frenzied crescendo.

...now, now, now, it must be now, the time is now, now, now, now, it must be now, the time is now, now, now, now, it must be now, the time is now, now, now, now, it must be now...

He leaned back in the chair, head back, mouth open, hands now clenched into fists, fully in the throes of a dark ecstasy.

He started breathing in time to the steady driving beat coming through the earbuds.

You know what you must do.

You must finish what you started.

You must release the one you summoned.

Rodney moaned, his breath coming in ragged gasps. The voices came faster and with more intensity. Dark shadows swirled along the walls, flowed across the floor and swept across his body like a dark tide. Dark tendrils of shadow caressed his face. The whispering built to a fever pitch and the last vestiges of any inhibitions were lost in a sea of dark longings. His head rocked back and Rodney cried out.

The shadows entered him through his mouth like a dark animal seeking its burrow.

You must finish what you started.

You must release the one you summoned.

You must release the one you summoned.

Then you must offer the final sacrifice…the final sacrifice…offer the final sacrifice. The ones who have kept you from your true heart's desire.

Rodney's parents' faces flashed through his mind and his rage threatened to consume him. They were keeping him from what he wanted. He knew what to do. As soon as he had finished what he started, he would deal with them.

…the final sacrifice…offer the final sacrifice.

The voices pounded their message through the earbuds.

The uncharged MP3 player, its batteries long dead, lay silent and unresponsive on the desktop.

IT WAS trapped.

Somewhere between Hell and earth.

Pulled from Its lair and transported to a place of limbo. Not fully ethereal, not corporeal, It felt the need to break through. Once more It strained against the force that held It captive.

It needed to feed. Needed to feel the power surge through Its body once again. It needed to spread Its black wings and track down prey.

Lesser entities had slipped through during the ritual. They were weak, but they were free. And they would find the ones who had spoken the ancient words and started the process of bringing It into the world. They would make the ones who spoke the words complete the ritual and pull It through into the mortal world.

And if not, It would find a way to pull Itself through.

Blood was the key.

Something flew against the house and hit a window. A bat. At the impact, It sent a surge of energy to the spot where the bat made contact. By the light of a fingernail moon, the flying mammal squirmed against the glass as blood seeped from a small cut in its wing.

The blood flowed against the glass, much more than should have been spilled by such a small cut. The blood seemed to pool in midair, then disappeared.

Drained from the bat, absorbed into the window glass, then gone. Slowly, the crack in the window receded. Like watching a movie played in reverse, the broken windowpane mended itself.

It wanted more, sent out psychic feelers, and found none. It was still weak. It wanted the people in the house, but It was not strong enough. Not yet. Frustration and rage over being stopped before It was fully through the deadlands consumed It, and It reached out into its surroundings. A shutter moved a few inches on its hinges, held its position, then fell back in place with a muffled thump.

The bat fell to the ground, its small body a dried husk.

With more blood came more power.

New power.

The woman had added to Its power earlier when she cut herself and It had tested Its expanding boundaries. It was not yet ready, but the time was drawing near.

It was patient.

It would wait.

The ones who had summoned It were nowhere near, and the ones who gathered in Its midst had the taint of the Holy One about them. The taint was strong at times. But no matter.

Three minor demons had escaped from the pit during the ceremony and were working their influence on those who had called It from the pit. It was not strong enough to sense them, to gauge their progress, but they were relentless and would urge the ones from before to come back and complete their task.

It was sentient enough to know It wanted to live apart from its prison. It must be free from the confinement that held it between two worlds.

It must walk in the world of men.

It was patient.

It would wait.

Soon, It thought.

Soon...

CHAPTER SEVENTEEN

KENNY RANDALL LOOKED at his cell phone in disbelief. How had things gotten this far out of control? It was bad enough he wasn't sleeping at night anymore. Bad enough that he was beginning to think he was losing his mind.

Ever since the night they went out to the house on Grant's Ridge with Rodney he had been hearing things.

Voices.

Or something that sounded like voices. They had become a constant hiss in the back of his mind, like faint static on an AM radio station late at night.

...now, now, now, it must be now, the time is now, now, now, now, it must be now, the time is now, now, now, now, it must be now, the time is now, now, now, now, it must be now...

He just wanted it to stop. Just wanted the voices to go away. His life was deteriorating more every day. He had not seen any of his friends in weeks and he was missing school for days at a time. Some days he would pretend to be sick and bury his head in his pillow for hours in an attempt to stop the constant whispering. Other days he would leave home and walk in the general direction of the school, then make his way over to Windsor Park and spend the day wandering in the woods.

At least there he didn't have to deal with the chorus of classmates and teachers wondering if he was OK, if he was sick, if he needed to call home, if there was something bothering him, if he was getting enough sleep, *if…if…if…*

In the end he had agreed to call Robin and Myra and tell them the plan. Actually, he had received his marching orders from Rodney and would dutifully call the girls and tell them what time he would be around to pick everybody up. He planned to take his parents' second car while they were out having dinner with a few members of their church covenant group.

He didn't want to call them, and he certainly didn't want to go. More than once since the fiasco at the house he had wished he had the guts Robin had when she walked (ran) out of the house. Sometimes at night he dreamed about the ceremony. In his dream, Rodney was standing behind an ebony altar and Myra stood beside him, swaying and chanting words he didn't understand, though he knew the feeling and intent behind them.

At first he didn't see himself in the dream. All he saw was the glow of candles, Myra's writhing, and Rodney's eyes.

In the dream, Rodney's eyes were red.

Always red.

As the ceremony reached its climax the scene shifted and Kenny was able to watch the action from high above the participants. He saw Myra dancing in full frenzy. Just to her right Rodney would unsheathe the curved blade and as it made its downward descent, he would see himself.

He was strapped to the altar.

He was the sacrifice.

He was the portent through which the entity would come.

And every night his own muffled scream would awaken him just before he was sacrificed to a nameless dark god and some minion of hell rose up to take his place.

He looked at the cell phone in his hand. He didn't want to call either of the girls. He didn't want anything else to do with any of it.

But he also didn't want to face Rodney if he chickened out. He dialed the first three digits of Robin's number.

Oh dear Lord Jesus, what am I--

The screams hit him like a solid wave of sound. He dropped the phone and grabbed the sides of his head. The voices in his head were no longer whispering. The whispers had turned to screams of pure, undiluted agony. The pain in his head came so fast and hard he threw up.

Please...

Before he could finish the sentence a second chorus of screams reverberated deep in his mind and a black wave of nausea wrung the last vestige of his breakfast from his already cramping stomach.

No...

His words came back to him hollow just before he blacked out.

KENNY OPENED his eyes and waited. He wanted to move but didn't dare. He couldn't bear the thought of triggering whatever had happened to him earlier.

He looked at the clock.

Had he really been out for two hours? And what was that smell?

Suddenly it all came back to him. He flinched, waiting for the second wave, but none came.

Only the voices.

Speak not the name of the Prince...speak not the name of the Prince... speak not the name of the Prince...

He looked at the clock again. Two hours. That meant his mom would be home in thirty minutes and he had a mess to clean up before she got there. But he had something to do first. Something that now seemed very important.

He looked around until he found his cell phone.

He had a call to make.

Then he had to go out before his mom got home.

CHAPTER EIGHTEEN

EN WALKED INTO Rachel's studio. She was working at an easel, painting the view from the bay window. She had said from the moment she selected the room as hers that she wanted to paint the view because it was a perfect fall study. Blazes of orange, burnt sienna, yellow, red, and gold spilled down the side of the ridge and on toward Pike's Crossing. And though it seemed the leaves were falling faster each day, the ridge was still awash in fall colors.

"How's it coming?"

Rachel looked up from her painting. "It's OK I guess. I'm just a little rusty after laying off for about a month."

Ben walked around behind her and saw the beginnings of the scene outside her window captured on canvas.

"If that's rusty, let me know when you get up to speed. I'll probably be able to hear the leaves rustling in the breeze right on the canvas."

Rachel grinned. "OK, Mr. Flattery, what do you want?"

He kissed her and grinned. "Just that. And I meant what I said about the picture. It doesn't look like you've lost a stroke since you packed everything up." He looked out the window at the landscape then back to her version of it on canvas again. "That really is good."

"In that case, here." She kissed him again. "Take one for the road." She cleaned the brush she had been using and wiped it on a piece of paper towel. "Oh, by the way, what were you looking for downstairs last night?"

"Huh?"

"You know, last night sometime after we went to bed."

"I wasn't looking for anything. Or if I did, I did it in my sleep because I was out the minute my head hit the pillow." He sat off to one side on the window seat so as not to obstruct her view. "What made you think I was looking for something?"

Rachel put the clean brush in a nearby jar and retrieved a fan brush. "When I went down to make coffee while you were in the shower, every cabinet in the kitchen was open. And I mean wide open." She mixed colors on her palette and started adding highlights to the groundcover in the painting. "I don't care if you were looking for something. Just remember to close the cabinets next time."

Ben stood. "Honey, I told you, I didn't go in the kitchen looking for anything after we went to bed. Between the hunt for Mario's dog and all the pasta I put away, I all but died the minute I went to sleep."

"Well, in that case, what happened down there?" She worked on a patch of ground.

"I don't know."

She reloaded her brush and paused before her next brush stroke. "Wait a minute. The day I cut my finger one of the cabinets kept inching open." She gestured with the brush; a brownish-gold teardrop of paint barely clung to the bristles. "I'll bet that's it. Those cabinets probably need to be adjusted, especially if the house is settling or something like that."

"That's probably it," Ben said. "So I guess I'm in the clear." He grinned at her.

"I guess," she said in his general direction. She returned to her painting.

Ben paused in case she wanted to say anything else; in case she wanted to apologize for accusing him of doing something he didn't do. When it was obvious she had nothing else to say, he started toward the door.

"Oh yeah," he said. "I'm going to take another drive around before I start writing. See if I can find Mario's dog."

Rachel gave a quick wave but didn't look up from her painting.

Ben waited another moment for any additional response. When none came, he left the studio.

He paused for a moment on the landing. There was something he couldn't quite place. Something in the air. Something different. He waited another moment, listening. Then it came to him.

A smell.

Faint.

Dark.

Like old, damp, mulched leaves. Barely discernable. Just a hint, but there nonetheless.

Ben ran a hand through his hair and descended the steps. He stopped again on the front steps and breathed deep.

The smell was gone. Out in the yard he smelled the smoke from a distant fire, probably somebody burning leaves, and the lingering scent of pine and cedar from the woods behind the house.

He inhaled the scents of autumn in all their glory.

"Lord, I'm still not sure what I've done to cause you to bless me like this," he prayed aloud while walking to the Jeep, "but I thank you just the same." He looked toward the studio window before he opened the door. Rachel was looking in his direction. He waved goodbye.

She turned back to her canvas.

He unlocked the door with his keyless remote but made no move to get in the vehicle. He continued to look toward the window a little longer. After a minute, he got in and started the motor.

"She probably just didn't see me," he said aloud. "She was probably rechecking the colors and shadows." He put the Jeep in gear and started down the driveway.

Ben covered the roads near the house and took every dirt road he came to. He drove slow and called for Tippy through the open window. He saw a half dozen rabbits, three times as many squirrels, three assorted dogs (none looked even remotely like the truant Border Collie), two foxes, and a deer.

A few times when he came to a likely field or patch of woods, he got out and called the dog. After his second circuit through the roads and pathways, he faced the fact that he was probably not going to find Mario's companion, and the next trip he made would be to the restaurant with the unpleasant news.

"Lord," he said, with equal parts desperation and reverence, "I don't suppose you'd consider giving me a hint where to look next."

The Lord's answer was wrapped in silence.

Ben made one more circuit of the roads he had already covered, this time expanding his area by a half dozen more state and county roads. He didn't really expect to find Tippy, but at least he could say he made as thorough a search as he could.

He drove home slowly. With his search for Mario's dog unsuccessful, now he wanted to figure out what happened earlier in the morning. Granted, Rachel had been at work on a painting when he went in the studio, but that had never bothered her before. She was able to stop at any time in a painting or other artistic project and pick it back up later just where she left off. In fact, she had commented to friends over the years that the only distraction they allowed themselves when working on a project was each other.

He could stop in the middle of a sentence and pick up his train of thought the next time he sat down to write. And even during the times that the writing seemed almost automatic and he was flowing with the process, if she came in and wanted to talk, he was always able to stop where he was, then get back to the process later with no hesitation.

Then again, it wasn't the abruptness that bothered him as much as it was the fact that she had accused him of something he didn't do, and was so cavalier about it later.

"Something's bound to be bothering her," he said to the vehicle's interior. "It's probably just the move finally catching up with her." He thought about the statement for a minute and decided that must be the reason. It had been a long, tiring move. And coming home to find two law enforcement officials at the house would be enough to rattle anybody.

He put a CD in the player and picked up his speed. The tight gospel harmony and up-tempo beat improved his frame of mind and, before the odometer registered a quarter of a mile, he was singing at full volume.

I saw a man who can walk on water,

And I am never going to be the same.

I saw a man who can walk on water,

He can cure the sick, raise the dead, and heal the lame…

Ben tapped the console between the bucket seats in time to the music and touched the replay button on the CD player when the song finished. The last notes of the song were fading for the second time as he pulled into his driveway. He let the last chord drift away completely before he got out of the Jeep.

The sky was turning a light shade of slate gray. Most likely they were in for some rain. Ben glanced toward the second story studio window but didn't go in the house. If it was going to rain, he wanted to go look in the woods one more time while it was still light out and there was no rain falling.

For the next fifteen minutes Ben walked through the woods, alternately calling the missing dog and stopping to listen for anything that sounded like a small animal moving around. If Tippy was hurt, he might be able to hear the dog trying to move.

As the first raindrops started to fall, Ben was certain he would not find Mario's dog. He had not seen a carcass beside the road during his drive, but that was no proof that Tippy had not been hit by a car. And if that was indeed the case, it was also possible the dog had been knocked into a ditch or had crawled into the edge of the woods by the road and died.

Ben didn't relish the idea of telling his new friend the bad news.

A cold, steady rain was falling, touching the landscape with streaks of gray. The rain smelled of fertile earth and carried within each drop a portent of the winter to come. Ben hunched against the building precipitation but did not hurry his pace. He made his way back to the house and entered through the back door. Once inside he removed his shoes and carried them so he wouldn't track dirt in.

He went upstairs and rummaged in his office trashcan until he found an old sheet of newspaper from the previous days unpacking. He laid the paper out and put his shoes on it. He would clean them up and put them away later.

"Ben, is that you?" Rachel called from the studio.

He walked down the hall and into her space. "Yep, it's me," he said. He looked around the room at the completed paintings displayed in various places around the room. She had a few ceramic pieces and a clay sculpture in a separate work area. He was always amazed at the detail her work contained, and in some ways he envied her talent.

"Hello, me," she said. "Did you have any luck finding Mario's dog?" She put the paintbrush down and stretched.

"No." He sighed. "And I don't look forward to calling him one little bit. He is going to be devastated." Ben looked out the window but the autumn panorama was little consolation. "But, I don't suppose I have much choice."

"I'm afraid not," she said, "and you may need to do it a little sooner than you planned because we've got to do something with the rest of the boxes this weekend. Either unpack them or hide them." She got up from her chair and walked to where Ben stood. "Remember, you've got an interview Monday afternoon."

Ben rubbed the bridge of his nose, then looked at Rachel. "I'm sure glad you remembered. I had completely forgotten it."

"Well," she said, "we've still got plenty of time. Didn't you say the writer wasn't supposed to be here until about two o'clock Monday?"

"Um-hum. Two or two thirty depending on the flight." Ben grinned. "I hope he likes little puddle jumper planes, because that's all that will be able to land at any airport around here."

"Atlanta it's not," Rachel said. She looked into Ben's eyes. "But then again, that's what we wanted. Right?"

"Definitely. I'm not complaining. Just still surprised at how different things are here. It's so quiet and the people are so friendly." He put his hands on her shoulders. "But what about you? Do you really like it here?"

"Of course I do. This is everything we have ever wanted." She stepped in closer to him. "What made you ask that?"

"Oh, nothing. Not really. You just seemed a little perturbed this morning and I just wondered if maybe the move had been a little much. I mean we've gotten a lot done in a pretty short time and you hadn't even been able to spend any time in your studio except for a little while yesterday and this morning."

"I guess I was a little out of sorts this morning. I don't know what that was all about. I think I was just a little aggravated about the cabinets. But we can get Jim to come out and take a look at them." She hugged him hard. "But no, I'm very happy here. Maybe a little tired, but very happy."

He held her a moment longer. "Good," he said. "Because that's the most important thing." He kissed the top of her head. "And as much as I would like to just stay here like this all day, I guess I had better go call Mario."

He headed down the hall to his office.

"Ben…"

He stopped and looked back over his shoulder.

"Maybe Tippy went home." She looked hopeful.

"Maybe so," he said with little conviction.

But, he thought, if Tippy had gone home, Mario would have called.

He went in the office, settled in his chair, and looked for the phone number. Ten minutes later, his bad news delivered, Ben went back to

Rachel's studio, but she was already gone. He found her downstairs in the kitchen.

"Hey" she said, "How was Mario? Did Tippy make it home?"

"He said he was OK, but I wouldn't bet on it." Ben filled a coffee mug. "He hasn't seen Tippy and if he doesn't find that dog soon, I think he is really going to be in a bad way."

Rachel leaned against the center island. "That poor man. Evidently his dog and his restaurant are all he has left."

"That and God," Ben said. "He seems to have a pretty strong faith."

"That's true. But even so..."

"*Mama.*"

The sound of Stacy's call startled them both, and the sense of urgency in her voice sent them rushing upstairs.

They found Stacy standing in the hall crying and pointing toward their bedroom.

"What did I do Mama? I haven't been bad. What did I do?" Tears washed down her cheeks and her breath came in ragged little gasps.

Stacy ran to her daughter and folded her in her arms. "What are you talking about, doodlebug? You haven't done anything at all." She squatted, smoothed Stacy's hair, and pulled her close. "You're the best girl in the world. What makes you think you've done something bad?"

Stacy pointed toward the master bedroom again. "In there," she sniffed. "You put Piggy Anne in there."

Rachel turned and looked at Ben. He shrugged and indicated he didn't know what she was talking about. Rachel held Stacy at arm's length and looked at the small tear-stained face. Her breath was still erratic and she continued to sob quietly. Rachel brushed Stacy's bangs away from her eyes and spoke in a softer voice.

"Honey, Daddy and I don't know what you're talking about. We haven't had Piggy Anne."

Stacy looked into her mother's eyes and tried unsuccessfully to stifle a sob. "But she's in your room, and I didn't put her there."

Ben went in the bedroom and looked around. He saw the doll in a corner of the room between the wall and the bedside table. It was on Rachel's side of the bed, and the angle at which the doll lay made it look like it was crouching.

Watching.

Waiting.

Ben shook off the notion and picked the doll up. There seemed to be some resistance. He checked to see if one of Piggy Anne's feet was caught on something or wrapped around a table leg, but the foot was simply lying on the hardwood portion of the floor in the space between the Oriental rug and the wall. Instead of wall to-wall-carpet, the bedroom had a large Persian rug on the side with the bed. The side nearest the master bath was all hardwood.

He pulled once more and the doll released whatever grip it had on the floor. He looked at the large rag doll, examined the feet, and shook his head.

Ben came back out with Piggy Anne. He knelt beside Rachel and Stacy. "Here she is, honey." He held the doll out. Stacy hesitated a moment and looked at her mother. Rachel smiled and nodded.

Stacy took the doll from her father.

"Where was it?" Rachel asked.

"It was sort of behind your bedside table."

"Sort of?" Rachel stood up but still kept one hand on Stacy's shoulder. "What do you mean, sort of?"

"Well…sort of…it was about half behind the table and half not." He pulled at the corners of his mouth. The action drew his face into a frown. "It almost looked like it was crawling behind the bedside table."

"Crawling? Ben, you're kidding."

"No, I don't mean it crawled back there. I just mean the position it was in made it look that way." Ben looked at Stacy. "Honey, have you been playing with Piggy Anne in our room?"

"No!" Stacy said. "I'm not supposed to play in your room." She looked from one parent to the other. Her lower lip trembled a little.

Rachel pushed the bangs away from her face again and held her face in her hands. "Stacy, honey, you're not in trouble. And you're right. You are not supposed to play in our room. Just tell us the truth. And if you were in there playing earlier, it's OK. We won't be mad. Just remember not to do that, because you have your own room to play in."

A single tear eased its way down her left cheek. "But I wasn't in there. Honest." Another tear followed. Then another. "I was a good girl." She hugged Piggy Anne and cried into the red yarn hair.

"We know you're a good girl," Rachel said, "but Piggy Anne got in there somehow. And it's OK if it you took her in there this time. But you need to tell us now. It's OK."

Stacy repeated her innocent pleas.

Ben squatted in front of her and pulled her close. "Baby, it's alright. If you say you didn't go in there, then we believe you." He stroked her hair. "But we didn't put her in there either. So we'll just have to think about this one and see if we can figure out what happened. OK?"

Stacy looked at her mother. Rachel smiled.

"OK Daddy." She looked at the doll in her arms. "How did you get in Mama and Daddy's room?"

How indeed, Ben wondered.

CHAPTER NINETEEN

THE DOORBELL FELT somehow wrong and Kenny snatched his hand away as if he'd been shocked.

He had cleaned up the mess at home as best he could and slipped out the back door just as his mother drove up. Too close for comfort. Then he'd pushed his bike through backyards until he felt it was safe to ride on side streets.

It had taken him another ten minutes to work up the nerve to go to the front door when he made it to the house on Grant's Ridge.

I've got to tell them. Got to tell them what happened. Maybe if I tell them the voices will go away. Maybe then it will stop. Got to tell them. Got to make it stop.

Kenny reached for the doorbell again and stopped. This was stupid. It was just a doorbell. Just a white button set in a brass plate on a regular front door.

No. It's the doorway to hell. He faltered. Reached out. Faltered again.

But I've got to tell them. Got to make it stop. Got to make it stop.

Something in the house moved.

Not something. Someone.

Kenny bolted from the porch and ran along the side of the house. Came to a window.

He fell on the ground and huddled next to the foundation. Waited for the front door to open.

Then he heard sounds on the other side of the window.

Kenny's stomach clenched. Released. He waited another moment and looked through the window and into the kitchen. The woman was pouring a mug of coffee. Then the man came in and poured himself a mug.

The Chalmerses.

He had to tell them. Needed to tell them.

Couldn't tell them.

The voices whispered as the couple walked out of the kitchen.

As Kenny rushed away from the house.

CHAPTER TWENTY

A COLD WIND SLIPPED around the corner of the gymnasium, moving candy wrappers, an old ragged tissue, and an errant page of someone's past due homework out of its way. Lifeless brown oak leaves chattered in its wake. The wind had teeth and brought with it the first bite of the coming winter.

Kenny shoved his hands deeper into the pockets of his denim jacket. He hunched his shoulders, trying to present as small a target as possible until the wind died down. He pulled his left hand out of its denim cocoon just far enough to see his watch. Lunch was almost over and Myra was fifteen minutes late. *If you're not here in the next few minutes...*

"That wind is nasty."

Kenny saw Myra coming around the corner of the building. He wasn't sure whether to be mad or relieved.

"Where have you been? You were supposed to be here fifteen minutes ago."

Myra crossed her arms and put her hands beneath her armpits. She hunched her shoulders forward and hugged her arms in tight to her body.

"I would have been here sooner, but I just spent the past ten minutes trying to get Robin to go with us." She shook her head. "She just won't do it. She wouldn't even come back here to talk about it." Myra looked at Kenny. It was the first time she had seen him in over a week.

"Kenny, what happened to you?" She stared at the face of the boy she once knew.

He had been shocked to see his own reflection earlier in the morning. His face had been drawn and hollow, his eyes lifeless. There was no sense of personality there. No animation. Just eyes that seemed to look out at the world but see nothing. He looked like an older version of himself. An older version close to death.

"Rodney happened to me," he said. "Rodney and you."

"Me?" Myra took a half step away from Kenny. "What did I do?"

"Nothing. That's what you did. Nothing at all. And maybe if you had, I would have left that night when Robin did."

"What? Kenny, slow down and make some sense. What do I have to do with you leaving anywhere?"

"I'm talking about that night at the house. That night when Robin ran off before everything got started." His voice was more animated but his affect remained flat. "The fact is, I didn't want to go. I was only out there to impress you. And when Robin left, I wanted to leave too, but I was too chicken."

His aborted attempt to warn the Chalmers family slashed through his mind like a razor. For a second, he thought he heard the faint sound of laughter.

"I've been thinking lately." He rasped an ugly laugh. "I've had a lot of time to think because I haven't slept in days, and when I am awake, I hear whispering. The only thing I can figure is maybe if you had started to leave when she did, or at least said something, I would have had the nerve to leave." He pulled his hands from his pockets and spread his arms. "I'm about to go out of my mind. I can't sleep, and don't know how much longer I can stay awake, and I'm afraid in another day or two I won't even care."

Myra took another step back. Kenny's desperation was as real as the cold wind whipping around them. But there was something else in his voice. Something even darker than his state of mind.

"Look," she said, "you can't put that off on me. I wanted to leave at first too, but after I got into it, I really wanted to be a part of it. I made my decision. And I'm going through with the new ceremony." She uncrossed her arms and pointed a finger at Kenny. "Now if you aren't man enough to make your own decisions, don't blame me."

Kenny's lips moved, but at first there was no sound. He tried again.

...*voices*...

"What?" Myra leaned toward him.

"Voices. I hear them everywhere. Don't you hear the voices?"

Myra nodded. "I hear them. I've heard them since the night at the house."

"Then how...how...do you stand them? I hear them everywhere. I can't sleep because they are worse when I close my eyes. And I see things. Horrible things."

"Like visions?" Myra cocked her head to the left and smiled. "Oh yes. I have those too. They have actually been very helpful."

"Helpful?" Kenny's face went slack, like a man who had just had a stroke. "How?"

Myra's smile broadened. "Oh, you'd be surprised."

Something flickered in Kenny's mind. A momentary ghost of the boy he used to be. "Myra, what are you talking about? The things I've seen are vile, evil things. What have you been seeing?"

Myra gave him a coy look. "Oh, I can't tell you just yet. Let's just say they showed me a way to send a message to all those foster families who shuffled me around all these years. All the fake families who said they wanted to give me a home but none of them wanted to keep me."

Kenny reminded her of some of the stories she had told about her previous foster families. "Maybe if you hadn't run away so much, or started staying out all night things might have been different."

Myra's face harbored an ugly smile. "Whatever." The smile broadened. "But you can believe one thing. Tonight they are going to get the message. Loud and clear."

Kenny just stared at her.

"But listen," she said, "you are still going aren't you? I mean after you called me and all, you're still going through with this aren't you?"

"I don't have much choice," Kenny said. "Rodney made it pretty clear that he expects us all to meet him here in the parking lot late this afternoon, and we'll all drive over together after we get some supplies. That's what he told me." He watched a paper cup skip along the gravel, carried along by a gust of wind. "He's gonna have a fit when Robin doesn't show up."

"Well, that's her problem." Myra looked around as if expecting someone to come by. "So you're sure you're coming?"

"I said I was," Kenny snapped. He lowered his voice. "This may be the only way I can make the voices stop." He looked into Myra's eyes. "If this keeps on, I don't know what I'll do…or what I won't be able to stop myself from doing."

Kenny turned and headed away from the gym and away from the school, the voices in his head his only companions.

CHAPTER TWENTY-ONE

*I*TS POWER WAS growing. Until now, each attempt to test Its abilities had left It drained. But each life taken had given It more power. So far there had been minute increases in power because of Its relatively small prey, but that was about to change.

It had new prey.

Something much larger. Not as large as the large beings housed within Its prison. Something smaller, but very much alive.

For now.

It was only a matter of time.

It was becoming more adept at manipulating Its prison. It was now able to manipulate anything in direct contact with Its surroundings. Moving the doll had taken a great deal of effort, but Its recovery had taken less time than with previous attempts. Soon It would feed again. Just as soon as It had recovered from moving the doll and the other tests of Its abilities.

Soon...

THE SLIVERS of light that seeped under the door did little more than add gray highlights to the swirling shadows. Dust motes swirled in the diffused light, perpetually suspended between heaven and earth.

Dark silhouettes drawn in contrast to the darker expanse that housed them stood as silent sentries. No windows offered the comfort of light. No skylight showed the passing heavens or the trek of the sun.

There was only gloom and shadow, twin sisters of despair.

Tippy lay huddled in a corner, terrified. The dark was deep and complete, punctuated only by the dog's sporadic whimpers. Around the dark expanse were the small, acrid puddles he had made, not from a need to relieve himself, but from abject fear.

The air in the room was charged like a summer sky just before a storm, and there was an almost tangible energy that pulsed through the enclosed space. The air grew thick and sluggish, and a second smell permeated the room. A sour smell like spoiled meat. Faint, but growing stronger as the shadows shifted and changed.

The room's occupant trembled and created another small puddle, never bothering to move from the spot to which he had resigned himself.

Something was coming.

And it was hungry.

CHAPTER TWENTY-TWO

KYLE ROTH TOOK in the autumn panorama that lay beyond the deck and whistled softly. The woods behind the house sloped down the side of a gentle hill, which led to a deeper ravine. Beyond that lay a vast expanse of fall-colored trees clothing the Blue Ridge Mountains in their seasonal finest.

"Wow. Would you look at that?" Kyle leaned against the deck rail. "A person could get used to seeing this view every day."

Ben sipped tea from a green stoneware mug but said nothing. He knew how Kyle felt. He had the same thought more than once. It was a beautiful spot, and a constant reminder of how God had blessed his family beyond his wildest expectations.

Since Kyle's arrival at the house a half hour earlier, Ben had made them both a cup of tea, had given him a tour of the downstairs portion of the house, and walked with him onto the deck to take in the view. They had spent the last ten minutes on the deck drinking tea, speculating about the coming winter, and making small talk. Occasionally Kyle made a note in a slim notebook.

Kyle scanned the landscape another moment, then pushed away from the rail. "Still, I suppose we'd better head in and get this interview started." He zipped his jacket a little higher.

Ben turned to go in the house and saw Kyle snapping a picture with a digital camera. "Hey, with a view like that so close, you are bound to have better things to take pictures of than me," he said.

The magazine writer laughed. "I plan to get a few shots of the view too, but I've got to have a picture or two of the subject of the story." He clicked off another shot. "If you don't mind, though, could we get a couple of shots of you in the house? Maybe some in the family room and a few up in your office?"

"Sure, if you think it will help." Ben opened the door and motioned for Kyle to go in. He followed and closed the door. The warmth of the house waited like an old friend.

"OK, where would you like me to do my writer pose?"

Kyle snickered and walked over to a leather wingback chair. "Would it be OK to move this chair a couple of feet and get a couple of pictures of you sitting here," he motioned toward the spot he had in mind, "and then get some shots of you by the picture window with the mountains in the background?"

"Sure, that would be fine." Ben moved the chair while Kyle checked the settings on his camera.

Kyle looked up and nodded when he saw the chair in position. "That's perfect. Now all you have to do is have a seat and look like a writer."

Ben put his tea mug on a side table and sat down. "How is this?" He had a serious look on his face and was sitting up straight with his legs crossed.

Kyle raised the camera and looked through the viewfinder. "You can relax for a minute or two. I'm still getting the settings calibrated. You know, taking light readings and that kind of thing." He turned the camera around, looked into the lens, then put the camera back into position. "This will take another minute or two. Just relax and I'll let you know when."

Ben settled back in the chair, took his mug, and looked toward the front entryway. He could see the place where Jim had repaired the panel and was surprised to see that the repair was all but invisible. "Well that's one," Kyle said. Ben focused on the magazine writer in time to see him click the shutter a second time. "And that's two." Kyle looked at the small LCD screen in the back of the camera. "Oh yes, that's the money shot." He turned the camera around so Ben could see the picture.

The image showed a relaxed Ben sitting in the chair, cradling the mug of tea. Ben was surprised at how well the picture had turned out. He had been so lost in thought that he forgot Kyle was in the room.

"Wow, that's actually pretty good as far as pictures of me go." He settled back in the chair again. "But you said you were going to tell me first."

"Oh, right." Kyle grinned and held up the camera. "Ben, I took your picture."

"Oh boy, a photographer *and* a comedian. I think you must be related to my wife. She's talented and funny too."

Kyle laughed and motioned toward the large window. "Now that you know how it's done, let's get a couple by the window just to be on the safe side. Just go stand by the window and look at the view. Kind of like you're contemplating your next masterpiece."

Ben grinned and walked toward the window. He didn't have to pretend to be interested in something outside because the view was beautiful. So much so that he was only marginally aware of the camera clicking softly in the background.

"OK Ben, I think that's got it down here. Where to next?"

Ben pulled himself away from the window and started toward the stairs. "Let's head upstairs and I'll introduce you to the one with the real talent during the second half of the grand tour."

"Good deal," Kyle said, "and after we get settled in the office, I'll trick you into another picture and we'll get to that interview." Kyle scrolled through the shots on his camera as he walked toward the stairs, then stopped with his foot on the first step.

"That's odd."

"Pardon?" Ben looked down at Kyle from the landing.

Startled, Kyle looked up. "Oh, uh…nothing. I just noticed a shadow in the background of one of the pictures. I'll check it later." He followed Ben up the steps. "Let's see the rest of this place. If it is anything like the downstairs, you've got a magnificent place on your hands."

"Better than I deserve," Ben said. "But you're right. It's a great house. I think we're going to be here a long time."

They arrived in the main upstairs hall. Ben showed his guest the master suite, guest room, guest bath, then stopped in the doorway of Stacy's room. Stacy was sitting on the edge of her bed leafing through a well-used Bible storybook. She had rearranged her animals once again.

"This is the animal sanctuary. We've got all kinds of creatures in here, and my daughter, Stacy, is the ringmaster for the whole menagerie."

Stacy looked up when she heard her father's voice. Piggy Anne lay sprawled against the pillows at the head of the bed, her fabric face buried between two Smurf pillows. "Hi, Daddy." She started to say something else, but stopped short when she saw Kyle. "Is this your company?"

"Yes," Ben said. "This is Mr. Roth. He came over to work on a magazine article. Can you say hello to him?"

"Hello, Mr. Roth. Are you writing an article because my daddy is famous?"

"Stacy…" Ben's face flushed from crimson to four-alarm red. "I told you, I'm not famous."

"I don't know," Kyle said. "If the numbers I keep hearing are right, if you're not famous now, it won't be long. Stores are placing some pretty hefty orders for this book, and the one you're working on has some pretty important tongues wagging." He smiled at Stacy. "But yes ma'am, I'm here to write a story about your daddy. And I'm with you," he winked at her conspiratorially, "I think he's probably getting a little famous."

"Well then," Ben said, "since you two are convinced I'm a full-fledged celebrity, I guess we'd better move along before I'm mobbed by stuffed animals wanting my autograph."

"Aw, Daddy." Stacy rolled her eyes. "You're silly."

"True," he said. "I forgot, they can't read, so they wouldn't want my autograph anyway." He looked at Kyle. "Shall we?" He motioned toward the hallway. "We'll wrap up the tour and get to the hard part."

Kyle told Stacy goodbye and went outside. Stacy grabbed her father's hand.

"What is it, doodlebug?"

"Tell Piggy Anne to stop playing so rough." She looked in the doll's direction. "She grabbed me a little while ago and it hurt."

"Really?" Ben stroked his chin with one hand. "What did you do when she did that?"

"I picked her up off the floor and threw her on the bed."

"Well," Ben said. "She probably learned her lesson after that." He tousled her hair. "But if she bothers you again, you just let me know."

"I don't know…" she looked in Piggy Anne's direction. Piggy Anne lay silent and still.

"You can handle her," Ben said. "And remember, your mom and I are just down the hall if she really gets rowdy."

"OK." Stacy pulled her bottom lip in against her teeth.

"That's my girl." Ben left the room and walked with Kyle toward the studio.

STACY SAT back down on the edge of the bed and pulled up her right pants leg. She touched the angry bruise forming on her ankle, winced, then reached over and punched Piggy Anne in the back.

"You heard what Daddy said. Now you leave me alone."

"RACHEL, THIS is Kyle Roth."

Rachel looked up from the canvas she was working on. "Oh, so you're the one Paul sent up here to inflate my husband's ego." She smiled and extended her hand.

"Yes ma'am, that's my assignment." He shook her hand, then looked around the room at the artwork on display. "Are all of these your work?" Kyle walked over to a seascape on the wall behind Rachel. It depicted a tremendous storm on the sea and was done in all blacks, grays, and blues.

"All except one," she said. She pointed to a framed Thomas Kinkade Christmas print. "I would like to think I could paint like that one day," she said, "but I'm not sure that's likely to happen."

"So you keep that around the studio for inspiration?" Kyle asked.

"Not really for inspiration," she said. "I just think it's very pretty. Plus it reminds me of the magical things that can be done with paint, a canvas, and a few brushes." She looked at her current project. "I don't have to try to duplicate someone else's style. It's just a sort of reminder when I feel a little down about a piece that the magic is there. You just have to put in the time to find it."

"That's rather profound," Kyle said. "I may need to come back and do a story on you. I think Paul said you are planning to open a small gallery."

"That will come later," she said. "First I've got to get back to my painting and sculpting and build up my collection a little more." She picked up a brush and started mixing pigments on the palette. "Till then I guess you'll just have to make do with the famous author."

"Here we go again," Ben said. "Come on, Kyle, let's get out of here. I think the paint thinner fumes are starting to affect her."

"OK. But Rachel, I'm serious. I'd love to come out after you open the gallery and do a story on the two artists living and working together."

"I'll think about it. As for living together, that we do. But he works in his own little world and I work in mine. That is time we have to set aside just for each of us alone." She highlighted a section of trees on the canvas. "But it works for us. And we couldn't be happier." She picked up more color on her brush. "So, you two go and talk writer talk while I try to make this look like a real painting."

Ben and Kyle went into the office. Kyle took a moment to look at the framed mementos on the wall. Amid the dust jackets of Ben's previous books, a few of Rachel's paintings, and one original painting for the cover of his first book was a framed photocopy of a check for twenty-five dollars.

"What is this?" Kyle asked.

Ben took the framed check down and looked at it. "This is a copy of the first check I ever received from a publisher. It was for a piece I had written for a Sunday school take-home paper." He handed the framed check to Kyle. "You know, the kind of thing you got in Sunday school when you were a kid. It usually had a story, a Bible crossword puzzle, and a craft to do in class?"

"Oh yeah, I remember those."

"Well, after I had been writing about three months I finally got the courage to send a story to a publisher who handles that kind of thing. I didn't really expect much, but about a month later I got a contract and this check in the mail."

Ben replaced the framed check. "I'll never forget how that felt. You would have thought the check had been made out for a quarter of a million dollars.

"My hands shook so bad when I picked up the phone to call Rachel I couldn't dial the number. It took me three tries to finally get through to the school where she was working as a substitute teacher. When I told her the news, we both cried."

Kyle had his notepad out and was writing in shorthand. "That sounds like a good place to start." He made another quick note. "Let's talk a while and then I'll see if I can trick you into another picture."

Ben got the rocking chair from the far corner of the office and placed it close to his office chair for Kyle.

For the next half hour they talked about Ben's career, the fact that he sold the first seven pieces he wrote, then went for almost a year and couldn't give his writing away. They discussed his move from short fiction and articles to novels, and the inspiration for his mystery series. Then they moved on to the newest book and the one in progress.

Ben told Kyle about his initial reservations and his agent's subsequent advice to skip the pen name and write both genres under his own name.

Halfway through the conversation, Ben noticed a slightly acrid smell, much like spoiled milk. Faint, but noticeable all the same.

As the interview progressed, Kyle asked why Ben chose to write Christian fiction.

"It just feels right," Ben said. "It gives me a chance to write the kind of things I love to read, but make sure the message of God's love is central to the story."

The spoiled milk smell intensified.

"For example, Stephen King wrote *The Stand* and, within a few years of its publication, there were college classes developed around the perceived theological significance of the book.

"I don't want people to have to wonder about the theological thrust of my books. For example, even in the new one, the first one in a more supernaturally driven line, I've attempted to make the message of the gospel evident without beating people over the head with it. Much like the book of Daniel where even in the very worst circumstances, the message from God was inescapable: no matter what happens to you in this life, I am with you, I love you, and I have a special place for you.

"Even when Jesus was dying on the cross, one thief who knew he was about to die in the most horrible way he could imagine, reached out to Jesus, and Jesus reached back."

Kyle nodded and made a quick note. "I think you accomplished that because the message comes through loud and clear... Hey, Ben, what's going on with your security panel?"

Ben looked toward the supposedly dormant security system. The panel featured a series of red LED lights, each one indicating motion sensors in every room of the house.

Every light was flashing.

"I have no clue. Shoot, the system isn't even active yet. The company is supposed to be sending somebody to activate it this week."

The smell washed over Ben in a putrid wave.

Craack

Kyle stopped in the middle of his next question. "What was that?"

"I don't know." Ben was already on his feet and headed for the hallway, the panel forgotten. Kyle put the notepad in his pocket and followed. Rachel and Stacy met them in the hall.

"What was that noise, Daddy?" Stacy's eyes were wide as she looked around the hallway.

"I don't know baby. It sounded like something broke." He looked at Rachel. "Is everything OK in the studio?"

"Yes," she said. "Everything's fine. I thought something had happened in the office." She pulled Stacy close to her. "Did anything fall over in your room, doodlebug?"

Stacy shook her head.

"Let's check the other rooms," Rachel said. "Maybe a picture or a mirror or something fell off the wall."

They searched each room, looking for anything out of place. They found no missing pictures, no bric-a-brac on the floor. Nothing in any of the rooms appeared to be broken or even out of place.

"That was weird," Kyle said. "That sounded for all the world like wood snapping. I heard the same sound once when I was doing a story in Morehead City. I found out too late there was a hurricane on the way."

"Did you get caught in it?" Rachel asked.

Kyle snickered. "Not really. I was stupid enough to think it would be cool to ride out a hurricane. I figured it would make a good story. So I wasn't trapped. I decided to stay."

"Was it worth it?" Ben asked.

"Well, I sold the story, but I almost got killed in the process. I got caught outside after the eye passed and almost didn't make it back in the shelter when the storm hit again."

"Man, you were lucky," Ben said.

Kyle nodded. "That's the truth. You know the old saying, God watches over drunks and fools, don't you? Well, since I don't drink, that narrows things down a bit." He folded his hands as if in prayer. "And I wouldn't be surprised if I said 'Thank You, Jesus' at least a hundred times before..."

Craack

"What in the world?" Kyle looked toward the end of the hallway.

Rachel flinched and stumbled a few steps when Stacy tried to pull her down the hall by her sweater sleeve.

"Mama, it came from down here. I heard it when it went off...it came from down here."

Rachel grabbed her daughter by the wrist and pulled her back. "Hang on Stacy. I heard it too, but let's be careful." She called to Ben and Kyle. They were already headed down the hall toward the stairway.

The men stopped and turned around. Ben saw a look of dread on his wife's face.

"Ben, remember the door?"

Fingers of cold glass bone gripped Ben Chalmers's spine.

He had almost put the incident out of his mind, but the events of that day came back in a rush. For an instant he was gripped by fear, but that emotion was quickly replaced by anger.

"Oh no." Ben took the stairs two at a time and almost tripped making the turn at the landing. He leaped over the last three steps and landed in the foyer. He looked toward the family room, but saw nothing out of place. He opened the front door, checked the immediate area outside, then scanned the area around the driveway.

Nothing.

No one.

He closed the door and was headed across the family room toward the deck when he heard Kyle call.

"Ben. I think you'd better come look at this."

Ben ran up to the landing and stopped. Kyle, Rachel, and Stacy were staring at the banister. The banister rail was broken almost in two just above the landing, and one of the spindles was snapped in half two steps farther down.

"I didn't do that, did I?" Ben looked from the damaged banister to Kyle.

"Ben, I think if you had done that, you'd have known it. That banister looks like solid oak, and it has to be a good three inches across." He stooped to look at the banister rail. "And that rail looks just as solid."

"What's going on with this house?" Rachel asked. She looked at Ben; her eyes were hard and her mouth was set in a firm line.

"You know," Kyle said, "it could be a defective piece of wood. If it had been twisted when the builder attached it, it's possible that the wood just snapped under the strain and took out a banister rail in the process."

"I guess that could happen," Rachel said. "Unless it's something like what happened with the door."

Ben's eyes widened. His mind raced, going over all the possibilities.

"Maybe," he said, "but if it had been something like that, we would have seen somebody this time. There is no way they could have gotten out of the house without me almost running into them."

Rachel's frown faded a bit. "I suppose so," she said, "but this is still awfully aggravating. A new house shouldn't be having problems like this." She fingered the jagged break in the banister. "We'll have to get Jim to look at this when he comes in tomorrow."

Stacy tugged on Rachel's sleeve. "What are you talking about, Mama? Who did we almost see?"

"Oh…um…Daddy had a visitor who came by while we were gone, and they didn't close the door all the way," Rachel said. She glanced at Ben. "When the wind slammed it back open and made a loud noise, it scared Daddy."

"Yep," Ben said, "I almost fainted." They weren't accustomed to lying, especially to their daughter, but this occasion seemed justified.

"I'll tell you what," Rachel said to Stacy as she gave Ben a more pointed glance. "How about if we go in the studio and you can help me work on my painting? Then Daddy and Kyle can go in the office and Daddy can tell him about the wind blowing the door open." She turned toward Ben. "How about that? You can tell him about the door and finish up the interview."

Ben nodded. "Yeah. Why don't we do that? I don't think there's anything else to see here. I'll call Jim and tell him so he can look at it when he comes tomorrow to put in the bookcase."

"And my animal shelves," Stacy said, all traces of apprehension gone.

"Yes ma'am, your animal shelves too," Ben said. "Come on, Kyle. Let's head in to the office, and I'll tell you all about the door. Then we can finish the interview while the two artists create a masterpiece."

THICK SHADOWS flowed across the floor, roiling in greasy black billows toward the corner of the room. A tendril of shadow slipped across the threshold, effectively blocking any light that might seep into the room.

The concrete floor rippled and bucked, throwing up minute sprays of concrete dust. It made a sound like giant's teeth clacking together. The movement lasted only a few seconds, but the room's occupant was beyond caring about time or space. All Tippy wanted to do was die.

The pain that flowed through his bones and sinews was like hot wax draining. He tried to howl once.

Twice.

The effort was like trying to swim against a river current.

He smelled the musty closed-in smells around him, but there was another smell. Something worse. Something bad.

He had smelled bad smells before. When the lady was dying, he smelled the disease. And the grief the man felt from her death had a bitter smell. He had smelled dead things, but this was worse. It was worse than the dead thing smell a hundred times over.

It smelled like fire and brimstone and death and hate and evil and rot and decay and all the bad things he had ever smelled plus a hundred more his brain could not comprehend.

Tippy was bleeding from his nose, and the floor absorbed the blood like a sponge.

His final memory was the smell of the lady when she died.

SOMETHING STIRS

KYLE CLOSED his notebook and put away his camera. Over the previous hour he had heard a remarkable story of God's grace at work in the life of a writer who wanted nothing more than to find a way to make the love of God real to those who read his work. He had also heard a story about one of the pitfalls of becoming a celebrity.

"Ben, I really appreciate your doing this interview on such short notice. I'll get started on the story on the plane and probably have it done by noon tomorrow." He flexed his fingers and stretched. "Boy, I'll tell you, that story about the door and having to call the sheriff was something. I think, though, I'm going to leave that out of the article if you don't mind. I don't want to give some other nut ideas."

"I appreciate that. One run-in like that is enough." He glanced toward the hallway. "I was afraid the same thing was happening again when that banister cracked, but if there had been somebody in the house, we would have had to have seen them when we ran to check on everything."

"Yeah," Kyle said, "but I don't mind telling you, that had me spooked for a while. What do you think happened to cause the wood to break like that?"

"There's no telling. But I'll call the fellow who is going to put in my bookcase tomorrow and have him take a look at it when he comes." Ben paused. "Then again, since he's already scheduled to come by, I don't see any real need to call him today. He can take a look…"

A high-pitched wail brought the conversation to an abrupt halt. The sound went straight through Kyle and made him flinch.

"Ben, what is *that?*"

Ben stood and listened, trying to pinpoint the origin of the keening. "I don't know. I've never heard…" A second cry, a little weaker than the first, but just as intense, pushed the men into motion.

"Come on," Ben said. "I think it came from outside."

Rachel stood in the hall outside her studio. "Ben, what was that sound? It sounded like something screaming."

179

"I don't know," he said, still moving with Kyle right behind. "Whatever it is, it sounded like it came from somewhere outside near the house." He saw Stacy behind her mother. "You two stay here, and we'll let you know what we find."

Ben and Kyle came to the foyer and stopped. "Did it sound like it was coming from the front of the house or the back?" Kyle asked. "I couldn't tell."

"Me either," Ben said. "Let's start at the front and work our way around."

They checked the yard then walked around the perimeter of the house, paying special attention to the area between any shrubs and the foundation of the house. If it was an animal, maybe it had been hurt and managed to drag itself to the house.

After making a complete circuit with no success, they walked through the edge of the woods. The late afternoon light filtered through the trees, touching them with soft fingers of autumn light. The woods were quiet. The only sounds were the leaves crunching underfoot and their own breathing.

"What could make a noise like that? I mean, I've heard a lot of things over the years, but that was the eeriest thing I have ever heard."

"Me too," Ben said. "It had to be an animal of some kind, but if it was, that animal was in a lot of pain. Maybe something a hunter wounded. I don't know." Ben glanced at his watch. "What I do know, though, is I need to quit holding you up and let you get on the road or you're going to miss your flight."

Kyle looked at his watch. "Yeah, I think you're right. But listen, let me know if you find whatever that was. I'm sort of curious, you know?"

"Um-hum." Ben scanned the leaves for signs of blood as they made their way out of the woods and back toward the house. "I'll do that." They walked around to the front of the house and Kyle stopped by the rental car.

"Ben, I really appreciate this. I'd normally go up and say goodbye to your wife, but I do need to hit the road." He opened the driver's side door. "But please tell her I was serious about coming back to do a story on her. I think my editor would go for it." He got in, closed the door, and lowered the window. "And it will be a good time to do a side story on the book you're finishing now, and take a look at how that one is doing then."

"OK, I'll tell her." He shook Kyle's hand through the open window. "And you take care."

Kyle nodded, started the car, and headed down the driveway. Ben watched until the car cleared the circle and headed toward the road below. Then he decided to look around the house one more time. The noise had seemed so close; it had to be between the house and the trees.

As he made his way behind the house, Ben saw Rachel standing on the deck.

"Any sign of whatever made all that racket?" she asked.

"No. Kyle and I checked around the house and just inside the woods. I'm going to look a little bit more." He looked toward the second floor windows. "How's Stacy?"

Rachel shook her head. "She's fine. Just before I came out here, she was upstairs playing with Piggy Anne." Rachel looked up toward the second floor windows as Ben had done. "She was giving her a good dressing down about something. When I walked by, she was saying, 'Quit grabbing me,' or something like that."

Ben looked at Rachel for a long moment. He started to say something, but she cut him off.

"Ben, don't say it." She pushed away from the rail and stood up straight. Her posture was suddenly stiff and formal. "I know we are going to have to do something about Piggy Anne. Stacy is getting too old to keep carrying her around. But we've just moved to a new house in a new town, and she needs a little time to adjust."

"OK," he said, "but we're going to have to talk about it sooner or later, and Dr. Halpern said…"

I know what Dr. Halpern said, and we'll do it. Just not now." She crossed her arms over her chest and waited.

Ben had seen that expression only a few times in their marriage, but he knew better than to carry that particular line of conversation much farther. Things were going along too well to purposely throw a monkey wrench in the works.

"Well, I don't suppose a little more time to get acclimated will hurt any of us, really." He looked for any sign that her mood was softening. "Besides, if she gets rid of Piggy Anne right now, next she'll probably want a dog."

The corners of Rachel's mouth curled upward a bit. Just a little, but enough.

"What harm can a few more days do?"

Rachel's posture shifted and the arms came down. Things were improving. She walked toward him, as far as the rail would allow. "Thank you, Ben. I know it's hard, but..." Rachel stopped and stood straight again, her head cocked to one side. "Honey, what's that sound?"

Ben listened. Heard nothing. He stood very still. So still he could feel his heart beating. Could feel the blood moving through his veins. Every nerve was attuned to one thing: trying to locate the phantom sound. When he turned his head to try a different angle, he heard minute popping sounds in his neck.

Just before he started to say he didn't hear anything, a sound came to him on the breeze. A small, breathy, terrified sound.

A whimper. Faint. Barely there at all.

"See? There it is again," Rachel said.

Ben turned his head again, trying to get his bearings. He heard it again, fainter this time, but it was enough.

"It's coming from the side of the house," he said. He ran to his right and stopped at the storage building. The 14x16 building was faced with the same stone as the rest of the house and was actually part of the house itself, but with the only entrance from the outside.

He looked around the base of the building but saw nothing. He listened for another moment. There was nothing there. He flinched when Rachel came up beside him and touched his arm.

"Sorry, honey," she said. "I didn't mean to scare you." She looked around. "Did you see anything?"

"No. Nothing." He stepped toward the door. "I know has been locked since we moved in, but I might as well look in here since we're right here." He pulled out the key, gripped the doorknob and pulled his hand back.

"Ow." He shook his hand.

"What is it?"

"I don't know." Ben looked at the palm of his hand. "That thing got hot all of a sudden." He gripped the knob and turned. At first he felt some resistance, then the door shuddered and opened inward.

The smell that assaulted him was his first shock.

Ben felt along the inside of the doorframe, his hand searching for the light switch. He found it and turned on the light. The darkness wasn't so much dispelled as it was just pushed aside. Ben stepped in the storage building and looked around the space. The room was empty except for a riding lawn mower and a floor stand containing an assortment of gardening tools: two rakes, a shovel, limb cutters, and a couple of hoes. He took another step inside and found a puddle of urine.

"Oh man," he said and looked at his shoe. "What did this…"

The rest of the sentence stuck in his throat like a splintered chicken bone. The second shock lay in the far corner of the room, off to his right.

It was the body of a dog.

A Border Collie.

And it looked like it had been dead for months.

CHAPTER TWENTY-THREE

RODNEY SPAT ON the pavement beside the Volvo station wagon. He had been waiting for fifteen minutes and he was not in the mood to wait much longer. If he hadn't needed the other three, he would have been gone long ago.

School was out for the day and the parking lot was vacant except for the cars belonging to a handful of teachers still dealing with paperwork, tests, and a PTA committee meeting. If anyone did happen to see the four of them getting into the car and driving off, there was nothing unusual about kids staying late for extracurricular activities on a Monday afternoon.

Rodney drummed his fingers on the car's hood. He was tired of waiting, and he planned to let them know how much when Kenny, Robin, and Myra got there.

The metal hooks on the flag rope clanged against the pole in front of the school. Pike's Crossing High was like many schools in the south. Leftovers from some previous decade, many of the buildings were in need of paint and the sign facing the road in front of the school needed to be replaced three years earlier, unlike the sign at the new magnet school just three miles away. Supposedly, it made more sense to spend seventeen million dollars for a new facility than to spend the two and a half million it would have cost to bring the high school back to its former glory, expansion included. So, it limped along on a shoestring budget with substandard facilities.

Rodney didn't care about the school politics. He was just ready to go. More than ready. He reached in his pocket and felt the piece of paper for the third time in fifteen minutes. It was a list of the items they would need for the ceremony.

He heard the crunch of tires on gravel and turned to see two figures on bicycles pulling up to the parking lot.

"Well you finally decided to show up, did you?" His voice was hard as flint. "Couldn't at least one of you tell time?"

"Look Rodney," Kenny said, his voice low, "we had to sneak out to get here, and it took me longer than I thought it would to get away, so I don't plan to stand here and answer a lot of stupid questions from you." He put down the kickstand and stepped off the bike. His steps were uncertain and he was having a difficult time walking.

Rodney stared in disbelief. Kenny had never shown any backbone before, and Rodney didn't like the current display a bit. He almost called Kenny on it until he saw how haggard the other boy looked. The sight of Kenny's gray face stopped him short.

"What happened to you?" Rodney looked at Kenny as if he was a bug in a science project. "You look like crap."

Kenny glared back at Rodney but didn't speak.

Myra parked her bike and joined the two boys. "Why couldn't you just come by and pick us up?" Myra asked. "You've got the car."

"I'm not running a chauffeur service. You come out here every day anyway, so I figured you could find it by yourselves." He paused and looked around the parking lot.

"Don't tell me we've got to wait for Robin." He looked at Kenny again, but with less curiosity. "Didn't I tell you to call her?"

Kenny raised his head slowly, as if it weighed twenty pounds and lifting it was an effort. "I did call her, and she said she's not coming."

"*She's what?*"

"She's not coming," Kenny said. "She said she didn't want anything else to do with this, and she is out of it completely."

Rodney's face went icy. "We'll see about that." He motioned toward the car with his head. "You two get in. We've got some errands to run before tonight."

"Errands? What kind of errands?" Myra glanced toward the car but didn't move.

"Errands," Rodney said. "We've got to get some stuff, and we don't have all afternoon. Now get in." He pressed the remote control button and all four doors clicked. He was already in the car before either one of his companions moved.

Rodney drummed his fingers on the steering wheel. "Hurry up. We've got a lot to do before tonight." He revved the motor and dropped the selector into drive as soon as both passengers were in the back. Kenny struggled to close the door.

"Nobody wants to sit up front?" Rodney spat out a mirthless laugh. "Well suit yourself."

"Where are we going?" Kenny asked.

Rodney turned to face him.

"Hey, keep your eyes on the road," Kenny said. He pressed himself into the leather seat and braced his feet on the floor.

Rodney laughed and turned his attention back to the road.

"We're going to a shop I know about in Boone to pick up what we'll need for the ceremony tonight. Then we're going to the SPCA and get another cat."

"Rodney, I don't know about this. You said we were going to get more supplies. You never said anything about getting an animal."

Rodney watched Kenny via the rear view mirror. "You don't look like you're in much shape to do anything about it." He glanced at the road ahead and looked at Kenny again. "What happened to you, anyway? You look like death eating onions."

Kenny looked down at the floorboard. "I can't take much more. I hear things all the time. Awful things." He raised his head and met the eyes watching him from the mirror. "I hear voices. And when I try to sleep, I see things."

"What's the matter? You getting spooked by a few nightmares?" Rodney grinned jack-o-lantern wide.

Kenny ignored the taunt. "No, these are worse. They're like visions." His head resumed its previous position. "If something doesn't happen tonight to make it stop, I don't know what I'll do."

He paused a moment and said in a softer voice, "Yes, I do. After tonight, I won't have any choice."

Rodney glanced at the clock in the dash. He needed to make better time if he was going to get everything he needed. The stores would be closing soon. He gunned the accelerator and the powerful wagon responded.

"How about you?" Rodney asked Myra. "Are you hearing spooky little voices too?" The venomous statement was designed to put her on edge as well, but her voice was dreamy and sounded far away.

"They're not so spooky." Myra twirled a strand of hair between her fingers and watched it take on a serpentine shape. "In fact, I have found them very helpful."

Kenny looked to his right. "How can that be helpful? How can you possibly say that? It's all I can do not to lose my mind." A single tear rolled down the craggy landscape of a face that appeared older than its few years.

"They're not just voices. They're spirits. They told me so. They are not the one Rodney was calling," she said, looking directly into the rearview mirror, "not nearly as powerful as that one. But they know things. Important things."

"Like what?" Rodney asked, his curiosity genuinely stirred for the moment. His attention drifted to the back seat as the car picked up velocity along the mountain road.

"They love me."

"What?" Kenny's body spasmed and he winced as he sat up. "Who loves you?"

"They do. The spirits. They said I would never be swapped from one family to another again. They said I was more than a tax write-off for some couple who could only feel adequate if they had a child in the house."

"Myra, what are you saying? The Webbs love you. I know they do."

"No, they don't. The spirits said they don't. They're just like all the other people who shuffled me around. And it's just a matter of time before Mr. Webb tries something funny with me. The spirits said so."

Kenny's face tightened. "You can't be serious. These things are not spirits. Not the kind you mean. They're...something else...they're..."

"Demons."

The voice came from the front seat. Rodney leaned back in the driver's seat and grinned. "They're probably demons. That's what we were summoning that night up at the house. At least we were trying to summon one in particular until Deputy Dawg came up and spoiled everything." Kenny punched the gas pedal a little harder, sending the Volvo whipping around the sweeping curves, now headed up a steep grade.

"Probably some minor demons slipped through during the ceremony. They're like a vanguard for the main attraction."

Kenny shook his head. "Myra, what did you do?"

"Yeah," Rodney said, "I'm curious too. What did you do? Have you been naughty?" The leer in his voice was nothing compared to the leer on his face. He turned around in the seat on a rare straight stretch of road and watched for her response.

"Let's just say I left them a message they will never forget." She smiled. "If they survive."

KENNY PLACED his hands on either side of his head and started to rock. "No, no, no, no." He continued to rock. "No, no...no." He looked at Rodney, who was now facing forward again and speeding on a downward grade toward Boone. The tires moaned in protest.

"Demons?" Kenny felt sick. In his head, the voices stopped whispering and began to laugh. The laughter was tinged with pure hate. With every breath he had left, he prayed.

Oh dear Jesus…

A spasm of pain unlike anything he had ever felt wracked every joint and muscle in his body. He started to convulse, but this time his prayer would not be denied.

I'm sorr…unngh…sorry.

Pain ripped through his gut like a rusty scalpel. Tears scalded his cheeks as he continued his prayer, teeth clenched. Gravity and excess speed rocked the car like a flag in a hurricane.

Jesus, puh…puh…please…

The voices in his head were screaming, louder than ever. Rodney reached back and hit him hard.

"Shut up!" Rodney's eyes were wild and his grip on the wheel was tenuous at best.

Jesuspleaseforgiveme.

The prayer came out in a rush of agony. It was followed by an explosion of blood and a viscous black substance from Kenny. He threw up violently, splashing the dashboard and the driver.

ALL RATIONAL thought now gone, Rodney released the wheel and turned in the driver's seat. He reached for Kenny with both hands, but Kenny had already slumped to the floor. Spent.

The Volvo hurtled into the guardrail, broke through, and was tossed back into the road when a portion of the axle tangled in the ravaged metal and concrete. It flipped, rolled sideways, and skidded on its roof in a shower of sparks. The car slammed into the solid granite face of the mountain a split second before a newlywed couple from Cranston, Rhode

Island, came around the curve from the opposite direction, narrowly missing the mangled wagon.

Joe Cherkes already had his cell phone out and was dialing 9-1-1 as his wife Cathy pulled their new Mercedes over and turned on the flashers.

The last thing Rodney Hardwick heard before slamming into oblivion was Myra Webb's shrill laugh.

AN EXPLOSION shattered the solitude of Barbary Court.

The upper story of Keith and Gayle Webb's Victorian house erupted in a concussive gout of fire. Neighbors on both sides of the street ran out of their houses amid a hail of flaming debris that covered the entire block. Black smoke lay like fog against the skin of the ruined house, extending tendrils here and there among the shocked onlookers.

In the distance, a fire truck screamed.

CHAPTER TWENTY-FOUR

BEN STOOD JUST inside the doorway to the storage room and looked at the mound in the corner. He found it hard to think of the pile of fur and bones as a dog, because there was little from this distance to indicate it had ever been alive. Even up close, had he not looked at the tag on the collar (and that had turned his stomach like nothing he had ever seen), he would not have been sure it was Tippy.

He couldn't bring himself to actually touch the dog, but he lifted the tag with an ink pen (which he doubted he'd use again) and read the name. He had seen hundreds of animals beside the road, road kill from every walk of animal life, and that was the closest thing he could think of to describe what lay in his storage room now.

Old road kill.

Two things puzzled him. One was the condition of the dog's body. The other was the question of how the dog had managed to get in the storage room in the first place. As best he knew, no one had been in the storage room since the moving men had put the lawn mower and the tool stand in there on moving day. And surely if the dog had been trapped in the room, it would have started barking when it got hungry or thirsty.

Then again, if he answered the question of how, there was still no explanation for the dog's emaciated appearance. Tippy had only been missing for a few days so there was no way the dog should have looked so wasted and atrophied in that length of time. Certainly not shriveled up and caving in on itself like this.

He moved a little closer, not really wanting to see, but unable to stop himself. Like a driver unable to pass a wrecked car on the highway without looking. The dog was a mass of matted fur and sharp angles. The hide seemed so thin that the bones were in danger of protruding through.

"Ben."

Ben jumped at the sound of Rachel's voice, like a kid at the end of the ghost story about the specter with the golden arm.

"Honey, I'm sorry. I didn't mean to scare you." Rachel touched Ben's shoulder. "I'm really sorry."

"It's OK," he said, covering her hand with his own. "I was just lost in thought." He glanced back toward what was left of the dog. "Still trying to figure out how this could have happened."

Rachel glanced in the same direction and shuddered. "Ugh. Honey, let's go back outside. I really don't like being in here with . . ." she glanced over one more time, then closed her eyes, "with *that*."

"Good idea." They left the room and Ben pulled the door until it was almost completely closed. "I'll just leave the door cracked a little."

They stood in the yard and spent a moment looking anywhere except at the room behind them. Ben finally broke the silence.

"Did you get Mario?"

"Yes." Rachel had offered to go in and make the phone call, more out of a need to get away from the aberration in the corner than a desire to be the bearer of bad news. "He's leaving the restaurant and coming right now." She brushed an imaginary piece of lint from her sweater. "I told him it could wait until tomorrow, but he was bound and determined to come right now." She brushed away another imaginary speck.

"He was crying when I hung up."

"Oh, man. This is going to kill him." Ben nudged a leaf with his foot. "You should have seen him with that dog." He sighed and shook his head.

Rachel looked back at the partially open door. "Honey, this hanging around outside feels a little morbid." She turned her attention back to Ben. "Let's go back inside and wait. This is just a little too strange for me."

He nodded and walked around to the front yard with her.

On the other side of the house, the storage room door clicked shut.

CHAPTER TWENTY-FIVE

ROBIN DAVIS LOOKED at the woman across the desk through a haze of tears. Things had been bad enough when she told her parents about what had happened at the house, but now to have to tell the sheriff. That just confirmed how wrong they had been that night.

That was the only way she could bring herself to refer to it anymore. *That night.*

The night she got on board a runaway emotional roller coaster.

"I'm s-so s-sorry," she stuttered, her throat seizing with every word. "I-I wanted to t-tell you s-so many times. I was just…just…" Robin broke down again. The tears came from a dark well that had been brimming for a while now. A swirl of emotion gripped her, and her sobs snatched the air from her lungs. The space between her shoulder blades ached with the effort, and her heart ached with guilt.

Her parents, one standing just behind her on either side of the chair, put their hands on her shoulders almost simultaneously. They kept them there until the sobs subsided.

"Honey, just tell the sheriff what you told us at home," Shirley Davis said. She stroked Robin's hair and rested her hand back on her shoulder. "I know it's hard, but you have to do this."

Her father squeezed her other shoulder gently. "I know this is hard for you. They were your friends. But don't worry pumpkin; we'll be right here with you."

Robin sat up and wiped her eyes with her hands. The sheriff reached in a desk drawer and handed Robin two tissues. She wiped her eyes again and blew her nose.

"Robin, are you ready to get started?"

Robin nodded and sniffed once more. "Yes ma'am. I guess so."

Elizabeth Cantrell leaned toward Robin slightly. "Robin, I want you to understand something. You're not in trouble. I know this is hard for you, and I think you are very brave to come forward the way you did. So what I need you to do is tell me the same thing you told your parents, and don't leave anything out. OK?"

Robin nodded and looked at the tissue in her lap.

"Robin?"

The girl looked up into the sheriff's face. She saw no trace of judgment or condescension. Just concern.

"Robin, what were you doing at the house that night?"

Robin glanced at each of her parents. Tom Davis nodded at his daughter. Robin sat up in her chair and took a deep breath.

"I thought we were going up there to make an occult circle." She looked at a spot on the sheriff's desk. "You know, just sort of fool around with a Ouija board and creep each other out. At least that's what Rodney told us we were going to do."

"Robin, exactly who went to the house that night," Elizabeth asked.

Another deep breath.

"It was me, Myra Webb, Kenny Randall, and Rodney Hardwick. The ones who were killed..." she looked out the window, "killed...in the... the accident." Her breathing was still ragged, and mentioning the wreck released another sob. Her mother started to say something, but the sheriff shook her head and waited for Robin to recover.

"We were going up to sit around and tell spooky stories and then fool around with a Ouija board. That kind of stuff. It's kind of like a club. Or at least that's what we thought we were doing. Just making an occult circle. But Rodney wanted to do something else."

"What did he want to do?" the sheriff asked.

"He wanted to conjure an entity."

"He wanted to do what?" The sheriff sat up in her chair.

"He wanted to conjure an entity. Or that's what he said." She closed her eyes and saw the events of the night once more. "He had some bowls and stuff to go in them. And he drew a five-pointed star on the floor and put candles around it. Then he lit the candles and started arranging all the stuff he brought.

"I was pretty scared by that time, and I just wanted to leave. And that's what I did a few minutes later. I ran out of the house." She turned and looked at her mother. "I'm sorry, Mama. I know I shouldn't have gone up there. It just seemed like something fun to do." She looked over at her father. "You know, like telling ghost stories at camp.

"But Rodney didn't want to do that. He wanted to do something wrong. Something really wrong." Robin looked from her father to her mother, then brought her hands up to her face and cried.

"Robin." The sheriff said her name with such tenderness that the tears stopped almost as quickly as they started. "Robin, why did Rodney want to conjure this thing he was talking about?"

"Sheriff!" Robin's mother interrupted the questions. She was no longer smiling. "You can't be serious. You don't actually believe that boy was going to conjure some kind of thing, do you?"

"No ma'am I don't believe anything of the kind. But I do want to know something about what he was thinking at the time. Maybe that way I can get a better handle on what went on that night." She turned her attention back to Robin.

"Robin, you're doing fine. Now tell me again, why did he say he was going to conjure this thing?"

"He said it would do whatever we wanted it to do. Said that he didn't want to have to wait for his trust fund, and how we shouldn't have to wait for things either.

"I...I...know it was wrong. And I'm so ashamed. I wanted to leave so bad when he started talking crazy. And I think Kenny wanted to leave too, but he wouldn't. And My...My...Myra wanted to stay." For the next few minutes Robin could hardly speak. She shook all over with a combination of guilt and grief. More tissues found their way into her hand and she used them all. Then she closed her fist around the sodden ball.

"Mama, that could have been me in that car. I...I was supposed to go today too." She lifted her head and looked at the sheriff for a moment. "And now they're dead. I'm the only one left."

"You're the only one left because you had the good sense to realize what you were doing and get out of that house," the sheriff said. "And I think you are very brave to be sitting here telling us all this. I really appreciate you doing this, because it may help somebody else at some point." She looked up at Robin's parents. "But I want to ask you another question. OK?" Robin nodded. "Do you remember anything else about that night? Anything you saw or anything you heard?"

Robin shook her head.

"Anything? Anything at all? Even if you think it's not important."

"Book."

"Pardon?"

"There was a book. An old-looking book that Rodney was going to use in his ceremony. I remember it because it felt like the room got colder when he took it out and showed it to us." She kneaded the ball of tissues in her hand. "I know that sounds stupid, but it seemed like that's what happened."

"And that's all you remember?"

"Yes, ma'am," Robin said. "I mean yes, Sheriff."

Elizabeth smiled. "Yes, ma'am is fine. And again, I really appreciate your coming forward like this. It took a lot of guts."

Robin looked down at the mangled tissue. "Yeah, but if I had said something sooner, they might not have been killed. Somebody might have been able to talk to them."

"Maybe," her father said, "and maybe not. That's one of those things we can't possibly know."

"Yes sir, but they were going to get more supplies so they could go back into the woods behind the house and finish the ceremony. That's what Kenny told me when he called and wanted me to go too." She wiped her eyes.

"Still," Tom said, "you don't know that anyone could have stopped them."

"He's right," the sheriff said. "If not today, it could have been some other day. No, now the thing I have to try and figure out is why a teenage girl would blow the top of her house off with a homemade bomb."

"What?" Shirley looked at the sheriff in disbelief.

"Somebody blew the Webbs' house almost in half a couple of hours ago. From the looks of it, Myra may have been the one who planted the bomb just before she went to meet the other kids at school. It was a miracle there was nobody home when it exploded because it destroyed the second story and caved in most of the first."

Tom rubbed the side of his face. "But what makes you think it was her? What makes you think it was Myra?"

"I really can't say why," the sheriff said, "other than there is some pretty strong evidence it was her. Now I've got to figure out why a teenage girl would do something like that."

Silence blanketed the room for a full minute. Then Robin spoke again.

"Maybe it was the voices."

CHAPTER TWENTY-SIX

POWER SURGED THROUGH *It*. More power than It had experienced since being trapped in the place called a house. But the imprisonment would not last much longer. It was gaining strength and abilities by the hour. Already It was starting to exert Its influence. Mostly in small ways, but that too would change.

There was much life in the house, and It meant to have it.

All of it.

The young one especially. Her life would be delicious.

There would be blood. So much blood. And It would revel in the power until It emerged from the wood and stone womb in which it now nurtured itself.

The minor demons had failed in their mission. It was not sure how It knew, but the knowledge itself was enough.

It sensed a presence nearby. A small presence to be sure, but a presence. It concentrated, expanded Its mind, and reached out psychically.

The being was not strong willed and soon succumbed to the call.

It fed.

Not a great amount this time. But It fed.

There would be more.

THE SQUIRREL stopped searching for the hickory nut it had buried in the vicinity months earlier and cocked its head.

Something was happening. Something that hurt.

The squirrel turned back to its digging, its forepaws moving frantically against the ground. It stopped in mid claw and stood on its hind legs. A bolt of pain lanced its skull and a gout of blood erupted from one eye socket.

The squirrel spun around and launched itself toward the foundation of the house. The force of its body hitting the concrete made a tiny thwapping sound.

It convulsed against the house for a full half minute, then fell away drained.

CHAPTER TWENTY-SEVEN

ACHEL WATCHED THE car pull onto the driveway. It had been a bright pearl gray coupe the first time its owner had visited the house, but now it seemed to be a dull, funeral parlor gray. A hazy overcast gray trick of the senses fueled by the unhappy work at hand.

She saw Mario Binelli get out of the car and walk toward the house. There was no beaming smile this time. No bounce in his step. No aura of joy surrounding his rotund frame. There was only the face of a man who has lost his best friend.

Rachel went out and met him on the front porch. She watched him mount the steps, trying with each step to keep his composure. The click of his shoes on the stone walkway seemed too loud in the late afternoon silence. The only other sounds were the ticking of his car's cooling engine and the whisper of her own breath.

He mounted the top step and stopped in front of her, eyes downcast like a little boy waiting for a parent's judgment.

Rachel broke the awkward silence.

"Mario, I am so sorry..."

Mario's shoulders hitched and a small sob hiccupped to the surface. He raised his head and looked into Rachel's face.

"How could this happen?" Mario wiped his eyes with the back of his hand. They were red and his complexion was blotchy. "He was such a good dog. He never ran away before, not even when he was a puppy." A tear traced a path along the smooth contour of his cheek. "And now..."

He broke down just as Ben came outside. Rachel glanced at her husband, and without a word, they put their arms around their grieving friend. They held him while the dam holding back his full grief broke. His anguish rolled out in a series of small, choked, staccato bursts.

They held him until he regained his composure. He put his arms around each of them and hugged them hard. Then he straightened up, wiped his eyes one more time, and exhaled.

"My good friends. I cannot thank you enough for what you have done."

"I'm not sure we have done very much," Rachel said.

"Nonsense. You and your husband went looking for my little Tippy, even in the rain. And you have both been so kind to an old man who grieves for something as silly to most people as a dog."

"A friend is a friend, two-legged or four-legged," Ben said.

"That's right," Rachel agreed. "And a good dog can be one of the best."

Mario nodded. "Yes, but I suppose it is time to face the inevitable." He turned and walked toward his car.

"Mario," Rachel called after him, "where are you going?"

He paused. "I have a large plastic bag in the car." His voice broke.

"Why don't you leave that in the car," Ben said. "I have a small moving blanket you can have. I think that would be more fitting."

Mario nodded and walked back to his former spot on the walkway. Ben disappeared in the house and returned a minute or two later with a pale blue blanket.

"Here we go," Ben said. "This will be more suitable." The trio went around the side of the house and walked toward the storage building. They stopped at the entrance.

Rachel looked at the door and frowned. Hadn't the door been open earlier? She shook her head.

"What is it?" Ben asked.

She closed her eyes for a second and reopened them. The uncertain feeling was still there. "Oh, nothing," she said. "I just…" She struggled to find something to say. Something that would seem plausible.

"I know," Ben said. "Let's go ahead and do what has to be done." He put a hand on Mario's shoulder. "You stay out here and I'll go in and get Tippy." Mario nodded but said nothing. "This will only take a minute."

HE TURNED the knob and opened the door. A cool draft clutched at his skin and drew goose bumps. He shuddered and stepped inside. Once inside the storage room he felt along the wall until he found the light switch. He switched on the overhead light, but it didn't seem as bright as it had earlier. Almost as if the room absorbed a portion of the illumination.

Ben took a deep breath and walked to the place where Mario's dog had died. He did not relish the idea of touching the dog, even through the blanket. But there was no way he was going to let the dog's owner come in and face the mass of bones and matted fur.

He spread a portion of the blanket over the corpse and let it drape over the dog and bunch up against the wall. He reached through the fabric in the crevice formed between the dog and the wall and rolled the animal toward himself. The corpse was stiff and made a crackling sound as it pulled away from the wall.

Bile pooled in the back of Ben's throat. His stomach revolted but held its contents. He turned his head to the left and took a deep breath. The air was thick and the room had developed a musty, almost fermented odor. He steeled himself and finished pulling what was left of the dog onto the blanket. The rabies tag clicked against the collar as the macabre bundle settled into place.

He folded the blanket around the dog, tucked in the corners, and left the storage building with the grisly package.

When Ben came out with the blanket, Rachel stepped a little closer to Mario. The chef stood tall, with little trace of the former sadness. Instead, his face was set with a grim determination.

Ben offered to place the dog in Mario's trunk, but he declined the offer. "Please," Mario said, "may I see him? My little Tippy."

Ben and Rachel exchanged a prolonged glance.

"Mario," she said, "do you really think that is a good idea? Wouldn't it be better to just leave him wrapped up like this?"

"No," Mario said. "You are both good friends, but I have to do this. I have to see him once more." He looked at the couple standing in front of him. Then he knelt down and unwrapped the bundle.

Ben opened his mouth to say something, then stopped. His words would have been too late.

Mario folded back the last flap and recoiled at the sight of the mass of matted fur and sharp angles on the ground in front of him. He looked up at Ben and Rachel, then back at the horror on the ground in front of him.

The dog looked like it had collapsed in on itself. There was a vague outline of what could have been a dog once; a sharp canine face structure with a protruding snout. The skin on the face had receded so far that the features were locked into a permanent snarl. The fur was drawn so tight to the dog's body that every bone showed through. The body itself lay at an unnatural angle, contorted as if in the throes of agony.

"How?" Mario looked at the abomination before him. "How could this have happened?" He looked at the couple standing over him. Rachel had a hand up to her mouth. Ben bit his lower lip but said nothing.

"Where did you find him?" Mario asked.

Ben motioned toward the storage building with his head. "He was in there."

Mario looked at Ben. "How did he get in there? We should have heard him when we walked around the house if he was in the storage room, shouldn't we?" His face was a storm of emotion.

Ben rubbed his hairline just above his left eyebrow. "I certainly would have thought so, but Mario, I didn't hear anything that sounded remotely like a dog or any other kind of animal." He rubbed the spot again.

"How long had he been in there?" Mario stood and walked over to the open door. He peered inside.

Rachel walked up beside him. "We don't know. The fact is, we're not even sure how he could have gotten in there in the first place. The only time the door has been open that we can remember was the day the movers put the lawn mower and the tool rack in there."

Mario walked back over to the lifeless form on the blanket.

"Then how could this happen?" He gestured toward the dog. "What could cause this kind of thing to happen? I just don't understand." He bent down and folded the blanket around his companion. A single tear dropped on the fabric, spread along a patchwork of threads the size of a dime, and was absorbed into the material.

Mario picked up the little bundle and stood, this time with more effort. His movements were slow and deliberate. He held the remains of his companion close to his chest and looked toward the open storage-building door.

"Come on, let's go back around to the front," Rachel said. "It's getting cold out here." She put a hand on Mario's shoulder. "And we can help you get Tippy in the car, then fix you a hot cup of coffee before you have to go back."

Ben walked toward the storage building. "Good idea. Just let me close this door."

As he approached the doorway, the door slammed in his face.

Ben jumped backwards and tripped over the edge of the flagstone pad in front of the doorway. He backpedaled three or four steps.

"Ben!" Rachel rushed forward and put her hand in the small of his back just as he regained his footing.

"Are you alright?" she asked. Ben's eyes were wide, and he was breathing hard.

"Yeah," he said. "Yeah, I'm OK." He looked at the closed door. "That just caught me off guard."

"Uh-huh," she said as she stared at the door. "Ben, how did that happen?"

"I don't have the slightest idea." He walked over and touched the door. It didn't budge. It was closed tight. "That is just weird."

"Come on," Rachel said. "Let's go."

"I will, in just a minute." He leaned in toward the door and sniffed. "Rachel, come here. Do you smell something?"

"Ben, come on and let's just go."

"No, really." He looked at her. "There's something else inside. There has to be."

Before Rachel could protest, Ben opened the door, disappeared inside the storage area, and closed the door behind himself.

A moment later, he emerged.

"Well?" she said.

"I don't know." He closed the door once more and checked to make sure it was closed. "I didn't see anything else. And I checked the hinges just in case something was wrong with them, but they seem OK. The floor and the threshold both seem pretty level, so I don't know why the door shut like that.

"But that smell. That's the thing. I noticed that same smell when Kyle and I went to check on the broken banister."

Mario shifted his burden and sighed.

"It's the smell of death."

CHAPTER TWENTY-EIGHT

NEAT STACKS OF wood lined the walls of the shop, and scores of power and hand tools occupied their specific places, ready to cut, bind, plane, and polish the fragrant oak, pine, and cedar planks. Plastic storage bins fixed to the walls held screws, nails, drill bits, router bits, brads, wood screws, and other smaller items in strategic locations.

Jim ran his hand over the various sections that would comprise Ben's bookcase and storage unit. He was always pleased when a project turned out the way he envisioned. It was at that moment that the hours of preparation, construction, and careful finishing all came together. He knew that his precise attention to every dovetail and mortise-and-tenon joint would go unnoticed by most of his customers.

But he would know.

Jim was running his finger along the face of a shelf, feeling for any minor imperfection, when the phone rang.

It was Sheriff Cantrell.

"Sheriff, this is a surprise." An image of Elizabeth Cantrell formed in his mind. "To what do I owe the pleasure?"

"Well, I don't know if you'll consider it a pleasure or not, but before I go any further, please, call me Liz."

Jim's heart beat a little faster. He paused a second, then answered. "OK Liz, what can I do for you?" His heart was skipping along at full throttle.

"I'm not sure, really. I just wanted to run something by you, but I need to ask you to keep it just between us if you will. At least for now."

Jim sat on a worktable, his heart moving back into its regular range. "OK, I can do that."

There was silence on the other end of the phone for a few seconds. Then she began.

"I'm really not sure where to start." Another pause. "And I may be reading things into what I know that aren't really there. But, here goes.

"I had a visit from Robin Davis and her parents. It turns out she was one of four kids who were up at the Chalmerses' house the night we found the occult paraphernalia out there. She said they were supposed to be going up there to have some kind of occult circle. You know, sitting around telling scary stories and fooling around with an Ouija board. But one of the kids had something else in mind."

There was silence on the other end of the line. Jim assumed she was gauging her words. "Liz, there is very little I haven't heard before, so don't worry about shocking me." He took a deep breath. "Was it sex?"

"I almost wish it was that simple. Then I would have an idea how to handle it. But from what Robin told me, one of the kids named Rodney Hardwick wanted to take things beyond that." He heard paper rustling on the other end of the line. "He wanted to conjure some kind of spirit, or entity."

"A what?" Jim stood again and gripped the telephone hard.

"She said he wanted to conjure some kind of entity to do things for them. That was when she told him he was crazy and left, before things got out of hand."

"Thank God she had the good sense to get out of there before anything bad happened," Jim said. "The occult is nothing to fool around with.

Even something as simple as a Ouija board can become a dangerous obsession." He measured his words. "Or worse."

"I'm not sure things can get much worse."

"How so? I thought you said she left before they started doing whatever they were going to do."

"She did. But evidently, the other three decided to finish what they started. So they were on their way to Boone to get what they needed for the ceremony, and the car they were in hit a guard rail, flipped over to the opposite side of the road, and smashed into the mountain."

"Oh no..."

"Oh yes. And that's not all." He heard a touch of fatigue in her voice. "While we were investigating the accident, Keith and Gayle Webb's house exploded."

"Exploded? How in the world...?"

"From everything we've been able to piece together, it looks like their foster daughter, Myra, planted a homemade bomb in the house before she went to meet the others. It blew the top of the house completely off."

"Oh, dear Lord. Please tell me nobody was hurt."

"Normally everybody would have been at home," she said, "but their son, Buddy, needed a new pair of sneakers, so they decided to head to the mall, get the shoes, and stop for pizza."

"And you say it looks like Myra did it?" Jim shook his head. He knew the Webbs, and he couldn't imagine why Myra would do something like that. The family had always seemed happy when he saw them out in the community. Of course, you never knew what lived in the dark corners of anyone's heart. He knew that all too well.

"I'm afraid so. We found some pretty convincing evidence."

"Oh man..." Jim switched the phone to his other hand. "What can I do to help?"

"I don't know of anything in particular," Liz said. "I think I just wanted to hear it all out loud and see if I could make any sense out of it. Something about all this doesn't seem right…I mean other than the obvious…and I just can't put my finger on it. Look, I'm sorry I bothered you."

"Liz, you're not bothering me in the least." He paced around the workshop. "I don't know that I've helped you very much, but if all you needed was a sounding board, then I'm glad I was here."

"Thank you, Jim. I really appreciate it. I think more than anything else, it's the fact that we go for such long stretches where nothing happens around here. The most we ever see is a little shoplifting, a few petty burglaries, and the occasional drunk getting a little too belligerent. After that, a day like this seems to really upset the balance.

"Still…" she fell silent.

"Well, tell me this," Jim said. "What did you find that night over at the house? You've mentioned that you found some occult items out there. What were they?"

"We found some bowls, a couple of sandwich bags with an odd assortment of items, a book of some kind that looks like it might be written in Latin, and a very wicked looking dagger."

"A dagger?" Jim gripped the phone tight.

"A nasty one. This thing has a serpentine blade and is sharp as a razor."

"What in the world were they going to do with a dagger like that…or any dagger for that matter?"

"My deputy thinks they intended to sacrifice a cat. He said he saw one huddled in the corner when he first investigated the scene. It came out of the corner like a bat out of…I mean…it was really moving. Like it was terrified." She paused. "He said it scared him so bad at first he almost shot it in self-defense."

"Poor cat. That's two lives down and seven to go." He barked a laugh at his own joke, and Liz did the same. But something was forming in the back of his mind. More a feeling than anything else, and he couldn't quite put a name to it. But it was there nonetheless.

"Liz, I've got to head up to the Chalmerses' house tomorrow to put in some bookcases. How much of this do they know?"

"They know about the pentagram we found on the floor, and they know we found some occult-related items. In fact, Mrs. Chalmers was concerned about it being done by a satanic cult at first. But after we explained to her that there has been no similar activity anywhere in this part of the state, she figured, as we did, that it was just kids out doing something they shouldn't have been doing, just like kids have always done. Playing with the occult."

Jim sighed. "That kind of thing is nothing to experiment with." He paused and looked at the bookcase sections. "While I'm over there tomorrow, I'll keep my ears open in case they bring up the subject. Hopefully, though, they have been able to get beyond it and get on with the business of settling in."

RACHEL STOOD at the kitchen sink and looked out the window. It was the same view she had from her studio, but being one floor down gave her a different perspective on the landscape. She drank a glass of water and thought about making another pot of coffee. There was something soothing about the aroma of mocha or hazelnut crème.

She glanced at the coffeemaker, but decided to wait. Maybe she would fix hot chocolate after supper. She returned her attention back to the landscape beyond the window.

Scritch...

scritch...scritch.

Scritch...

The noise pulled her attention back to the kitchen. The sound was soft, urgent, and vaguely familiar.

Scritch...

There it was again. She couldn't place it. The noise seemed to come from the walls, from the ceiling, from...

"Mama!"

Stacy's shout pushed the noise into the background. Rachel ran from the kitchen toward the sound of her daughter's voice. Stacy stood in the family room, staring at the floor.

"What's wrong honey?" Rachel stopped next to Stacy and looked where her daughter was looking.

The floor was covered with fungus. Lazy loops and arrow straight tendrils of grayish-green covered the floor. Intertwining. Intersecting. Mingling.

"What is it?" Stacy asked, not looking away from the bizarre display.

"I don't know. It looks like some kind of mold or fungus or something." She took a step back. Stacy remained where she was.

"Eww, Mama, it stinks."

Rachel pulled Stacy back, then realized her daughter was right. Whatever was on the floor was pungent. Like spoiled food and ammonia. And the shape seemed to continue under the end table and under the couch.

Rachel's throat clutched.

"Stacy, help me move this stuff," she said. They moved the end table off to the side and struggled with the sofa until it was at a ninety-degree angle to its former position. They stepped back to see how far the fungus damage had spread.

Rachel looked at the anomaly in its entirety and gasped. The putrid tendrils formed a perfect pentagram.

"Oh my dear Lord Jesus."

The moment she said the words, it sounded like the kitchen exploded. Stacy screamed and grabbed Rachel around the waist.

"Mama, what's happening? What's happening?"

Rachel squatted down and held Stacy by the shoulders. She made sure she had her daughter's complete attention. "Honey, you run upstairs and get Daddy. I'm going to go see what happened." She gave her shoulders a slight squeeze. "Go now."

Stacy turned and ran.

Rachel moved toward the kitchen.

Broken plates, glasses, platters, and mugs created an alien landscape on the kitchen floor. Serving pieces, trivets, and sundry plastic storage containers lay in clusters among the rubble. Rachel put a hand to her mouth and stifled a scream.

She looked at the cabinets and gasped.

They were pulled away from the wall and hanging at a crazy angle. Almost as if they had been wrenched out of the wall and left dangling. All seven doors hung open and all the cabinets' contents lay shattered on the floor.

Rachel jumped when she heard Ben's voice.

"What in the world..."

She pivoted around to face him. "What in the world? Is that all you can say? What in the world?" Tears cascaded down her cheeks. "Well I'll tell you what in the world." She gestured toward the shattered tableware. "This house is coming apart, and we're just lucky somebody hasn't been hurt."

Ben moved back a step. "Hey, calm down. I--"

"Calm down?" She choked back a sob. "Don't tell me to calm down. There is just about every dish we own shattered all over the floor." She wiped her eyes with the backs of her hands and pointed. "Look at the cabinets."

Ben stepped around her and walked in the kitchen as far as he could without stepping on a shard of stoneware or china.

The two cabinets above the refrigerator jerked away from the wall and vomited their contents behind him.

Ben scrambled toward the doorway. Rachel grabbed his shirt and pulled him through. Gleaming shards of glass glittered wickedly from the debris that had once held their meals and snacks.

"Ben, are you alright?"

"Yeah, I think so."

Scritch...scritch.

Ben looked around the room.

Scritch...

"What is that sound?"

"I don't have the slightest idea," Rachel said. "I heard it earlier but then the dishes fell, and..." She stopped and looked around the room.

"What is it now?" Ben asked.

"Where's Stacy?"

"Huh?"

"Stacy. Where's Stacy? Didn't she come downstairs with you?"

"Yeah. She was right behind me."

They looked around the room again, then peered into the kitchen.

"Maybe in all the confusion, she went upstairs," Ben said.

Rachel turned and ran toward the stairs, calling Stacy's name. Ben was two steps behind her. Rachel topped the steps and continued to call. She checked each room as she came to it, then stopped in front of Stacy's room.

Stacy cowered in the far corner of her room. She clutched Piggy Anne tight to her chest and looked up with wide eyes.

"Is it over, Mommy?"

Rachel ran to her and gathered her in her arms. Piggy Anne was squeezed between them like a rag doll sandwich.

"I think so, baby. I think so." She hugged Stacy again and held her. "Why didn't you stay downstairs with us? You could have been hurt."

"I'm sorry," she sniffed. Tears rimmed her eyes. "I got scared so I ran up here and found Piggy Anne. She was almost under the bed." She turned her wet eyes toward her father. "I'm sorry."

Ben looked at Rachel, then back to his daughter. He knelt down and smoothed her hair. "It's OK, doodlebug. You just had us worried, that's all."

Rachel nodded. "That's right honey; we just didn't want you to get hurt." She released her daughter and looked her over. Stacy still held Piggy Anne to her chest, but not as tight. "Are you sure you're OK?" Rachel asked. Stacy nodded. She put Piggy Anne on the bed. "I'm OK." She looked at Piggy Anne for a long moment.

"What's with you and Piggy Anne?" Ben said. "You look like you're expecting her to do a cartwheel or something."

"No, just making sure she stays on the bed."

"Why?" Ben asked. "Does she have a habit of jumping off the bed and running around the room?"

"No sir. I don't think she's running around."

Ben nodded.

"I think she might be crawling, though."

Rachel wrinkled her brow. "Now why would Piggy Anne be crawling around? Has she lost a contact or something?"

"I don't know why," Stacy said. "I just keep putting her up, and she keeps trying to crawl under the bed."

"I think she's probably just falling off of her perch on the headboard," Rachel said. "If the cabinets can be pulled out of the wall like that, I don't think it will be too hard for a doll to fall on the floor."

"I think she jumps down when I'm not looking."

Rachel sat on the edge of Stacy's bed. "Stacy, there are a lot of strange things happening right now, but I don't think Piggy Anne is one of them. Sometimes things just fall down. Sometimes strange things happen. But there's always an explanation.

"Now maybe you didn't put her on the headboard good, or maybe you dropped her on the floor and just thought you put her up because you were sleepy. But that's all it is." She picked Piggy Anne up and held her at arm's length. "She is a pretty big doll, and she could fall over during the night." Rachel looked at Piggy Anne and wrinkled her forehead again. A thought tried to form in her mind. Failed. And she put the doll back on the bed.

"Speaking of strange things, I'm going to go back downstairs with Daddy and show him what we found beside the couch. You stay up here and play, and maybe in a little while we'll go out to see Mario and get some pizza. How about that?"

Stacy glanced at her doll. "OK."

"Come on," Rachel said to Ben. "There's something else you need to see down here. Then I want you to call Jim. This house is not right."

They went downstairs.

The moment Rachel saw the pentagram on the floor, the thought she had been searching for surfaced.

The fabric on Piggy Anne's hands and knees was scuffed and threadbare.

≡

JIM PUT the telephone back in its charger and closed his eyes. The story Ben and Rachel had just told him was troubling. First, the physical problems with the house didn't sound right. The banister shouldn't break, even if the wood was twisted. It would twist in the brackets and pull them away from the wall, but they shouldn't snap. And there was no way those cabinets would pull out of the wall. Of that, he was certain.

He had designed them so the bracing inside the cabinets lined up with the studs in the wall, and each bracing strip had eight heavy-duty wood screws going through the brace, through the half inch back of the cabinet, and almost two inches into the stud itself. Those cabinets would be a major pain to remove even for a professional demolition crew, so a family's stoneware couldn't pull them off the walls.

But the thing that really bothered him was the fungus on the floor. Fungus, or mold, or whatever, didn't grow in a design pattern. It just wasn't natural. And Ben and Rachel Chalmers didn't seem to be the kind of folks who saw the face of Jesus on a moldy piece of bread…or satanic symbols formed by fungus on a new hardwood floor.

And there was something else. Something he couldn't put his finger on. He opened his eyes and looked around the room. It didn't look much like the kind of room a man would design. But then again, Gwen had selected all the furniture, made the ruffled country curtains, and even painted the room a soft, pastel shade of blue.

It had been their family room—he couldn't bring himself to call it a den with all the ruffles and knick-knacks—back when they had hopes of having a family of their own. Back before the accident.

He sighed and turned his mind back to the Chalmerses. Something else about their conversation nagged at him, but he couldn't place it. He told Ben and Rachel he would come out earlier than he originally planned tomorrow so he could look things over and see about reattaching the cabinets.

But something was wrong. Something Rachel said.

Something…

It was about the same time I saw that nasty fungus on the floor. I remember I said, "Oh my dear Lord Jesus" because the stuff on the floor just shocked me. Then all of a sudden, it sounded like World War II in the kitchen.

Jim sat up in his chair. His breath caught in his lungs. His mind raced from conclusion to conclusion, weighing, examining, evaluating. He exhaled, gripped the telephone again, and dialed the sheriff's office.

The dispatcher answered on the second ring and promptly transferred him to the sheriff's phone. She said she was sure the sheriff would be glad to talk to him. Then she said something else that he filed away in his mind for later. Right now, he had to talk to Sheriff Cantrell, not Liz.

The sheriff answered on the first ring and sounded happy to hear from him. He hoped that was still the case after he told her what he wanted to do.

Jim told her about the conversation he'd just had with Ben and Rachel. Then came the favor he needed.

"The thing is," he said, "I have a huge favor to ask. I need to see if you'll let me photocopy the book you found at the house. The one with the Latin writing in it."

The sheriff asked why he wanted the copies.

"This is going to sound a little strange, but I want to fax them to a friend of mine in Atlanta. He is a professor at Emory University. I'd like to see if he'll translate them for me."

"What does the translation have to do with what is happening at the house?"

"Nothing I hope," he said, "but there may be something there that could shed a little light on what those kids were doing out there that night." He kept his ultimate fear to himself, partially because he didn't want Liz to think he was going off the deep end.

And partially because if he didn't give the thought utterance, then maybe he would be wrong.

Liz's voice cut through the connection. "Jim, I'm sorry. As much as I'd like to, I can't let you photocopy evidence."

He closed his eyes and sighed.

"But," she continued, "There's nothing to say I can't photocopy it for you. Will about half an hour be OK?"

Jim thanked her and hung up the phone. He breathed a silent prayer, then turned his attention back to the last thing the dispatcher said to him.

"I think she kind of likes you."

CHAPTER TWENTY-NINE

*I*T SUMMONED THEM by the dozens and they came. It was growing stronger by the hour, and soon it would have enough life to break free. The smell of human flesh was growing stronger. The smell of sacrifice was growing stronger.

It found that by manipulating the young human's doll, It could follow the human flesh through Its prison. It had also found that it was possible to use the doll to gather small items.

Sharp items.

Items It would need in time.

It had been surprised by the extent of Its reaction to the name of the Prince. The name was terrifying, and when the female human uttered it, the reaction was almost instantaneous. When the other human used it, the lesser response was equally instantaneous, and it was taking less time to recoup Its strength.

The minor demons were wandering aimlessly since their hosts were dead. Eventually they would seek new hosts or be recalled to the pit.

But it made no matter. Soon It would be free.

And the next time the humans uttered the name of the Prince, It may very well kill them all.

KYLE ROTH looked at the image in the view screen of his camera again. There was no way in the world he could be seeing what he thought he saw.

Things like that didn't exist.

What was more disturbing was the fact that he knew there was nothing in the viewfinder other than Ben Chalmers when he took the picture. Granted, he took a few quick shots in succession, but he would have remembered seeing something like this.

It looked like a living nightmare. Something out of Lovecraft.

He downloaded the picture to his computer, attached it to an e-mail, and then reached for the phone. Ben needed to see this.

Kyle paced while the phone rang. "Come on Ben, pick up."

The phone rang seven times.

"Hello."

"Thank goodness you're home," he said. "Rachel, could I speak to…"

"We're not in right now, and we're really sorry we missed your call…"

"No!" Kyle said. "Come on, Ben. It's Kyle Roth. If you're there, pick up please."

"…but if you'll leave a message, we'll call you as soon as we are able. God Bless You."

Beeep.

"Ben, this is Kyle. I just sent a photograph to your e-mail address. I have no idea what in the Sam Hill the thing in the picture is, but I think you really need to take a look at it." He clenched his fist in frustration. "Call me when you've had a chance to look at it."

Kyle left his number and severed the connection.

Then, for the first time in years, he prayed.

CHAPTER THIRTY

IM LOOKED OVER the photocopied pages and put them back in the folder on Liz Cantrell's desk. She had the copies finished and waiting for him when he arrived.

"Liz, I really appreciate this. I hope it doesn't get you into any kind of trouble."

"I don't think it will. Just tell the professor or whoever you're sending them to not to be passing them around. In fact, if he'd file them away, or better yet, shred them when he's through translating them for you, I think it'll be fine." She was sitting on the edge of her desk while Jim occupied the same chair he had used on his previous visit.

"I'm sure he will be very discreet." Jim dug through his shirt pocket and came up with a piece of paper. "I hate to keep imposing, but would it be possible for me to fax them from here? I don't have a fax machine at home, and I'm not sure the library is still open. I'll be glad to pay for them."

"I don't think that will be a problem."

Jim stood up, reached in his pants pocket, and brought out a cell phone. "I'll call and let him know the pages are coming."

"OK, you call and I'll start faxing the pages." She took the paper from him and walked to the fax machine. "Do you need a cover sheet?"

Jim looked up from the phone. "No, this is his home fax number. He'll know what they are as soon as he sees them."

The ancient text traveled through the phone line and spooled itself out as Jim finished his call.

"Thanks Liz. He said the first page was just arriving as we were finishing up." Jim slipped the phone in his shirt pocket. "Now, how much do I owe you for the fax?"

She grinned. "Hmmm, for a fax traveling all the way to Atlanta, that could be pretty pricey. It could cost you as much as a cup of coffee."

Jim smiled at her and noticed again how the uniform didn't hide one bit of her beauty. He imagined she would look wonderful in just about anything. "Well, considering they went all the way to Atlanta, how about if we make it coffee and dessert at Casa Binelli's one night? Or maybe even dinner followed by coffee and dessert." He held his breath, afraid he had said too much.

Liz looked at him for a few seconds without speaking. It was the equivalent of a lifetime of silence.

"That sounds nice."

Jim nodded. "Really? Ah, good." He shifted foot-to-foot like a teenager asking for a first date. "What night is good for you?"

Liz glanced at the desk calendar. "I've got to be on duty about twelve hours tomorrow. How about the night after that?"

"That's great. Say about seven? And I can come by and pick you up if you want me to."

"Seven is fine with me." She wrote something on a piece of paper and handed it to him. "Here is my address. I'll be ready."

Their fingers brushed during the exchange, a gossamer-light touch. Neither one spoke, but they looked at each other a little longer than would normally have been comfortable.

Normally.

After a moment, Liz broke the silence.

"Jim, what does that batch of pages we just faxed over have to do with the Chalmerses? Are they in some kind of trouble?"

"I honestly don't know. I hope not, but when I talked to Rachel and Ben earlier, they both told me some things that just don't add up. There are some pretty strange things going on over there, and as much as I'd like to think there are natural causes, I don't know."

Liz cocked her head to one side. "What kind of things?"

"There are a lot of little things, but the ones that have me worried are the most recent things. Just today, two sets of cabinets were almost pulled out of the wall in the kitchen. And Rachel found some kind of mold or fungus or something growing in the family room."

Liz sat on the edge of the desk again and motioned for him to take the chair. "So? I know a cabinet almost coming down is unusual, but it's not impossible, is it? And lots of people have mold problems." A fine line formed on her forehead.

"In itself, no. It's not impossible." He sat down and leaned forward in the chair. "But I put these cabinets in myself, and while I'm not infallible by any stretch of the imagination, I know for a fact that the way these cabinets were braced and attached to the wall, it would have taken a demolition crew to rip them out." He sat back and made a quick calculation. "There were over sixty heavy duty screws holding those cabinets on the wall, and each one was attached to a stud."

Liz made a low whistling sound. "It sure sounds like they're up there to stay. But hypothetically, isn't it possible that the cabinets could fall on their own? No offense intended."

"Oh sure, anything's possible. But I'm wondering if it happened on its own. I think it's possible those cabinets had some help."

"Are you saying the Chalmerses did it?"

"No, no. Nothing like that. But I do think—and here's the part where you are probably going to call the county psychiatrist—that something else did." He closed his eyes, took a deep breath, and took a chance.

"I think something in the house did it. Something they can't see."

"Are you saying the house is…is haunted?" The fine line developed into a furrow.

"I don't know exactly what I'm saying. I'm not sure if haunted is even the right word, but I think there is something in there with them. Something dangerous." He saw a shadow pass across her features. "Just hear me out. Remember the mold on the floor? Well it wasn't just growing in a clump. Rachel said it was growing in the shape of a pentagram."

Liz's mouth hung open. Jim waited for the full impact of the statement to sink in and continued. "And the cabinets didn't just fall off the wall. Rachel used the name of Jesus and almost immediately, she heard a big crash in the kitchen. The exact same thing happened to Ben not five minutes later."

"Jim, you can't be serious." Liz rubbed the right side of her face lightly. "This sounds like something out of a Stephen King story. Fungus growing in the shape of a pentagram, cabinets flying off the wall. It's all just a bit much to take in."

"I hope I'm wrong about all this. But I don't know what else to think. Maybe tomorrow when I go by the house I'll see that they were exaggerating, or that there is some rational explanation for everything."

"You're going by there tomorrow?"

"Uh-huh. I am supposed to put in a bookcase and hang some shelves. So that will give me a chance to see what's going on."

Liz bit her lower lip. "If they've had all that trouble today, is it safe for them to stay there?"

Jim shrugged. "It depends on what's actually going on. But when I talked to them earlier, Ben said they were going to Casa Binelli's for pizza, then they were headed to a hotel for the night. Rachel said she just couldn't face having to clean everything up with all that had happened."

"That may be for the best." She stood and walked to Jim's side of the desk. "Jim." She hesitated for a moment, then continued. "Are things like what you described really possible? I mean, this is the twenty-first century."

"Oh it's possible. You don't hear much about it because we have become so enlightened that we can always attribute such things to our imagination, or find some rational explanation." He made a quotation mark sign with his fingers on the word rational. "But regardless of the times or the amount of enlightenment we claim to have, evil has always been present, and it always will be.

"There are things we don't understand, and our lack of understanding acts like a cloak of invisibility for them. Ignorance is bliss, and modernity is camouflage."

Liz shuddered. "Jim, what kind of things could be in the house?"

Jim stood up.

"I'm hoping that's what Dr. Ward can tell me."

CHAPTER THIRTY-ONE

DAVID WARD RETRIEVED he pages from his printer and sat down at his desk. He had been surprised to hear from Jim Perry, even though they'd had many stimulating conversations over the years. As a student, Jim had always shown a desire to examine issues from every angle in an attempt to discover the underlying truth. As his ministry progressed, he had tended his flocks with compassion.

David had always liked discussing theology with Jim, and as their relationship developed from professional to one of friendship, he came to respect Jim's keen mind and strong faith.

Then Jim's wife died in that horrible accident and he retreated into himself. He had almost shut down completely while he tried to deal with the tragedy. Maybe this request for help with a translation was the beginning of Jim's coming back into the world.

"Let's see what you've got for me tonight Jim, old boy," Dr. Ward said as he settled back into the leather desk chair and looked at the first page.

The first two lines startled him. He re-read them twice to be certain of what he was seeing.

"Good Lord, Jim, what have you sent me?"

He worked through the first page slowly, making notes in the margins, and pausing more than once to pull books from their respective shelves to check a reference or an obscure word.

The one that bothered him the most was a not-so-obscure word.

Ashmedai.

Had Jim really said someone had been using this? He hoped not. That would be tantamount to using napalm to get rid of dandelions in the back yard.

David looked at the clock in his study. It had taken about an hour to translate the first page. Not bad, but what he had found caused him to be more cautious than usual, rechecking words and phrases he knew to be correct, and using more source materials than normal in the hopes he had missed some shade of meaning or regional dialect anomaly. If his translation was accurate, the ritual he was uncovering was dangerous at best—perhaps even deadly.

He went to the kitchen, put on a pot of coffee, and waited for the coffee to brew. The few minutes it took for the coffeemaker to run through the cycle gave him time to think.

Ashmedai. That name was bad news. Surely someone wouldn't be foolish enough to use that creature's name in the kind of ritual it looked like he was dealing with. Ashmedai was evil personified. A demonic destructive force with no rival.

David closed his eyes and breathed a silent prayer.

Father, give me the ability to translate these words correctly. What they have shown so far has me scared, and I am afraid of what else I may find. There is terrible danger in these words. Father, please, be with Jim and those on whose behalf he is working. Surround them with your love and place around them a hedge of protection from whatever they may encounter. In Jesus' name, I pray. Amen.

When the coffee finished brewing, he poured a cup for himself, then poured the rest in a thermal carafe and returned to his study. For the first time in his career, he hoped his translation was wrong.

David sighed and got back to work.

It was going to be a long night.

RACHEL STARED at the ceiling. The first time they had stayed in this motel there was an air of excitement about the new house. Now, it seemed like the house was turning against them. She had wondered in the beginning if they were moving too fast. Buying a house in a place they had never heard of before. But she had kept her reservations to herself because Ben seemed so happy.

Now, she wondered. Couldn't he see what was happening? He couldn't be that oblivious. Could he?

And what about Stacy? How much more could she take? Hadn't she been through enough pain for a lifetime already?

Rachel stared at the ceiling. Sleep proved to be an elusive butterfly, flitting teasingly close, then fluttering just out of reach.

She stared at the ceiling and wondered what tomorrow would be like when they walked through the door and confronted the mess in the kitchen. Would there be more damage, or was the house through throwing out its structural surprises? To his credit, Ben had been the one to suggest they come out to the motel and face everything tomorrow when Jim came to look things over.

Maybe it was a good idea, and maybe he was just avoiding the fact that there was something wrong with their "dream house."

She looked across the room in the second queen-sized bed. Stacy was asleep in a tangle of sheets, her arm draped across Piggy Anne.

That was something they were going to have to address soon, too. She was compensating with the doll. And it was about time for her to let Piggy Anne go. A couple of times over the past week or two it almost seemed as if she was going to do it on her own. But from the time they left the driveway, Stacy had returned to holding on to her stuffed friend.

Even Mario had commented on how close she seemed to be with Piggy Anne when they went to his restaurant for supper. He had looked very tired, and much of the old sparkle had faded from his eyes. But the subject of Tippy had not surfaced, and the small talk seemed a little strained.

Maybe tomorrow would be better. At least she sincerely hoped so. She wasn't sure how much more she could take.

Rachel closed her eyes.

It was going to be a long night.

ASHMEDAI CALLED out and they came. *It* was not able to reach out far, but the woods nearby provided a sufficient supply for the time being. Later there would be more and larger prey, but for now, it was enough.

The cloth doll was gone, but Ashmedai had enough of a sense of *Its* surroundings to move from room-to-room. Still trapped, Ashmedai was learning to interact with *Its* surroundings more forcefully with each passing hour.

Ashmedai willed itself along the walls and into the lair of the male. It reached out along the floor, across the walls, along the work area. The surfaces rippled and settled back to their normal state.

It lingered a few moments more, then returned to Its own lair. But Ashmedai would be trapped only a short time longer. Soon there would be sufficient blood spilled to make the transposition complete.

CHAPTER THIRTY-TWO

JIM SAT IN his truck and looked at the house. He was about fifteen minutes early on purpose. He wanted a chance to walk around and see if there was any evidence from the outside that the house had some sort of structural problems. Maybe if he could find some rational explanation for what the family had experienced so far, he could discount his "other" theory.

He got out of the truck and walked up the circular drive. "I'd really like to find some problem with you," he said to the house. "Maybe they were exaggerating."

Jim walked around the corner of the house, stopping every few feet to look at an exterior wall, the foundation of the house, or the angle of the roofline.

Everything looked the way it should.

He came to the storage building attached to the house. He tried the door but it was locked. He looked at the seam that ran between the house and the building. The mortar was smooth and even. There was no sign of settling or the smaller building pulling away from the house. He walked up on the deck and looked in through the glass doors.

Everything seemed to be in order. He couldn't see far enough to see into the kitchen—the angle it sat from the doors made that impossible—but from all he could tell, it was just a large, well-appointed house. He looked a moment longer, then went back to the ground level. He continued walking, still stopping every few feet, until he had made a complete circuit of the structure.

He walked up to the front door again and stood in front of it as if he were waiting for someone to answer and invite him in. He waited a little longer then started to turn away. A stray sound caught his attention. He stood still and listened.

The air was still. At first, the only sound he heard was that of his boot shifting on the porch. A dry, rasp of leather on stone. No dogs barked in the distance. No crows cawed, no squirrels made a raceway of the dry leaves scattered across the landscape.

The silence was eerie. There should have been something moving this time of year. And now the phantom sound he heard was gone. Jim moved a step closer to the door. Maybe it had been some appliance coming on inside the house or the heat pump switching itself on.

He listened to the air. Nothing.

Just quiet.

Jim turned to leave again. There it was.

He put his ear to the door and listened. The door seemed to vibrate slightly, and there was a low, thrumming sound. It seemed to come from the door itself. He straightened up, then leaned in and listened again.

Nothing.

No vibration. No sound. Just a heavy wooden door. Jim touched the door. Again, nothing.

Just a door.

He stepped off the porch and walked back toward his truck. He looked up at the roofline once again. "Are you what you seem to be? Are you just a house, or is there something else going on with you?"

He opened the tailgate and sat down on it. Jim decided to wait for the Chalmerses to come home and see what was going on inside the house. He didn't have to wait long. Within five minutes, the Jeep pulled up in the driveway. Jim could tell there was an animated conversation taking place in the SUV, so he stayed where he was and didn't go to meet the family.

After about half a minute, three doors opened and the family piled out and made a beeline for the door.

"Ben, all I'm saying is that we might have moved a little too fast is all. Got a little too much money and went a little crazy for a day or so. That's all I'm saying. You know, this did all happen pretty fast once the ball started rolling."

Ben kept walking. He didn't acknowledge Rachel's argument. Just kept walking. And Stacy brought up the rear, her doll clasped to her chest. She didn't smile. She did little more than glance toward Jim, and kept walking. She didn't seem to be in a hurry to catch up, but at the same time, she kept her parents within eyesight.

Jim frowned. This wasn't the family he had visited with on previous occasions. These people seemed like strangers. Even to each other. And in the short time he'd known them, he never imagined they would get so caught up in a squabble that they would shut each other out.

The voices grew in intensity. He heard them from where he sat out in the driveway.

"Look at this mess! Does this look like the kind of thing that just happens? It looks like just another in a series of mistakes…mistakes that cost us dearly!" The angry voice belonged to Rachel.

"Uh-uh," Jim said to no one in particular. "Not today. Not if I can help it." He jogged up on the porch and let himself in. It was easy since the door was standing open.

Rachel and Ben stood in the doorway leading to the kitchen. She was gesturing and Ben was looking off into space.

"Have you seen this? Really seen it?" Rachel shouted. "Look at this mess and tell me buying this house wasn't a mistake!"

Ben glanced at Jim and mumbled. "We have company."

Rachel turned around and saw Jim. Her voice dropped in volume, but not intensity. "Hello Jim," she said. "We were just discussing what to do about the kitchen."

Jim looked at her for a moment. Then he looked at Ben. From their body language, they may as well have been in two different houses.

"Really?" he asked. "It sounded like you were fighting to me."

The shock on their faces was exactly what he had hoped for. Years of counseling people, breaking up fights, and listening to parishioners talk about how wrong their spouses were had left him with a pretty deep bag of counseling techniques, and from what he could tell, he was going to have to shock Ben and Rachel out of whatever it was they were fighting over... and fast.

The stakes were excessively high.

"What?" Ben was the first to speak.

"Listen," Jim said. "I don't know what happened to the folks I saw here just a few days ago, but you two are not the same people."

Ben spoke, but Jim cut him off. "No, before you say anything, answer one question for me." He watched them for any sign they were going to challenge him. But his change in demeanor had them off balance enough that he pressed on. "Without looking around, where is Stacy?"

They looked at each other and around the room.

"Uh-uh, I said without looking. Where is she?"

They looked at him with shock and shame on their faces.

"The couple I know who moved into this house would have known where their daughter was because they would have seen her come in the house and would have spent at least a few minutes talking to her and joking with her.

"The couple I know wouldn't have embarrassed themselves by walking past a friend, one looking like he wants to be anywhere else in the world but here, and the other yelling for all the world to hear." He took a deep breath. "That little girl looked like someone had sucked the last bit of joy out of her life, and I would suggest you need to go upstairs and comfort her." He put a hand on each of their shoulders. "You need to go let her know her parents haven't lost their minds. Then we need to talk."

Something in their eyes changed. A flicker of the light that once lived there was coming back. They began to apologize, but he waved them off.

"Go to her. Then we'll talk."

They ran up the stairs calling Stacy's name. In the meantime, Jim walked over and looked at the pentagram on the floor. This was the spot where the kids had marked out the symbol, of that he was sure. He shuddered and moved away fast. He needed to call David Ward more than ever.

Next, he walked into the ruins that had once been the kitchen. Stoneware and glass crunched underfoot as he made his way to the cabinets. From the angle the cabinets were hanging, fully two thirds of the long screws that held the cabinets in place had to have been ripped out of the wall. He brushed away some of the debris and boosted himself up on the sink. He craned his neck and looked behind one section of cabinet.

The screw holes he could see were splintered. Great shards of wood had pulled away from the anchor points. It wasn't the look of screws that had slipped out or been gradually pulled away from the wall.

It took a lot of force to rip the cabinets away. An unimaginable amount of force.

He looked at the two single cabinets over the refrigerator. If he reached up and pulled on one, he had no doubt it would come off the wall easily.

There couldn't be more than five or six screws holding them up.

Scritch...scritch...scritch...scritch...scritch, scritch...scritch, scritch... scritch...

scritch...

Jim listened to the sounds coming from the walls, the ceiling, from every corner of the kitchen. It sounded like tiny scampering feet.

"Jim."

He recognized Rachel's voice. And this time it sounded a lot more like the old Rachel.

"In here," he said as he made his way toward the doorway. "I was just looking at these cabinets."

Rachel and Stacy met him in the family room. Stacy looked better than she had when she walked by him earlier.

"Hi, Stacy," he said. "How's your mom doing?"

Stacy looked at her mother, then back to Jim. "I think she's better. She was just really scared."

Jim looked back toward the kitchen. "Yeah, I'll bet. I'd be out buying new underwear if that had happened to me." Stacy giggled and he grinned back at her. Then he turned his attention back to Rachel. "How about it, Mom? Are you OK?"

"Well, I'm better." She hung her head. "I'm also pretty ashamed. We've never acted like that before." She looked up. "I've never even raised my voice to Ben before. Much less screamed like a banshee." She looked at Stacy. "And I'm sorry you had to see all that, honey." She knelt down. "I'm so sorry." She hugged Stacy hard and made no pretense about the tears that flowed freely.

Stacy stroked her mother's back with her free hand. Piggy Anne was held captive by the other. "It's OK, Mama. I was a little scared too."

They hugged a moment longer.

Rachel stood again. "Jim, what's happening? I find it hard to believe we're having these kinds of problems with a new house."

Jim wanted to see the extent of the damage they had experienced. Maybe that would give him a clue. Anything to dispel the notion that kept growing in the back of his mind, although the pentagram had all but ruled out every other possibility.

"Rachel, show me where the banister broke." He followed her to the stairs. She pointed to the landing and he walked up.

He examined the breaks and scratched his head. He looked at the bracket that held the banister rail and came back down stairs.

"That's odd." He looked back up toward the landing. "That's really odd."

"What's odd?" Rachel started up the stairs, then stopped.

"The railing," Jim said. "The way it is designed, there is room for the rail to turn inside the mounting bracket. That way if the rail had been twisted, it shouldn't have been bound up against the bracket and pulled against it. It would float in the bracket."

"What does that translate to in English?" Rachel asked.

"It means it shouldn't have broken like that, even if the wood was twisted. And the brackets aren't pulled away from the wall. The rail is just broken."

"It doesn't make sense."

"What doesn't make sense?" Ben made his way into the room.

"That banister rail," Jim said. "I was just telling Rachel that if the wood had been twisted or formed wrong, that kind of pressure would have pulled the mounting brackets away from the wall. But that didn't happen."

"Oh, OK." Ben walked over and stood next to Rachel. No one spoke for a moment. The unspoken question of the couple's behavior hung like a pall all around them. Finally, Ben broke the silence.

"Jim, I'm afraid we owe you an apology. What you saw earlier was not like us at all, although I have to admit, your approach was something of a surprise too. But we were really out of line."

"Well, I'll admit, I was shocked," Jim said. "You two remind me so much of Gwen and me when she was still alive, and I guess that's what prompted me to come in and give you both barrels."

He waited for a reply. When none came, he continued. "When Gwen died, I felt like a part of my heart had been ripped away. And while I didn't blame God, I did blame the drunk that hit her. I wanted him to be the one who died. Sometimes I wished for it. I had the hardest time trying to figure out why God would take somebody like Gwen and let some stupid drunk walk away from the accident with little more than a bruised arm and a hangover."

Ben spoke up. "How *did* you deal with that?" There was something pleading in the question.

"I finally came to terms with an explanation that makes sense to me. I don't think God really had a lot to do with it."

Ben and Rachel looked puzzled. "How could God not have anything to do with who lives and dies?" Rachel asked.

"I think God is more concerned with being there when we grieve than causing the grief. The hard cold truth is that we are all going to die. And death comes in every form from lingering disease to a gentle drifting away in your sleep…or at the hands of a drunk driver.

"What I finally began to realize, even though I was working hard to build a shell around myself, is that there were people coming out of the woodwork to offer comfort, bring food, hold my hand, offer encouragement, and otherwise just be there for me. Even months after the accident. And many of them were not even members of my former church.

"That's where God was in all of this. Not deciding who lived and died. Alcohol and the laws of physics took care of that. But once it happened, God set about seeing to it that I was constantly reminded that He works through His people. And even though I pushed them away in order to wrap myself in grief, they gave me space, but never let me forget they were there." He paused a moment and let the words sink in. "Even when I turned to woodworking and started working in other people's homes, they constantly reminded me of two things; how sad they were that Gwen had died, and how happy we had always seemed together."

A tear touched the corner of his eye. "She was God's great gift to me. And when I saw you two earlier, I knew I had to do something before you lost sight of the same thing."

"We know about losing something precious," Ben said. He sat on the couch and looked at a spot between his feet. Then he glanced up at Stacy. Rachel caught his glance.

"Hey, doodlebug, how about if you go to up your room and play," Rachel said. Stacy said OK and scampered off. Rachel turned her attention back to her husband.

"Ben, you don't have to do this," she said. "You really don't."

Ben looked up. "Yes, I do." He looked at Jim. "We lost something precious once. One of the most precious things you can imagine."

Jim held the younger man's gaze. "Ben, I know you lost a child in an accident. You told me that much before. But that's all you ever said about it.

"It was our son. Brandon. He…" Ben stopped and swallowed hard. Rachel sat next to him and touched his arm.

"…we were at a neighbor's house. At a birthday party. There were a lot of people there, lots of adults and children. And the people who owned the house had a pool." He closed his eyes hard. "There was a gate leading to the pool and it was supposed to be locked. But it wasn't…"

Ben kept his eyes closed, squeezed them tighter. "…and somehow Brandon got inside the…inside the fence. And he fell in the pool."

Ben's shoulders hitched and the nightmare poured out through his sobs. Rachel held him close.

"Jim, when we realized Brandon had wandered off, we started looking for him. One minute he was playing with some of the other children, and the next minute he was…" Rachel rubbed her eyes with her sleeve. Before she could continue, Ben cried out.

"Oh God, he was in the water. I ran to the edge of the pool, and he was in the water." He looked up through red-rimmed eyes. "I reached out but I couldn't grab him, and then I froze. I couldn't move." He looked at Jim through pleading eyes, his face a tortured mask.

"The next thing I knew, I was in the water flailing around. I don't even remember jumping in the pool. Then I felt an arm around my chest. Someone was pulling me out of the water. I kept screaming for Brandon, but they were pulling me out of the water."

"Why were they pulling you out?" The shock registered in Jim's voice. "What about your son?"

Ben tried to breathe around the sobs, but could not. Rachel finished for him.

"Ben never learned to swim. And by the time he jumped in the water to try and save Brandon, he was already dead.

"Two men from the party jumped in the pool. One grabbed Ben, and the other brought Brandon's body out."

"Oh my…" Jim sat on the chair across from the shaken couple. "I had no idea."

"Not many people do," Rachel said. "We don't talk about him very much. Our pastor at the time said we should be glad that we had him for a time, and that we shouldn't grieve. God evidently had a place for Brandon and was ready for him."

Jim's jaw dropped. "What?"

"Yeah," Ben said. "He said there was really no need for us to grieve. We still had a beautiful daughter, and grief would only slow the healing process. He said we should pray regularly and let God help us deal with the loss privately, because Brandon had evidently served his purpose here on earth."

Jim gripped the arms of the chair. "What a load of bullshit."

"What did you say?" Rachel's eyes were wide.

"That's a theological phrase I use once in a while," Jim said. "It means whoever that alleged preacher is, needs to have his head examined. Just as soon as he pulls it out of his backside." Jim shook his head. "Of all the unmitigated, unfeeling bullshit I have ever heard in my life, that takes the cake. What were you supposed to do, just cut your grief off like a spigot and get on with living your life as if nothing happened? That's the most insensitive, hurtful thing I've ever heard."

"Well then, how do you deal with it?" Ben looked at Jim, his eyes wet. "How do you square God's plan against your own?"

Jim walked over and sat on the sofa beside Ben. "First, you have to look at it from God's perspective." He turned to face Ben. "You see, I'm not convinced God decided it was time for Brandon to die."

Rachel leaned forward.

"No, I think when your son drowned that God was as heartbroken as you were. Remember, He had a son who died too. And I think when Brandon got to heaven that God held him in His arms and told him it would be all right. That his mommy and daddy would be there for him one day. That's what I think.

"That's what kept me sane when I lost everything precious to me."

"Then where was God in that pool?" Ben asked. "My son was dying and all I could do was stand there and watch. Where was God then?"

Before Jim could speak, Rachel turned her husband's head toward her. "I think I know," she said, tears of grief mixed with tears of joy. "He was in the heart of a man willing to risk his life to save his son." She smiled at him. "You didn't just stand there. You jumped in, knowing you couldn't swim, and you almost died trying to save our son."

They fell into each other's arms and cried for their son. A few minutes later, Ben looked up and wiped his eyes. They were still red, but the haunted look was less evident.

"In our effort not to dredge up the past and get on with our lives, somewhere along the way we also expected Stacy to do the same thing. You see, she saw Brandon being pulled from the pool. And then when we didn't talk about it, neither did she."

"Instead," Rachel said, "my sister gave her Piggy Anne in an effort to help cheer her up. And she has substituted Piggy Anne for Brandon." Rachel took a deep breath. "Piggy Anne became to her what our respective artistic endeavors became to us--A poor substitute."

They sat in silence a few more minutes.

Scritch...scritch.

Jim looked around the room, listening for the source of the noise. "Hmmm. Sounds like you've got squirrels in the attic." He looked at the fungus-encrusted symbol. The two-ton elephant in the room. "And you've got a stain on the floor that needs to come up as soon as possible." Jim checked his watch, then looked at his friends. The pentagram unnerved him, but the last thing he needed to do was start a panic.

"Look," Jim said, "if you don't mind, what if I wait to put in the bookcase until later? I know this sounds like an excuse, but I really need to go home and make a phone call." He stood up. "Plus, I think you may have some things to finish talking over."

Ben and Rachel nodded.

"But listen, it might be a good idea for you to get out of the house for another day or two. I need to check on something that may have a real bearing on this situation, and you may be safer somewhere else until this is all cleared up."

"What do you mean?" Rachel stood to face him. "If we need to wait on the bookcases, that's fine. But do you really think the house is that dangerous?"

Jim opened his mouth, danced on the verge of telling them his real fear, but stopped short. "I'm not sure just yet," he said. "But I should have some answers soon. That's what the phone call is about." He looked at Ben. "If you'd be willing to give me your cell phone number, I'll call you as soon as I know something."

"Sure," Ben said. "I don't mind giving you the number, but we should be OK here. The only reason we stayed away last night was that it all just seemed a little much to deal with after the fact. We should be OK here."

Jim shook his head. "I really think it would be better if you took Stacy and Rachel out of here for a day or two."

Rachel rubbed the side of her face. "If you think it's not safe, we could go back to the Daystar motel for a day or so." She looked at Ben. "Stacy loves motel rooms and restaurant food. She thinks it means we're on a vacation."

Ben smiled. "I guess another night or two won't hurt anything."

"Good." Jim wrote down the phone number Ben gave him. "I'll call you as soon as I have an answer."

The three friends hugged at the door and as they joined hands, Jim offered a prayer.

"Please dear Lord, give these brave children of yours a sense of your peace. Hold them in the palm of your hand, dry their tears, and touch their lives with the joy that comes from loving you. Bless their memories of their son Brandon, and thank you for bringing him back into their lives. Help them deal with their loss, and in so doing, draw them closer together"— Ben and Rachel squeezed his hands—"and closer to you. Amen."

"Thank you." Rachel kissed his cheek and Ben hugged him once more.

"You're welcome. I'll call you as soon as I can."

Jim headed to his truck while Ben and Rachel went back in the house.

"BEN, I'M so sorry. I said some pretty awful things last night and earlier today…"

Ben's kiss caught her by surprise. "Honey, that's all in the past. I didn't help the situation by shutting you out. So let's just let it go and concentrate on getting our family back on track." He hugged her and she hugged him back. "I think Jim was right. We need to let Brandon's memory back into our lives. God didn't take him, and he didn't pack his pictures away in a box."

Rachel nodded. "You're right. And maybe if we start by talking to Stacy about what happened, let her know it's OK to talk about Brandon, she can start to let that doll go."

Ben kissed her forehead. "I hope so. I tell you what. You go get the munchkin and I'll go get the Jeep."

"OK." Rachel paused. "Hey, before you get the Jeep, would you mind taking a look up in the attic and see if there really are squirrels up there?"

"Squirrels?

"Yeah. I kept hearing this noise off and on this week and couldn't for the life of me figure out what it was. But I think Jim just put his finger on it. We may have squirrels in the attic."

"OK, you get Stacy and I'll look up in the attic real quick."

BEN STOPPED at the door that hid the pull-down steps in the ceiling. He reached up and pulled the door down, followed by the folding steps.

He flipped the switch on the wall that activated the lights in the attic, and went up. When his head cleared the floor level of the attic, he gasped. He was looking at a miniature version of the valley of the shadow of death.

The floor was littered with animal corpses. There were squirrels, bats, birds, snakes, chipmunks, field mice, a few raccoons, and half a dozen possums. All dead. All dried to the stage of mummification. There must have been three or four dozen at least.

"Oh man." He turned away from the necropolis that had formed along the length of the attic, gagged, and half tripped down the folding stairs.

Rachel came back with Stacy in tow. "Are you OK?" Rachel steadied him on the last two steps.

Ben folded the stairs up. "Yeah, just a little shaken up is all."

Rachel looked puzzled. "Was it squirrels?"

"Yeah," Ben said as he walked to the office, "and before we leave, I'm going to call Norm Scott and find out when he can come over and fix the hole where they are coming in. I figure this is a job for the contractor. Plus, he should really be the one to take care of all the other problems too, since he built the house. We don't need to drop all that on Jim."

He found the number, dialed it, and prayed that Rachel wouldn't want to look in the attic.

CHAPTER THIRTY-THREE

JIM WALKED IN the house and grabbed his cell phone. He couldn't believe he had given Dr. Ward the number then walked out this morning and left the phone behind. He flipped the top open, and sure enough, there was one message. He keyed in his PIN and waited.

"Jim, it's David. Please tell me this is some kind of research you are doing, although I don't know why you would be researching something like this. In fact, please call me as soon as you get this message, even if it means pulling me out of class.

"Jim, I'm really serious. This is some scary stuff, and I want you to be sure about whatever it is you've found. I'm leaving my cell number so you can call anytime."

Jim made a mental note of the number and punched it into his own phone. David picked up on the first ring.

"Hello. Jim?"

"Yes, it's me. How are you, David?"

"I'm well, or at least I was until I saw those pages you faxed over last night." There was a brief pause. "Jim, what is this?"

"That's what I was hoping you could tell me." Jim walked into the kitchen and sat at the table. He glanced at the clock over the doorway. "Look, before you get into this, I'm not pulling you away from a class or anything, am I?"

"Actually, you are, but that's OK. They'll leave in fifteen minutes and thank me later for a day off. So now, let me ask you something. How do you fit into all this? I know you've got a naturally curious nature, but I have to admit, this is the last thing I ever expected to get from you. And I couldn't help noticing the fax came from the County Sheriff's office."

Jim related the story of the kids' interrupted attempt at a ritual in the house and Robin's subsequent admission of what happened there. He also related the story of the other three teenagers' deaths.

"Jim, does anybody live in the house?"

"Yes, the family moved in a couple of months after the event at the house."

"Get them out of that house." There was an unmistakable urgency in the professor's voice. "Get them out now."

"I've already told them they need to leave for a day or two. I wanted to have a chance to talk to you and see what is going on."

"Thank heavens for that. But a day or two may not be enough."

Jim remained silent.

"Let me tell you what you're dealing with. The pages you sent me are a ritual for summoning demons. It is written in Latin, but the Latin seems to be a translation from the Ugaritic language."

Jim inhaled sharply but said nothing.

"In the spring of 1928 a Syrian farmer was plowing his field when he uncovered a stone over a grave. A team of archaeologists was called in, and soon they discovered the nearby ancient city of Ugarit, what we know as modern-day Ras Shamra.

"During the following years as they excavated the site, they found a number of clay tablets written in cuneiform in Ugaritic. Part of the find included a number of texts grouped together called the Baal Cycle.

The texts provided a lot of otherwise unknown information about the Canaanite religion.

"It was also rumored that there were a few other, much darker texts unearthed. Banned rituals and some unholy writings. I think what you've got here is a translation of one of those other rituals."

"I was afraid of something like this," Jim said.

"What makes you say that? This is not exactly the kind of idea that lends itself to wide acceptance in the modern world. Most people, even ministers, pooh-pooh the idea of demons and supernatural manifestations."

"Well, if there is a God who represents all that is good and holy, then there has to be some opposing force. There has to be evil. And remember, there are still some ministers left—even former ministers—who take the notion that there is a battle between good and evil being waged everyday very seriously.

"Add to that something the woman who lives in the house said, and the evidence is strong that this is not just a construction problem. According to her, when she simply mentioned the name of Jesus, a cabinet was ripped out of the wall. And the same thing happened when her husband mentioned the name of Jesus. And add to that the fact that there is a nasty fungus growing in their family room in the shape of a pentagram, and it's sort of hard to discount the idea. The only thing I don't know yet is *how* it happened. What is causing all this?"

"Oh man. Jim, did you say they have left the house?"

"They were supposed to be leaving right after I headed here to call you."

"Good, because there's more bad news. You said the kids had to stop the ceremony before they were finished?"

"Yes. A local deputy almost walked in on them."

"Depending on how far they got in the ritual, it is possible they have suspended a demon called Ashmedai between hell and earth. In fact, it sounds like it is trapped in the very fabric of the house."

"What is an Ashmedai?"

"In Hebrew, demons are known as Shedim, and Ashmedai is the chief of all demons. The Shedim are thought to live in deserted and or unclean places. Ashmedai is the worst of the lot, and from the pages you sent, those kids were trying to call Ashmedai out to do their bidding. But what would have happened is after a large enough blood sacrifice, it would have taken over one of them as a host until it could shed the body like a skin and return in full force.

"And, Jim, make no mistake. Ashmedai is a killing machine."

"So how do we stop it?" Jim gripped the phone so hard his hand cramped. He switched hands and worked the stiff fingers of his right hand.

"Short of burning down the house and salting the ground, I don't know. But what I do know is, if they had completed the ceremony you gave me, that town you live in would have been doomed."

"What about some kind of exorcism? Is there something like that we could do?"

"You mean driving demons out with holy water and religious relics? I don't think so. The only thing that can drive out a demon is Christ himself. There is no place in the Bible where a demon was driven out by any physical item or talisman. It is always through the power of Jesus. But as for how to do it, I have no idea."

Jim thought a moment, and shifted the phone back to his other hand. "David, I appreciate the help. I don't know what I'm going to do, but I know I need to call the Chalmerses and tell them to stay away from that house at all costs."

"Jim, you be careful. This is serious business, and as I said, I have no idea what to tell you as far as finding a solution. I'll do some more research and see what I can find out, so keep your cell phone handy."

"I will. And thank you, David."

"God go with you, Jim. God go with you."

CHAPTER THIRTY-FOUR

EN ENDED HIS call and put his phone back in his pocket. "Rachel, I just talked to Norm Scott. I missed him at the office, but his secretary gave me his cell phone number, and I caught up with him in his truck. He said he's on the way to another job, but he has to come within a mile of here, so he's going to swing by in a few minutes."

"That's the best news I've heard in a while. I guess we can wait until he's been by before we head back to the Daystar Motel." She stood looking into the kitchen.

"Penny for your thoughts," Ben said. He wrapped his arms around her and rested his chin on her shoulder.

"I was just wondering how to go about getting the kitchen cleaned up, but I think I'm going to leave that to Norm and his crew. If it was their fault, they can clean up the mess." She leaned her head to the left until she made contact with Ben's cheek. "He can also haul out any little animals he finds in the attic if that's what was causing the scraping noise."

Ben's mind returned to the graveyard above them, and he shuddered.

Rachel turned to face her husband. "Are you OK?"

"Yes, I'm fine," Ben lied. "A goose just ran across my grave."

Rachel was quiet for a moment. "Ben? I think Jim was right about how we handled Brandon's death." She pushed her hair away from her forehead. "We just went on with our lives as if nothing had happened. Just put our feelings and emotions on hold and toughed it out. He was our own son, and we acted like he was just away at camp, or staying with some relative."

Her eyes glistened. "Ben, how could we have let that happen? We didn't even question it when the preacher said we weren't supposed to grieve. We just moved on as if…as if…"

Ben held her and told her that things would be different. That they would make the memory of their son a real part of their lives. "And I think it's finally time to do something about Piggy Anne," Ben said. Rachel agreed.

The doorbell interrupted their conversation. Ben went to the door and ushered Norm Scott into the room.

"Good morning, Ben. I'm glad you caught me when you did, otherwise I may have been on my way to Wilmington. I've got to meet with the city manager about a contract to refurbish a suite of offices in the city government complex out there."

"I appreciate your coming out on such short notice." They made their way into the family room. Rachel was waiting for them.

"Good morning, Norm."

"Good morning, Mrs. Chalmers. How are…" His voice trailed off when he saw the fungal design. "What is that?" Norm craned his neck to get a better look, but didn't move toward the pentagram.

"We were sort of hoping you could tell us," Rachel said. "It's been growing like that for the last day or so, and from what the sheriff told us a while back, this is the spot where those kids drew their occult symbol the night they were fooling around in the house."

Norm moved toward the pentagram, still keeping his distance. "I know Hank Turnage came out here at the sheriff's request and cleaned all that up, and we put the flooring down over it, but it was all but invisible when we did it. You could hardly see where it had been unless you knew where to look." He moved closer to the design. "I guess it's possible there was something in the paint or whatever they used that has allowed this stuff to grow like this. Maybe like a medium or something." He moved closer to the design.

"Maybe that's what it is. Something they used when they drew their design has attracted the mold or whatever it is." He straightened up and rubbed his chin.

"While you're looking," Rachel said, "there are a few more things you need to see." She showed him the banister rail and told him the circumstances around their finding it broken.

"That's the strangest thing," Norm said. "How does a banister break like that? I would be willing to declare in court that that rail was as true as could be." He motioned for them to look at the rail. "There is not a twist in the grain that I can see. It looks like it was snapped in half." He turned his attention back to the couple peering over his shoulder. "And you say nobody was near it when it broke?"

"No, we were all up in the upstairs hall," Ben said. "Nobody was even close to it at the time."

"If it can wait a day or two, I'll come see to it personally after I finish with the Wilmington meeting. I'll get back late tomorrow."

"That's fine," Rachel said. "And I have another project for you to take a look at. We are having a problem with the cabinets in the kitchen too." She led the way. When the contractor saw the kitchen, he cursed under his breath.

"How did this happen?" He looked incredulous.

"We don't know," Ben said. "They pulled away from the wall yesterday. We thought they were not fastened securely, but Jim Perry came out and looked at them. He said it would have been a job for a demolition crew to pull them down. He couldn't explain it either."

Norm walked through the shattered dinnerware and looked in the cabinets. All solid wood, plenty of braces. He pulled a multi-tool from a case on his hip, pulled up a Phillips head screwdriver attachment, and took out one of the screws. It was as straight as the day it was installed. And it was more than long enough to have secured the cabinet.

He pulled three more screws out at random. All four were identical.

"I don't understand it," Norm said. He jingled the screws in his hand. "This doesn't make a bit of sense." He turned to face Ben and Rachel. "I'll talk to Jim and see when he can come back out and reattach them. I'll plan to come out with him so I can check the walls and see if there was a problem there, but I really don't think there is."

"That's fine," Ben said. "We're going to be at the Daystar for a couple of days. I don't think it's entirely necessary, but Jim thought for some reason we should get out for a while until somebody can check the house over."

"Look," Norm said. "If it turns out all this is due to faulty workmanship, or if we find any structural problems with the house, I'll pay for you to stay there while we get it cleared up."

"That's very generous," Rachel said. "Thank you."

"You're welcome. And I can promise you, if this is the result of one of my crews taking shortcuts, I'll have their hide. I hope that's not the case, but there is always some joker on a site who knows a dozen ways to beat the system. I try to weed them out, but you never know one hundred percent. Especially with subs.

"Now Ben, if you'll show me what you found in the attic, I'll see if I can find a hole that a squirrel could use to get in."

Ben led the way to the attic door. When he was sure they were out of earshot, he told Norm what he had seen earlier.

"Norm, this isn't just squirrels getting in. It looks like an animal graveyard up there. There are carcasses everywhere. And not just squirrels." The contractor grimaced, but said nothing. "I just thought you ought to be prepared," Ben said. "It's pretty bad up there."

Norm reached up, pulled down the stair assembly, and paused. "It's that bad?"

Ben nodded.

Norm went up the stairs. He stopped half way up and grunted.

Norm backed down a few steps. "Ben, how about flipping on the lights up here." He disappeared up the steps as Ben turned on the attic lights. Ben followed the contractor into the attic. Dust motes floated along slanted shafts of sunlight coming through the gable vent and swirled around the dried husks of a squirrel and a cat. Almost directly in front of them lay the mummified corpse of a raccoon.

Norm stood in the attic and looked around him. There were animal bodies everywhere, contorted husks with limbs akimbo. He nudged the remains of a chipmunk with the toe of his boot. It rustled like parchment and pulled away from the floor. A small patch of skin and fur remained attached to the plywood.

Ben stepped up beside him and whistled softly. "It looks like there are more now than there were when I called you."

"What in the precious name of Jesus…"

A wave of bone-numbing cold hit both men like a polar wind off the mountain. The stench that rode the blast was unlike anything either of them had ever experienced.

A second later there was an ear-splitting crack followed by a sharp, wrenching noise. Ben looked up to see a brace nailed between two trusses rip away and launch itself across the attic. The section of two-by-four pinwheeled in midair and flew past him at an unbelievable rate of speed. He felt the breeze created by the moving timber.

The four nails, each over four inches long, which protruded from the ends of the board, found their mark in the contractor. They made a hollow *thonk* as the two nails on one end pierced his chest and the two on the other end drove themselves deep into his thigh.

Ben looked on in stunned disbelief. His muscles felt like they had turned to wood and all he could do was watch in horror. His mind screamed at him, telling him what he had just seen was impossible. All he could do was stare—until the contractor screamed.

Norm Scott jerked like a man holding a live wire. He stood in one spot, vibrating, his mouth opening and closing like a fish out of water.

He touched the board that had impaled itself on him. That's when he screamed. It came out as a high-pitched crying sound.

Ben forced himself to move. He put a hand on Norm's shoulder and wrapped his other hand around the wood.

NO!

nuh…nuh…no…don't pu…pull it out.

"Norm, we've got to."

"NO…NO…hurts. Hurts bad." Norm tried to move on his free leg, but that gave way and he fell. Ben was able to break his fall somewhat, but the movement must have thrown the contractor into new realms of agony. He passed out before he hit the floor.

Norm's blue shirt was almost black where the blood was seeping out around the nails. His left khaki pants leg was almost black at the thigh.

Ben stood and yelled down the stairs for Rachel. She was already on the way.

"Ben what is all that screaming?"

"Honey, call 911. Norm's been hurt."

"Hurt? How?" She started to come up to see.

"Honey, just call, now. He has two big nails stuck in his chest and I don't know if he has passed out or if he's dead."

Rachel ran to the nearest phone and started dialing.

JIM DIALED Ben's cell phone number again and got no answer. "Stupid technology," he said. "You're supposed to make my life easier." He walked over to the telephone stand and took the phonebook from its cubbyhole. He found the number he wanted and dialed.

"Thank you for calling the Daystar Motel. This is Barb. How can I help you?"

"Hello, Barb. Could you connect me to Ben Chalmers's room please?"

"Do you know him?" she asked. "He's that famous writer, right?"

"Yes, that's him. This is Jim Perry, and I've been doing some work for him. He said he was going to be staying there a few days, and I just need to talk to him for a minute."

"I'd like to help you Mr. Perry, but he's not here."

Jim inhaled through his teeth and closed his eyes. "What time do you expect him back?" He heard computer keys click over the phone line. Then Barb came back on the line.

"I really have no idea, Mr. Perry. I'd like to think it will be soon, though. Do you know he signed one of the menus from the restaurant for us while he was here? He is the nicest man. And his family is nice too."

"Yes, they're all very nice." He squeezed his eyes shut tighter. "Well, can I leave a message for him?"

"I don't see how. They checked out this morning."

Jim got up and paced around the room. "I know, but they should have checked back in again."

"Oh, I hope so," Barb said. "He is such a nice man. Not a real pinhead like some famous people." More key clicks. "No sir, they haven't been back, and we don't have a reservation for them either."

Jim thanked her for checking and abruptly cut off the phone. He dialed their home number and waited. There was no ringing, nor a busy signal.

The sound coming from the phone sounded like laughter.

Jim said a word he hadn't said since before his seminary days and ran to his truck.

SHERIFF CANTRELL was leading a tour of fourth graders through the office when she heard the scanner bleat out something about an ambulance in route to the home on Grant's Ridge. Mrs. Ruth Moss always brought her civics class to take a tour of the sheriff's office. They saw the patrol car, turned on the siren, were fingerprinted, and walked through a real jail cell. Then the sheriff would talk to them about the importance of being good citizens.

Today, she caught Steve Hughes on his way to the bathroom and asked him to take over. He looked pained, but she didn't give him a chance to answer.

"Kids, today you're in for a special treat. Deputy Hughes is going to show you his handcuffs and talk to you about being good citizens."

She leaned over and whispered, "Thanks, Steve. I owe you one."

Once she was out of the children's sight, she ran to her cruiser. She wasn't sure what she expected to find, but she knew one thing. Jim was supposed to be at the Chalmerses' house.

She floored the accelerator.

CHAPTER THIRTY-FIVE

ASHMEDAI CRINGED AT the mention of the Prince's name. *It* moved along the beams, and in a fit of rage, hurled the first object It could wrench free, and impaled the blasphemer.

The blood that touched the floor was ambrosia. And soon there would be more.

Much more.

It had stashed the items needed to make the blood flow and finally had enough power to move at will and manipulate the prison without requiring rest.

The demon had fed well, and soon would not settle for animal lives. Soon Ashmedai would feed on the inhabitants of Its prison and would take one of them for a host.

Yes…the small one.

Ashmedai decided to take the small one first. Then after entering the host, kill the others and gorge Itself with their blood. Through the small host, It would spill enough blood to complete the sacrifice and allow Itself to shed the host and walk free.

Then It would feed for pleasure.

Ashmedai moved along the framework of the house until It had located the small one.

The host.

CHAPTER THIRTY-SIX

EN SAT BESIDE the wounded contractor. He felt helpless and bewildered. How could he have seen what he just saw? Norm had not lost his footing and fallen on a nail. He had not tripped and stuck a pair of exposed nails in his chest and leg.

No, he saw the piece of wood hurl itself half way across the attic. And that wasn't possible. It just wasn't possible.

Ben began rocking back and forth, beating his fists against his legs. *I did not see that. I did not see that.*

"Ben, the ambulance is on the way."

He heard a voice but had no desire to answer. Too much was happening. Too much. And if things didn't start making sense soon, he was going to just shut down. Boards don't just fly around and--

"Ben!"

The voice penetrated his foggy brain. It was Rachel. Rachel was calling him. That jarred something inside him. She couldn't come up here. She just couldn't.

Too late.

"What is all this?" Rachel stood on the steps, looked around the attic, and saw the tiny corpses. Then she saw Norm.

"Ben. What happened to him?" She scrambled up into the attic and went to Norm. "How did this happen?"

"I think it was the house."

"The house?" She looked at Norm and bit her lower lip. "How does a house do this?" She reached for the board to remove it. Ben stopped her.

"No honey. Don't. It's stuck in him with four big nails." He dropped his voice. "And I think the house did it." He paused. "No, I *saw* the house do it."

"Ben, what are you telling me? Are you saying the house can do things?"

"All I know is one minute we were talking, and the next minute this board flew across the attic and hit him in the chest."

Norm groaned but didn't open his eyes.

"Ben, we've got to get him downstairs."

"Honey, we don't dare move him. He will go ballistic, and I think he stands a better chance if the paramedics move him than if we try." Ben rubbed his forehead and started walking around the attic. Small rodents crunched underfoot.

Rachel winced. "Where did all these animals come from? Could this be what I've been hearing the last few days?" She looked around at the carnage. "They look like the dog."

"What?" Ben stopped pacing.

"These animals. They look like Tippy did when we found him. And he certainly hadn't been in the storage room long enough to end up in the condition he was in. And look at these animals. The look like they've been up here for months." She made a sweeping motion with her arm. "Whatever happened to Tippy happened to them."

Rachel looked around the attic again, then moved toward the stairs. "Come on, we'd probably better get down there so we'll be ready when the ambulance gets here. We'll stay close to the stairs in case Norm comes to."

Ben nodded and followed her. Once they were down, Ben noticed she was holding something. "What's that?"

Rachel glanced at the paper in her hand. "Oh yeah. How could I forget this?" She handed the paper to him. "While I was upstairs earlier I noticed the light on the answering machine was flashing, so, I listened to the message. It was from Kyle. He said he was sending you an e-mail attachment and you really needed to look at it."

Ben looked at the paper the way a scientist would look at a new microbe.

"I went to my computer and pulled up your e-mail account," she continued, "and this is what he sent." She moved closer to her husband and looked at the paper he held.

At the top of the page was a picture of Ben standing in front of the picture window in the family room. Reflected in the glass was an impossibility.

The image in the glass had a long, narrow face. Its mouth seemed to be lined with needle-like teeth that protruded beyond its lips. It had a long, bony frame, a pair of what appeared to be massive wings, and it was snarling at the camera. Below the image was the e-mail message.

Ben, I don't know what this is, but I didn't see it in the viewfinder when I snapped the picture. Any explanations?

"What in the world is that thing, and where was it when he took the picture?" Ben asked. "What can make a reflection like that?"

Rachel took the picture back and looked closer. "Honey, that doesn't look like a reflection. That thing looks like it is in the glass."

"Hello, is anybody home?"

Ben and Rachel jumped at the same time. They recognized the sheriff's voice, but not until they had almost cried out.

"We're up here," Ben called out. "We'll be right down."

When they reached the bottom level, the sheriff was looking at the pentagram. "I'm sorry if I scared you," she said. "I just heard on the scanner that an ambulance was on the way, and I wanted to see if I could help." She looked around the room. "What happened?"

Ben explained as best he could without saying the house seemed to attack Norm. Then the two of them took her to the attic.

LIZ CLIMBED the steps, made her way over to Norm, and placed her fingers against the side of his neck. "He has a pulse. It's thin, but there," she called to Ben and Rachel who waited at the bottom of the steps. She examined the immediate area. "He's lost a little blood, but I expected to see more." She checked his pulse again then made her way back down the attic steps.

"You were wise to leave him there. If you move him with those nails in that area, you could puncture his heart, if it's not punctured already." The sheriff looked around the room. "Mrs. Chalmers, where is your little girl?"

"Stacy is in her room. I told her to stay there until we came to get her. Jim said it would be a good idea for us to go to the Daystar Motel for a few days while he and Norm checked the house. But now...."

"That's probably a good idea anyway," Sheriff Cantrell said. "In fact, once the ambulance gets here and they get Norm down, why don't you get ready and go on?" She watched the relief on their faces as they agreed. "Oh, by the way. Is Jim still here?" She couldn't hide the emotion in her voice.

"No," Ben said. "He had to make a phone call, and I don't know if he was even coming back today."

"Oh." Now she couldn't hide the disappointment. "Well, I'll tell you what. I'll go out and wait for the ambulance. You two get that little girl ready to go." Sheriff Cantrell opened the front door to leave.

Something wrenched the door from her grasp and slammed it shut.

Rachel gasped.

"What?" The sheriff drew her gun and motioned for the Chalmerses to go upstairs. "Whoever did that is about to get a wake-up call." She reached for the door handle and pulled her hand back.

"Ow." She examined the red welt that was already forming. She had burned her hand when she touched the handle. "What the...?" she touched the handle again with her index finger and pulled it away again. "What's wrong with this door?"

"Sheriff, maybe you'd better come up here too. There are some strange things going on around here and maybe we don't need to be separated," Rachel said.

"Yeah," Ben said. "I'll go up and check on Norm again. You two go in with Stacy."

BEN STEPPED on the bottom step, then the next. Suddenly, the stairway bucked and shuddered. He fell off and the overhead door snapped up, pinning the portable stairs against the ceiling.

Ben stood and ran toward Stacy's room. The hallway seemed twice as long as it had only a minute ago, and the floor seemed slightly out of level. The walls undulated like ripples on a pond.

Ben lurched forward, and tried to keep his balance. He half stumbled, half fell into Stacy's room. None of the rooms' occupants paid any attention to him. "Hey, did you see that?" He walked over to them, but their eyes were fixed straight ahead. "What's going on over..." The last word died in his throat when he saw what had their attention.

Piggy Anne stood on an exposed portion of hardwood floor between the area rug and the wall. And Piggy Anne had a box cutter.

The small, flat blade made a lazy arc back and forth. Piggy Anne looked at them with unseeing eyes, but not one of the room's occupants doubted for a minute that the doll knew where they were.

Before any of them could speak, the doll lunged.

CHAPTER THIRTY-SEVEN

JIM FLOORED THE accelerator and climbed the hill leading to Grant's Ridge. Surely to goodness those folks weren't still in that house.

The truck's tires squealed with every turn of the steering wheel. He was going way too fast for driving in the mountains, and if he met anyone coming from the opposite direction, he could be the next guest of honor at the county morgue.

"Father God, please, let them be alright. And let me get them out of there in time."

Jim glanced at the speedometer and set his face toward the house on Grant's Ridge. He just had to be in time.

He had to be.

CHAPTER THIRTY-EIGHT

THE DOLL LANDED on the wall closest to the door and scrabbled sideways like a crab.

"Shoot it!" Rachel yelled. The sheriff pointed the gun at the retreating figure just as it rounded the doorframe and disappeared.

Stacy had her arms wrapped tightly around Ben's leg, her face scrunched up and her eyes closed tight. Rachel stood staring at the spot where they had last seen the doll before it crawled around the doorframe.

"Would somebody like to explain to me what I just saw?" Sheriff Cantrell was visibly shaken. She started to reholster her gun, but hesitated. Instead, she pointed it toward the floor, but did not engage the safety. She looked to Ben and Rachel for answers.

They had none.

Ben pulled Stacy from his leg and knelt down in front of her. "Doodlebug, did Piggy Anne hurt you?"

"No sir. But she scared me. She scared me a lot."

"Honey, I think she scared all of us a lot. But listen. I need to ask you something else." Ben looked at the two women in the room. "Was Piggy Anne in your room when you came up here earlier?"

"I didn't see her up here, so I figured she was in another closet some-where." Stacy wiped away a tear. "I told you she kept running away."

"I know you did, honey, and I'm sorry," Rachel said. She stroked Stacy's hair, then turned to the sheriff. "OK, what now? What do you want us to do?"

She motioned for them to stay put and walked to the doorway oppo-site the side the doll had crawled around. If Piggy Anne was lurking on the other side of the doorframe, she didn't want to be within easy reach. She took a deep breath and moved into the hallway, gun drawn. She kept to the right, watching for any sign of movement. After she checked the hallway, she moved where the Chalmerses could see her and motioned them into the hall.

"Listen," the sheriff whispered once they were all together, "I think we need to move downstairs quietly and see if we can get out through the front door again. If not, maybe we can get out through the deck doors." She raised her pistol upward into the ready position and checked the hall once more. "I'll go first, then let you know when it's OK to move."

Ben and Rachel each took one of Stacy's hands in theirs and waited for the sheriff to signal them to come. Ben glanced toward the ceiling. "I hope he's OK." Rachel nodded and gripped Stacy's hand tighter.

The sheriff disappeared onto the first landing, then came back up and waved them on. They followed, making as little noise as possible.

They stopped on the landing, where the sheriff made them stay until she checked things all the way down. Her footfalls were soft on the steps, but the one creak of wood about halfway down seemed to echo forever. They all flinched as one, like a shared involuntary response.

Once they were on the main floor, the sheriff shifted the gun to her left hand and winced. The place she had been burned hurt like blazes. She touched the door handle lightly and pulled her hand away quickly. No burn-ing. She grabbed the handle, pressed the release mechanism, and tugged.

The door didn't move.

She pressed down on the leaf shaped release again and pulled harder. She felt the dead bolt move, so by all rights, the door should swing open. Instead, it held fast.

Or something was holding it.

Either way, they weren't getting out through the front door. The sheriff told them to stay by the door, but be alert. She moved out into the middle of the room slowly. She watched for any sign of movement, taking one slow step at a time.

Though there were windows in the front of the house and two glass doors in the rear, the room seemed dark. It was as if a storm cloud was rolling past the sun. But outside the autumn day was bright and clear.

The sheriff made it across the room and over to the doors without incident. She reached for the brass knob of the right hand door and turned it. The latch moved as it should.

There was a faint padding sound—followed by silence. Then a sliding, scrabbling sound. Faster, and more urgent.

The sheriff heard Stacy's cry a split second before she saw the box cutter flash. White-hot pain seared the back of her gun hand and she dropped the Glock. Throwing herself backward, she instinctively searched for the pistol with her uninjured hand, never losing sight of the doll standing on the wall at an impossible angle, holding the box cutter at the ready.

Blood coated the sheriff's hand and a rivulet landed on the floor with a sizzle. A second later, it was gone.

ASHMEDAI WATCHED the human scamper for the weapon she had been holding. The demon had made contact with a weapon of Its own and was able to shed more blood through the doll. Even now, It could smell the sacrifice. Could smell the blood. When the blood made contact with the floor, even so small an amount, Ashmedai sent out a tendril and absorbed it.

When Ashmedai finished with this one, It would go after the others.

THE WALLS in the family room rippled from top to bottom. Light bulbs popped in their sockets and plunged the room into more gloom. The temperature seemed to have dropped by ten degrees, and a foul stench permeated the room.

Rachel looked at Ben but said nothing. Stacy held onto her mother's waist and looked on in horror. Then, she began to scream.

"Kill her! Kill Piggy Anne! Kill her now!"

Sheriff Cantrell moved the gun around, ignoring the pain in her right hand, and put the demon doll in her sights.

Then Piggy Anne was gone.

Elizabeth searched the walls and the floor. Nothing. No flash of flannel and curly red hair.

"There it is!"

The sheriff spun around and saw where Rachel was pointing. The walls appeared to be buckling, but it didn't seem to slow the creature down. The doll launched itself from the wall to the ceiling like a possessed Spider-Man. Only this was no comic book, and the doll was not concerned with rescuing a single person in the room.

It was planning to kill them.

Piggy Anne skittered across the ceiling toward the fireplace. It paused for a second, and Elizabeth took the shot. The side of Piggy Anne's head exploded in a cloud of fluff. The doll didn't flinch. It just reversed its direction and moved toward the sheriff.

BEN DASHED toward the fireplace to grab the poker. Stacy screamed for somebody to kill Piggy Anne, and Rachel yelled for Ben to stop. But he went anyway.

The coffee table skidded across the room and caught Ben directly in the side of his right kneecap. He felt something rip in the back of his knee and went down hard. The pain was so intense it made him want to throw up, but he pulled himself to the hearth and grabbed the long brass poker.

"Ben!" Rachel moved a step toward him and a dozen brass candlesticks hurled themselves off the mantle, one of the smaller ones glanced off her head. She dropped to the ground, pulling Stacy with her.

Stacy was crying constantly now. "Honey, did you get hit?" Stacy shook her head, her sobs escaping in little gasps.

"Mama, make it stop. Please make it stop."

Rachel held her tight and raised her head enough to see Ben. He had the poker in his hand and was hobbling toward the sheriff. He barely let his right foot touch the ground, and every step was agony.

"Ben, what are you doing?"

He stopped and leaned on the poker for support. It was too short for him to stand erect, but even stooped over he was able to take some of the pressure off his knee.

"I'm going to help the sheriff."

"Stay put," the sheriff commanded. She was tracking the doll's movements with her gun. "You're hurt."

At that instant, the window exploded.

CHAPTER THIRTY-NINE

JIM PERRY PUSHED the truck as fast as he dared. The house was less than a quarter of a mile away. He had tried to redial the Chalmers' number three times, and each time he got a guttural hiss, or something that sounded like a clown's laugh.

He had dialed the sheriff's number, and the dispatcher said she was not available.

Things didn't look good.

Lord, please be with the Chalmers family right now. Protect them with your heavenly power. He paused. *And please don't let me be too late.*

Jim hit the driveway doing sixty and slowed to forty-five for the curve. He slammed on the brakes and threw the truck in park. He jumped from the vehicle, the motor still running, and bolted to the porch. He tried the front door and it was locked.

He ran along the front porch to the garden window that would have been next to the fireplace and looked in.

Stacy's doll was standing on the opposite wall waving some kind of knife. It looked like half of its head was missing. Ben was leaning on a fireplace poker, and Elizabeth was standing in the middle of the room with her gun trained on the doll.

Elizabeth. His heart threatened to jump out of his chest when he saw her. Then a thought hit him hard.

Where were Stacy and Rachel?

He couldn't see them. But he heard a clatter of metal somewhere inside the room. Adrenaline slammed his system like a freight train. He had to do something.

Jim looked around for something heavy. There were no concrete planters. No rocking chairs. In desperation, he ran to the end of the porch, turned, then ran back along the porch at full speed. When he came even with the garden window, he planted his left foot and pushed off hard to the right.

He crashed through the window in a hail of glass and broken wood.

CHAPTER FORTY

WHEN THE WINDOW shattered, things happened in a blur.

Piggy Anne launched itself from the wall toward the ceiling again, its ruined head lolling behind it. Elizabeth fired wide and missed. But Ben managed to lurch forward and swing the poker in a tight arc. He caught Piggy Anne in mid-leap and knocked the doll across the room.

It landed on the windowsill, impaled on a shard of glass.

Jim stood up and stared at the writhing, thrashing abomination. Piggy Anne whipped the box cutter around behind itself and tried to cut Jim.

Jim dodged the cutter and turned to see Liz running toward him, gun drawn.

"Move!"

He sidestepped as she moved into position. At point blank range, she blew Piggy Anne's knife arm off completely at the shoulder, then blew the other arm off for good measure.

She looked at Jim. "Nice entrance. Do you think we can get out the same way? Something has the doors blocked."

"I think so. Let's find Stacy and Rachel and get you all out of here." Liz pointed toward mother and daughter. They moved toward them, then stopped.

The glass shards on the floor rattled and cracked against each other. A tremor ran through the floor, and the glass erupted into a whirlwind. Glass spiraled around in a deadly vortex in front of the window.

"Jim, what's going on here?" It was Rachel. She was supporting Ben on one side, and he used the poker as a kind of crutch. Stacy held onto his pocket.

"What's going on here is a demon named Ashmedai. It's trapped in the wood and stone of this house, and it wants out."

At the mention of Its name, the doll stopped thrashing and went rigid. The glass cyclone increased in intensity.

And a shadow passed through the glass doors.

Jim's face went hard, and a second jolt of adrenaline hit his system. Adrenaline and something else.

"Ashmedai, in the powerful name of Jesus, I rebuke you."

In that instant, every piece of furniture in the house slammed against the walls. The heating system groaned like something possessed, and a stench unlike anything they had ever encountered hung thick and heavy in the room.

Stacy gagged.

Piggy Anne whipped itself into a frenzy on the glass shard, its half a head flapping like a broken bat wing.

The floorboards buckled and popped, throwing everyone in the room to the floor. Ben screamed in agony when he landed on his ravaged knee. Pictures hurled themselves from the wall and shattered against each other in midair.

The couch jumped and bucked in place, and the chandelier overhead crashed to the floor. The walls thrummed and vibrated.

Bum Bump. Bum bump. Bum Bump. Bum bump.

Like a giant heartbeat.

SOMETHING STIRS

In the midst of the chaos, Jim Perry stood and prayed. "Father God, I know this unholy abomination is not of you, and I ask that you protect your children." His breath turned to frost. The room was frigid. "Father God, show me the way to defeat this evil, in JESUS' name, Amen."

The house screamed and shook down to its foundation. Jim stood in the midst of the chaos and watched as the kitchen door slammed shut so hard the moldings around the doorframe cracked. Behind the door, he heard the refrigerator jumping and drawers being pulled from their respective resting places and hurled across the room. Seconds later, he saw the blades of several knives and two Chinese cleavers erupt through the door like the fangs of a viper released from their resting place. He heard his cabinets splinter and crack. Then he heard them rip away from the walls completely.

He could only imagine the destruction.

"Jim, what do we do now?" Elizabeth had holstered her weapon and was standing guard over the Chalmers family as best she could. But supernatural assailants were something the academy hadn't prepared her for. "There's no way out." She ducked as a lamp flew past her and shattered against the wall.

Jim glanced at the door and remembered David Ward's warning.

"...*after a large enough blood sacrifice, it would have taken over one of them as a host until it could shed the body like a skin, and return in full force...*"

"There's only one way to drive this thing out. And we've got to deal with it before it takes one of us as a host," Jim shouted over the noise of the maelstrom. Then he turned his attention to the door.

The exposed blades gleamed.

There was only one answer.

"You want a host?" he yelled. "Well you've got one. But I don't think you're going to like it."

Jim ran toward the door and the ruined doll arm that still clutched the box cutter launched itself across the room. The blade bit deep and sliced him from elbow to shoulder. Jim dropped to his knees, grabbed his arm, felt bone, and howled in pain.

BEN LEANED on the poker in the center of the chaos, and the full impact of what Jim said hit home. This thing intended to use one of them as a host then kill the rest of them, and at that point, all hell would break loose. Literally.

Ben took two agonizing steps toward his wife and daughter and a brass paperweight hurled itself into his knee. The pain was white-hot. He called out to Rachel, but before she could answer, he was assaulted by the vilest odor he had ever smelled. Like rotted meat, infected sores, and stagnant water.

It was the smell of death.

The walls began to quiver. What few framed items that remained fell and shattered. And a voice, guttural and dark, seemed to issue from the air around them.

I have come to take a host. And when I have taken my host, I will kill you all and bathe in your blood.

Rachel screamed and pulled Stacy close, and Jim struggled to stand again. Elizabeth scanned the room, her gun at the ready. Suddenly, the gun was wrenched from her hand and sent spinning across the room.

The stench intensified and the voice grew louder. *I have come for a host, and I claim the small one.*

Ben froze. He saw Rachel draw Stacy in even closer, trying to shield their daughter with her body. Saw her thrown aside. Heard her scream. He saw Stacy start to crawl toward her mother.

Saw his son in the pool.

Saw the door. The blades. And he understood what Jim had intended to do.

What he must now do.

Ben roared *NOT AGAIN*, lurched toward the kitchen door, and slammed his palms into the two largest blades full force.

The last thing he heard before the darkness enveloped him was Rachel's scream.

CHAPTER FORTY-ONE

THE DARKNESS RECEDED in a swirl of slick, muted color. Like oil and gas residue on a rain-slick road. The swirl resolved into a dirty burnt-orange landscape, barren and twisted, like a Salvador Dali vision of hell. Rock outcroppings shoved their way through the hard packed surface at impossible angles. Mangled trees unlike anything he had ever seen thrust up through the dead landscape, their stubby, leafless branches reaching out toward the bleak landscape in a posture of alien supplication.

Ben lay on the ground, his hands aching like a rotten tooth. The first thing he realized was, despite its inhospitable desert appearance, the air was cold. Frigid. A soul- numbing cold that gnawed at his lungs and made him breathe in short ragged gasps. The next thing he noticed was he was able to function somewhat despite his injuries.

The final thing he realized was that he was tired, on the verge of collapse. Coupled with the oppressive atmosphere and his growing disorientation, he knew that whatever his next move, he would have to do it and do it fast, while he could still function.

He pushed himself to his knees, then moved slowly to his feet.

"ASHMEDAI."

A familiar stench assaulted him from behind. He had encountered it in the house. A smell like spoiled meat, rancid milk, an abscessed sore. He turned, and the thing that faced him was a culmination of every nightmare he had ever had.

The creature was easily eight feet tall. Leathery wings flared from its back, and it hissed at him through a mouth full of needle-sharp teeth. It had wicked talon-like appendages at the end of its long, powerful arms. The thing regarded him, Its reptile-like eyes never blinking.

You are not the host. The small one is the host.

He had never heard the language before, but he understood it. And Ashmedai's statement chilled him to the bone.

"You cannot have my child or anyone else," he said. "In the name of Je…"

Ashmedai moved quickly. It leapt at Ben and slammed him against a stone outcropping, ripping at him with Its talons in the same movement.

Blasphemer, you will not speak the name of the Nazarene in my presence. I will use you as a host and tear the others limb from limb.

Pain, white-hot and liquid, erupted with every slash. The speed and ferocity of the attack stunned him. Jim felt a rib crack. Then another. The pain seared his torso, and his brain responded with a flood of adrenaline.

"You will have to kill me first, and I'm not about to let that--"

Before he could finish, the nightmare increased its attack, ripping and tearing in a frenzy of bloodlust. Ben tried to defend himself from the blows, and the surge of adrenaline had little effect in the face of the ongoing damage to his body. He was growing weaker by the moment. The pain was too intense and his few punches were ineffective. He felt flesh separate from bone, and saw bits of gristle fly from the wounds. When he lifted his left hand to ward off a blow, the demon snapped his wrist like a twig.

Ben screamed with nothing but the patchwork landscape and the demon to hear.

Neither of them cared.

Ashmedai rose to *Its* full height to deliver the final blow. The demon wavered in and out of focus, and Ben's eyelids felt like they weighed five pounds. Blood flowed from a score of deep gashes, and he was dimly aware that whatever he was able to do before the demon unleashed the next attack would likely be the last thing he ever did.

Just as the demon slashed with its talon/fingers, Ben pushed out from the rock with the remaining strength in his legs and rammed the thing's midsection. The demon, caught off guard, staggered back. Ben fought on sheer instinct and will. Every punch ripped his own ravaged flesh, but he fought on. He clawed at the demon's eyes, and it threw him aside like a child.

He remembered Stacy. He had already lost one child because of his inability to act. He could not let this unholy thing touch her.

But in his condition, he also couldn't prevent it.

"The only thing that can drive out a demon is Christ himself."

Ashmedai came for him. Ben struggled to get off the ground, and could only reach his knees. He was dying. He felt it. And he was about to fail the people he had set out to protect. The people his pride was about to slaughter.

His daughter.

The demon set itself for the killing blow.

Ben bowed his head. All pride drained away just as his life was draining away.

Precious Jesus, I can't do this alone. Forgive my arrogance for thinking I could prevail here. Please Lord Jesus, protect them. In your holy name, I pray...

Before he could say *Amen*, the world erupted in a flash of white light.

Then darkness.

CHAPTER FORTY-TWO

EN HEARD VOICES.

Faint.

But voices still.

Felt a presence.

He opened his eyes and saw two angels. One was holding his hand and the other was praying softly. After a moment, the praying angel smiled at him.

Then, darkness again.

LIGHT.

Just a bit.

Then a bit more. Ben squinted against the light until his eyes began to adjust.

"Welcome back."

Ben looked into his wife's eyes. "Rachel, where am I?"

You're in room 1010 at M. E. Watauga Medical Center in Boone."

"How long have I been here?" He was thirsty and his voice was more of a croak than a real voice.

"Two days." She smiled again.

He loved it when she smiled like that.

"How long have you been here?"

"Two days." She squeezed his hand gently.

He tried to sit up, panic gripping his chest, but the monitor lines pulled against him.

"Stacy, where is Stacy?"

Rachel put a hand on his shoulder and guided him back down. "Stacy's fine. She's outside with Liz."

"Liz?"

Rachel laughed. "Sheriff Cantrell. I've gotten to know her pretty well over the past couple of days."

Ben leaned back and closed his eyes for a moment.

"Could I have some water?" Rachel passed him a cup with a bent straw. He sipped at first, then drank in full swallows as his throat accepted it. He emptied half the glass and his eyes widened. "Norm, and Jim. What happened…?"

"They're fine," she said. "Norm is in intensive care, but the doctors expect him to make a full recovery. He doesn't remember what happened exactly. He thinks he fell and hurt himself and has been very apologetic for any trouble he caused." She grinned. "I didn't tell him any different. As for Jim, the box cutter ripped him open, so it took about a hundred and eight stitches, and he's pretty sore. But otherwise, he's OK."

"What about you?" Ben asked, his concern as evident on his face as in his voice.

"I'm fine. They checked me out here to make sure I didn't have a concussion. Fortunately, it was just a really nasty bump from the candlestick."

She helped him adjust his position in the bed. "You, however, tore your ACL almost completely out, so you're in for a little arthroscopic surgery in a few days. The doctor said you'll be fine in a few weeks. He also said it was a good thing you make your living sitting down."

Her laughter touched his heart in a place that had been closed for many years.

She put her right hand back on his. That's where it had been for two days.

"Well you two look pretty cozy."

Liz Cantrell walked in the room with Jim and Stacy. Rachel stood and hugged Jim and Liz. Stacy ran to her father's bedside and stopped.

"Is it OK if I hug you, daddy?"

A tear welled in the corner of his eye as he reached for his daughter. "You'd better believe it, doodlebug." He savored the feeling of his daughter in his arms. He had come so close to...

"Sheriff," Ben said, noticing her bandaged hand, "Are you OK?"

"I'm fine," she said. "I burned my left hand on your door handle, but oddly enough, the scar looks almost exactly like a rose. The doll from hell cut the back of my right hand, but it just needed a few stitches." She lifted her hand. "It stings a little. Otherwise, it's no big deal."

Then he noticed that Jim held Liz's other hand.

"Well, Jim, other than that long bandage, which I assume is covering up about a million stitches, you two look pretty cozy yourselves." He raised one eyebrow and grinned.

"It's hard to be very cozy here in Grand Central Station, what with folks coming by to take your temperature, stick you with needles, and spend the better part of two hours practicing their sewing skills on you. In fact, I think I'll probably have to take this lovely law enforcement officer out for dinner and dessert before we get much privacy any time soon."

Liz looked at Ben and said, "You heard that didn't you?"

Rachel grinned, "You have a room full of witnesses."

"Speaking of witnesses," Ben said, "what happened in there, after, um..."

"After you scared us to death?" Rachel said. "I saw you slam your hands on those knife blades and I freaked out. Then we tried to get over to you, but it was like the floor had been coated with glue. It felt like it took forever to get to where you were."

"Liz tried to pull your hands off the door, but you were bucking and fighting against her," Jim said. "Then all of a sudden, you started bleeding through your shirt, front and back. These nasty, long gashes started forming, and you kept mumbling something about Ashmedai and the gashes got worse. Then your wrist flipped to one side and snapped." Ben looked at the cast on his left wrist.

Jim continued. "The next thing we knew, you screamed, 'Help me Jesus' and it was like a bomb went off. White light flooded the room, and everything stopped. Piggy Anne sort of, well, sort of died I guess you'd call it. And the glass tornado fizzled. It was almost peaceful."

"Where did the light come from?" Ben asked.

Rachel sat back down and took his hand. "It came from your wounds."

Ben lifted the sheet to look at his chest and gasped.

"You'd better look quick," Rachel said. "They've been healing steadily since you got here and they're almost completely healed now. And the bones in your wrist are doing the same thing, though not quite as fast. They took two x-rays and your doctor thought there had been a mistake, so he ordered another one to be on the safe side." Ben glanced at his wrist. "He's been ordering them regularly, but I don't think anyone else has seen them. Not all together." Rachel chuckled. "As a matter of fact, it's safe to say you're freaking your doctor out as we speak."

"From what you've told me I'm surprised he's not in here right now," Ben said.

"When we came in, Liz told him we had all been involved in an accident and that she is handling the follow-up. He doesn't buy it completely because of what is happening to you. But what he does know is that nobody would believe it if he told them. So, he is just monitoring you closely, shaking his head, and mumbling something about miracles. And he is going to want to have a long talk with you at some point now that you're awake."

The room was silent. Then Stacy took her father's hand. "Daddy, I'm glad you didn't die."

Ben hugged Stacy again around the monitor lines. His tears washed away the last of the crust that had formed around his heart. "Oh baby, I'm glad you didn't die too."

AFTER THEY said their goodbyes, Jim and Liz started toward the door. Liz stopped and turned back to the Chalmers family.

"Where will you go?" she asked.

"We're going to the motel!" Stacy was all smiles at the prospect.

"That sounds like fun," Jim said. "How long will you be there?"

"However long it takes us to get the house back in order," Rachel said. "And that could be a while because it was hammered pretty hard. But once we have the OK from the inspector and the contractor, we're moving back in and having one whale of a dinner party for our new friends."

"You can bring a date if you like," Ben said, and winked at Liz.

"You're moving back in the house?" Jim looked puzzled.

"Well sure," Rachel said. "The most dangerous things I'll have to worry about now will be dust bunnies." She nudged Stacy. "And maybe a real dog to replace the one we don't have."

"Really?" Stacy said. "Can we go pick it out now?"

Ben laughed, "You might want to wait until you have a dog house."

Stacy looked at Jim. "You could build us one, couldn't you?"

Jim nodded thoughtfully. "I suppose I could. But I think I had better take the Sheriff out to dinner first before she has me arrested."

Liz looked at Stacy and winked. "Will you let me borrow him that long?"

"I guess so," she said. "But don't let him forget about the dog house."

Liz looked at Rachel and they both began to laugh. Then she wiped her eyes and turned back to Stacy. "I've got an idea. It's still a little early for supper, so why don't we head down to the lobby for a while, and you can tell Jim what kind of dog house you want while your mom and dad talk a while." She looked at Ben. "Is that OK?"

Ben nodded. "Sounds like a good idea. Just don't let her talk you into a pink and purple polka dot paint job."

Ben listened to the laughter as the new couple walked down the hall hand-in-hand with Stacy.

Ben looked at his wife. "I was going to ask how she was handling all this, but it looks like she's doing OK."

Rachel sat on the edge of the bed and took his hand. "I think so too." She looked into her husband's eyes and continued. "You know, Stacy and I sat here for the past two days and waited for you to wake up. You were in and out of consciousness the whole time, but you never fully came to until just now. And the funny thing is Stacy didn't talk much the whole time. She just sat there and watched you.

"Then sometime early this morning, she looked at me and said, 'He saved me mommy. He saved all of us.' Then she went back to her vigil." Rachel held his hand to her lips for a moment then continued.

"You did, didn't you? You saved us."

Ben shook his head. "No, it wasn't me."

"Then who? What happened?"

"I'm not sure I'll ever be able to completely describe what happened." Ben closed his eyes. "The minute I hit those blades I felt like I was transported somewhere else. Some bleak and terrible place unlike anything you can imagine." He opened his eyes. "Then, I saw it. I saw Ashmedai. Fought him…fought it." Ben shuddered.

"Honey, don't." Rachel put a hand on his forehead. "It can wait."

Ben reached up and took her hand. "No, it can't. You need to know, and I need to talk about it." He reached for the water cup and Rachel helped him. "Anyway, this place was little more than rock and sand, but it was cold. So cold. So dead." He paused a moment. "I've never experienced anything like that in my life." She squeezed his hand but said nothing.

"I think I almost died. It sure felt like it. But during the fight I realized I had already lost one child because I couldn't act, and that I was about to lose my entire family because I was trying to act on my own." Twin trails of tears burned his cheeks. "And in that instant, I realized I have lived every day since Brandon's death by losing myself in the work, denying my real feelings, going through the motions, and acting like I had everything under control. When that realization hit me, I stopped fighting and prayed. Prayed with everything I have in me. I admitted I couldn't do what had to be done. That only the power of Christ could defeat this thing that had invaded our home and our lives." He squeezed her hand. "I realized I just dove into another pool without knowing how to swim. But this time I asked for help.

"Then the world exploded, I blacked out, and here we are."

Ben tried to hold the remaining tears back, but the flood would not be denied. They held each other as their tears created new reservoirs of love for each other. After a moment, Rachel sat up and took both her husband's hands.

"I want you to know I never blamed you for Brandon's death. Not for one moment. In fact, I wondered just how you could manage all that pain alone."

"I know you didn't. I was doing enough of that for both of us. It's just that I was so helpless, then so embarrassed. I almost died trying to save my son."

"That's right. You almost died *trying to save our son*. Then you almost died trying to save our daughter and everybody else in that room. Ben, how much more can you love someone than that?"

She kissed him softly.

"Now you get some rest. Stacy and I are going out for pizza. We'll stop in again for a little while later today. Tomorrow I'm going to meet with the inspector to see the extent of any structural damage, and once you are discharged and any work has been completed, we're going to start the process of making that house our home."

Rachel squeezed his hand, kissed it, and went to get their daughter.

Once she was out of the room, Ben lowered the sheet covering his chest and watched as the last of his wounds faded away.

SPECIAL BONUS STORY:

THE HEART IS A DETERMINED HUNTER

Originally published in Gothic Ghosts, edited by Charles L. Grant, 1997

———————

THE MOMENT LLOYD McPherson dialed the telephone the world went dark. At least that was the illusion created by the first dark clouds of the coming storm as they pushed the October sun out of the way. As it was, Lloyd barely noticed. His connection had already failed twice and the one that was coaxing the second ring from the phone on the other end was tenuous at best.

He had debated the idea of calling the Steadman Resort for almost two days and, right or wrong, he had finally placed the call. The line popped and crackled; the ghosts of past conversations unaware they were long finished. Lloyd's finger hovered over the tiny plunger that held the power to terminate the connection. Twice he had pulled back at the last second. An instant away from the comforting buzz of a new dial tone. He was still not too sure.

"Thank you for calling the Steadman Resort. How may I be of service this afternoon?"

"What?" The world swam back into focus in one large wave." Oh ...yes, I'm sorry. I was a little preoccupied."

"Of course sir. How may I be of service?" The voice was steady. That sort of well bred, professionally aloof hotel voice. A voice that implied the sort of patience gained after a lifetime of serving the public's whims and fancies.

Lloyd stopped drumming his fingers long enough to pick up a pen and start tapping the capped end on a weekly organizer pad. Stupid Stuff I Gotta Do This Week. He tapped number three. Call the Steadman."Yes, I was calling on the off chance you might have a room available for the next two or three days. I know this is rather short notice, but this was a spur of the moment idea." The lie tasted funny.

"If you'll allow me just one moment, I'll be happy to check for you sir. I believe we may have a room available tonight. Could you hold please?"

"Yes."

The line went silent. At that moment the idea of severing the connection before the reservations clerk returned was overwhelming. Though he needed to go back, this might not be the time. Maybe in a couple of months. That's it, he thought. I'll wait a little longer.

With that thought in mind he reached for the plunger. Just as the voice returned."Sir we have an ocean view room available, and I will be more than happy to hold it for you if you'd like."

Lloyd hesitated. He was still not one hundred per cent sure about this decision.

"Sir..."

"Oh, right. That will be fine." He fished for his American Express card."I'm sorry if I sound a little out of it. To tell you the truth, I wasn't sure you would even be open. I thought I remembered someone telling me you were in the process of remodeling."

"No sir, that's all finished. We are right here and ready for your visit."

"OK, that sounds fine. My name is Lloyd McPherson, and my American Express number is…"

"Mr. McPherson, you of all people don't need to secure a room. You're a valued guest here, and it will be our pleasure to have you stay with us again. As a matter of fact, I look forward to serving you personally."

Lloyd sat back in his chair."Thank you, that's very kind. I'm looking forward to staying…

another lie?

…for a few days. I will probably arrive sometime after nine tonight."

The voice, smooth as polished wood."We'll be waiting. Have a pleasant trip."

The world went dark again."Thank you."

"Good bye then Mr. McPherson."

"Goodbye."

Lloyd replaced the receiver and stared at the telephone. Stared like a man waiting for the next word from God Himself.

THE OPEN road and the subliminal hint of salt in the air cleared his head a little. Lloyd had been driving for almost an hour and a half before he so much as sighed. He hadn't sung with the radio, hadn't even yelled at the Volkswagen full of college kids that pulled out in front of him earlier. His grief had been gray and deep, just like the weather. But even with the thickening clouds overhead, the sea air began to work its magic.

Slowly.

So slowly.

He and Carrington had always loved the beach. Before they could afford a place on the ocean, they dreamed of having their own place. Then, when money was no problem, they found they enjoyed going to various hotels or renting a condo for a week or two. That way they could enjoy one another and somebody else could worry about maintenance, cutting the grass, and all the other little headaches that would go with owning their own place.

And now the ocean was starting to soothe him somewhat. But not before he had replayed the events of their last day together.

They had read about the Steadman Resort in a regional travel magazine and immediately fell in love with it. The tennis courts, racquetball courts, ocean view, bicycle trails, and attentive staff were just the tip of the iceberg. The location--the Outer Banks of North Carolina--was secluded enough to afford them privacy when they wanted it, but they were close enough to the quaint shops and historic sights of the surrounding area to immerse themselves to their heart's delight. And immerse themselves they had.

Their days had been filled with walks on secluded beaches, picnics on the shore, treks to such exotic places as Duck and Nags Head, and wonderful evenings of dinner, dancing, and romance. The resort had a grand ballroom and an orchestra that played big band and swing music until the wee hours of the morning. They had enjoyed their first trip so much they had spent the past five Thanksgivings there.

Almost five.

Every newspaper in the state ran a story about the fire. Due to the tragic outcome it even made the wire services. Fifty people lost their lives and a dozen more went to the hospital with various cuts, burns, and broken bones. The news people said they were lucky anybody survived at all.

But Lloyd hadn't felt lucky.

The fire started on the outside of the building and effectively trapped everyone in the ballroom from the start. At first no one noticed. It was Thanksgiving and the Steadman was hosting its annual black tie charity dinner and dance. Champaign. Party favors. The works. The orchestra had been playing a jumping arrangement of Woodchopper's Ball that had two thirds of the couples in attendance on the dance floor. The large hearth at one end of the room so big you could roast an entire pig in it - crackled and snapped while the celebrants whirled and glided across the room.

Blanche Lee was the first to notice that something was wrong. She noticed the moment the window next to her shattered from the heat outside. An eighteen-inch dagger of glass pinned her to her chair and claimed the first casualty of the night.

The first of many.

Marge Newland, Blanche's newfound friend and fellow antique shop aficionado, screamed as the shards of glass fell around her. She watched her companion die in horrible slow motion. Time was molasses thick and through it all Marge could neither move nor breathe. The scream siphoned all the air from her lungs and the effort to refill them was thwarted by panic. She started to hyperventilate.

At the same time Marge screamed, Joe Ramey burned his hand on the door which lead to the outer hallway and on to the main building. The massive oak door blistered his hand, but his yelp of pain had been lost in Marge's scream. Later that night Joe would tell district fire chief Walt Richards about the ensuing pandemonium. Other witnesses would tell the chief about Joe rescuing five people from the blazing ruin.

All Lloyd remembered from that point on was trying to get himself and Carrington out of the building. When the severity of the situation became apparent, the herd instinct took over and the occupants of the room all headed for the nearest exit in a giant cluster. Joe waved them away from the door which had devoured two layers of skin moments earlier and part of the crowd shifted toward the next exit. Caught in the crush, he and Carrington had been swept along with the tide. Stumbling, sweat soaked hands slipping but never completely losing contact, they scanned the room for another way out.

When the line that fed the gas jets in the fireplace ruptured, the orchestra were dead where they sat. The resulting explosion unfolded a fan of solid blue flame that covered the entire bandstand. So intense was the blaze that the lead trumpet player's valve oil bottle erupted in his hand and created a blue hot formal length glove of flame from elbow to fingertips.

Nobody heard him scream.

Overhead a beam exploded and several others ignited as if by an unseen hand. The crowd, now very much like stampeding cattle, managed to find an exit and began to trample one another in an effort to leave the microcosm of hell. Pushing and shoving. Trampling anything and anyone in their path.

That's when the beam above Lloyd fell.

His first instinct had been to pull Carrington to safety and he had pulled with all his might.

He had pulled against the tide of terrified humanity.

He had pulled against the tide of the inevitable.

In the seconds that seemed to stretch into months he saw her face. Saw the look of horror on that smudged, perfect face. Somehow her cheek had been cut and the blood seemed to have been painted on in a long thin line from ear to chin. Then time sped up, a demon train on its way to oblivion. He remembered screaming her name, remembered being shoved deeper into the crowd, and remembered the feeling as her fingers slipped away.

And he remembered the beam falling.

An oaken inferno, close to a thousand pounds of flame and timber, came crashing down with an ear splitting roar. It sounded like a victory cry straight out of Hell. In the end, it had killed four people. Carrington and three others.

He knew that he screamed and tried to wade against the frightened, cow-eyed mass of people, but he couldn't remember how he managed to get out.

And as he sat watching the world through a haze of tears, he didn't know how long he had been in the Steadman parking area.

Lloyd switched off the Jaguar's engine, unbuckled his seat belt, and got out of the car. The last half hour was a blur. He still thought about that night often enough, but it had been a while since the memory had been that vivid. Was that an omen? A message to retreat for a while longer? He didn't know. Couldn't bring himself to think about it now.

The first thing he noticed when he entered the lobby was the sameness of it. It hadn't changed. The wood, the furnishings, the plants, even the smell. Brass polish and heart pine. It was as if the Steadman had never burned.

He stared at the polished oak and gleaming brass. Everything was the picture of perfection. The hotel had been resurrected. As if the fire had never happened.

Something slick and terrible caressed his insides.

The sound of the bellman's voice jolted him back to reality."May I be of service sir?" A voice accustomed to helping travelers caught up in the spell of the Steadman. No impatience. Just waiting to do his job; a job he had no doubt performed since the Steadman's opening.

"No...I mean yes. I need to check in. My reservation is in the name McPherson."

The bellman took the lone suitcase."Of course Mr. McPherson, we've been expecting you." He bowed ever so slightly."Please follow me."

The bellman escorted Lloyd to the front desk where he was greeted like an old friend."Mr. McPherson," the desk clerk said."I trust you had an enjoyable drive." He nodded to the bellman. "Take Mr. McPherson's case to his room."

He turned to tell his escort he would be glad to handle his own bag, but the bellman and his suitcase were gone.

"Mr. McPherson, here is the key. You will be in room one thirty-nine. If there is anything else you need, please don't hesitate to ring the desk." Lloyd turned and accepted the brass key. He looked at it, trying to find the answer to a question as yet unformed.

"Mr. McPherson, is there a problem?"

"No. No, I was just..." He looked at the desk manager."Just trying to take in how perfect everything is. It's almost as if the Steadman never, well, never—"

The desk manager smiled."I know. It is quite astounding what can be done when you want it badly enough."

"True enough I suppose. It's funny though." Lloyd looked at the key again. Noticed how the light rippled across the polished brass."I didn't realize you had rebuilt the entire complex."

The desk manager, he of the smooth, polished wood voice, smiled."Well, you have been rather preoccupied if I may be so bold." The smile changed ever so slightly.

"No," Lloyd answered, "you're absolutely right." He pocketed the key and stepped back from the desk."I think a few days here might actually be just the thing I need to…"

The desk manager cut him off. "Of course. We understand completely. This cannot be an easy journey for you." The smile slipped away." So sad. So tragic and so needless."

Lloyd nodded but said nothing. Another sound had captured his attention.

Music.

Big band music. He looked around to his left then back again."You really have made a comeback." He looked in the direction from which strains of I Can't Get Started flowed.

"Maybe you'd care to have a drink and listen to the orchestra for a while before you turn in Mr. McPherson. I believe you will find it beneficial."

Lloyd started to refuse the suggestion and go straight to his room. The trip had been long and he wasn't sure he was ready to go in the ballroom just yet. He was just now becoming accustomed to the idea that he was here and having a conversation with the desk manager in a place that represented the darkest day of his life. In fact, he had been so taken aback by the experience so far, he realized his credit card had not been imprinted. He hadn't even inquired about the desk manager's name.

He turned to raise the issues with the desk manager but was stopped short. The blond man behind the counter extended his hand, and Lloyd shook it automatically. "Now Mr. McPherson, you go right in, order a drink, and make yourself comfortable. Don't be concerned about your room. We will take perfect care of you. And should you need anything, ask for me personally. My name is Paul."

The room seemed to tilt slightly and he followed the tilt toward the room where the orchestra played. He turned back just long enough for Paul to say, "Go ahead in sir. This is the reason you came."

Before he could respond his hand was on the brass door handle and he was walking inside.

The room was exactly the way he remembered it. The long mahogany bar to his right was polished to a high sheen. The brass rails and sparkling glass and crystal ware reflected in the long mirror behind the bar created the illusion of a huge double bar. And the single bar was plenty large for the room.

The tables were arranged in clusters around a pristine dance floor, recently polished to a high gloss. There were already about fifty couples in various sections of the room. The orchestra played as if there was a New Year's Eve party in full swing. The bandleader threw a two-fingered salute in Lloyd's direction while giving the downbeat for Satin Doll.

"How many in your party sir?"

Lloyd turned to the woman who had addressed him. Her platinum hair and fair skin was a perfect contrast to her night black dress.

"Just one thank you."

"Will anyone be joining you later?"

Lloyd cocked his head as if he hadn't understood. "No, I'm alone this evening." That's the truth if I ever told it, he thought as he was escorted to a table close to the bandstand. When he was seated, the platinum vision in black took his drink order and went back to the bar.

For the first time since his arrival Lloyd had a chance to really look and take everything in. It was the same. From the exposed beams right down to the design in the carpet. It was exactly the same. Like the desk manager had said, it was amazing what you could do if you wanted to badly enough.

If only that were really true.

A slight movement at his right elbow interrupted his thoughts. "That didn't take very long," he said as he turned to take his drink.

"No, not long at all," Carrington said in response.

Carrington.

The room shifted, went slightly out of focus. Lloyd could see nothing except the face of his beloved Carrington.

Carrington was his life. Carrington was the exhale to his every inhaled breath.

Carrington was dead.

She died here.

This was impossible.

Heart hammering. Hard to breathe. Room spinning.

Lloyd's heart jackhammered his ribs.

Cold.

Oh dear God, he thought. I'm losing it.

He closed his eyes and tried to bring his breathing under control. Calm. Deeper, deeper. He opened his eyes. The specter of his dead wife was gone. Stress, he thought. That's what it is. I just came out too soon.

He turned to pick up his glass. If he ever needed a drink, he needed one now.

"Lloyd."

The sound of his name turned his spine to ice.

Carrington sat across from him looking for all the world the way she had looked the night they first came to the Steadman.

He looked at her. Saw without fully comprehending. Her face was the same. The same delicate nose; the same bright green eyes. The same porcelain skin. It was Carrington.

But it couldn't be.

"What's happening to me?" Lloyd asked no one in particular. A last attempt to hold his emotions in their precarious safety net."What's happening?"

Carrington smiled."Don't you know? Really?"

Lloyd slid his chair back and jerked his hands away from the table as if it had carried a two-twenty charge. "This is not happening. It's not." A tear formed in the corner of one eye. "It's not."

The smile changed ever so slightly. "Yes it is Lloyd. This is happening. Everything here is perfect. Just the way you wanted it.

"Just the way it was that night."

Her words were lost on him.

"How? I mean…" He looked around the room. The orchestra played—had never stopped playing—while couples danced, or sat and listened. Ice tinkled in glasses. Smoke from a dozen cigarettes ambled toward the ceiling.

Smoke.

Fire.

Then.

Now.

"No. This is wrong. All wrong."

"Why," she asked. "It's what you wanted isn't it?"

"What I wanted?" He turned to face what had once been his partner in life. "What do you mean wasn't this what I wanted?"

"Lloyd, I know you've been hurting. Every day since—"

"No." He cut her off and shook his head. "I came here to come to terms with what happened." He sent a less than steady hand to fetch his drink.

"Is that really why you came?"

The bourbon was tasteless. There was no reassuring jolt of fire from throat to belly. He looked at the glass, then at his wife. "What?"

"You came here hoping to find it had all been a dream. You wanted the impossible to happen, and now it has." She held out a hand. "So now you have to accept it."

He moved his chair toward the table. Hesitated. His heart was a thoroughbred straining against the gate.

"Carrington?"

The tear traced its way down his cheek. Many more followed the path it blazed.

"Carrington …how …I mean …how did …?"

"You did it."

The words hit him with the force of a sledge hammer. "How did I do this? How could I possibly have done this?"

"If you want something bad enough." She smiled again. The smile he had seen a thousand times. The smile that had buoyed his heart every day of their married life. The smile that now brought the reality of his situation home.

He reached for her hand. "It really is you. You're really here." Now it was his turn to smile. "It's impossible, and insane, but you're here."

She nodded. "I told you so."

He looked at her. He couldn't help himself. She was exactly as she had always been. Perfect.

He released her hand and wiped the tears from his eyes. The orchestra played and couples swirled around the floor. But as far as he was concerned, there was no one else in the world but Carrington. His Carrington. It was absolutely impossible and absolutely true. He stood and walked around the table.

"Can I hold you?"

The orchestra played a slow Glenn Miller tune. Carrington stood and held out her arms to him.

"Yes."

Lloyd took her in his arms. Savored the feel of her. He buried his face in the soft junction of her neck and shoulder. Pulled her closer. All the memories and all the suppressed feelings rushed back in a solid wave of emotion.

She was here. They were together. And she felt

If you want something bad enough.

different.

He held her tighter.

She didn't respond.

He held her at arm's length. "Carrington, what's wrong?"

She smiled again. The same smile he had loved for years. But not the same? Almost the same.

"Just then when I held you. Didn't you feel anything at all?"

"No. We don't feel anything here."

He bit his lower lip. Partly habit and partly for the pain. He needed the pain. He needed to clear his head. "What do you mean you don't feel anything here?"

She motioned for him to sit. "When I died I saw the fire, the smoke, the crush of people. And I saw others around me watching the same thing. Then there was a kind of nothing for a while. I knew what was happening, but it didn't matter."

Lloyd's head was throbbing like a rotten nerve in an abscessed tooth. The orchestra continued to play and the couples continued to swirl. Then he realized what had bothered him from the moment he walked in. With the exception of the desk manager and the hostess, no one had spoken. The couples at the tables smoked and drank but never uttered a word. The orchestra played but there was no banter between songs from the bandleader.

"You see, we know everything we need to know here. This is a different level of existence, so the physical amenities of the other existence really aren't necessary."

"If you don't have any feelings for me then why did you come back?" The tears started again but this time there was no trickle.

"Lloyd, I didn't come back. You came to me. What you see is the essence of who I was. Much like it was frozen in time. We do not age, we do not feel. We know what we need to know. We exist, and existence is enough."

He attempted to understand."Then this is Heaven?"

"No."

"Is it Hell?"

"No."

Lloyd felt the first stirring of anger push his fear off to the side. "Then where are we?"

"We're at the Steadman. Your Steadman."

The black dawning of complete realization struck him like a fist.

"Carrington, you said there were others watching the events of that night with you. Do you mean these people too?"

She nodded.

He began to shiver. The air had grown suddenly cold and the fire in the hearth provided no warmth. He watched the couples swirl soundlessly. The orchestra played on, no longer burned by the inferno, no longer feeling the music. Just shades of musicians playing shades of feelings long forgotten.

"If what you say is true then I'm going back home. If I can't hold you--the real you--then I won't settle for an empty substitute. I just can't." He stood and turned to go.

She took his arm. "You can't leave."

Another smile. Mirthless. The memory of a smile. "Those who haven't crossed over know so little. You assume it is always those from this side who cross over. Hauntings you call them." She paused

if you want something bad enough, you can make it happen

"Sometimes one of you crosses over to here. That's what you did." She sounded so matter-of-fact now.

"There is no front desk. No Steadman. And tomorrow or the day after someone will find your car parked where you left it. In front of the charred foundation of what used to be the Steadman Resort."

Lloyd's breath caught in his throat. The room grew colder. The band played louder. He grabbed her shoulders and shouted to be heard above the increasing din of the orchestra. "What are you saying? Do you mean I'll just stay here, never age, and keep company with a room full of what used to be?"

"Not exactly. You'll age, but since time has so little meaning here, you will age slowly.

"But you will never die."

She smiled her dead smile.

The horror of the situation bloomed, a blood rose opening in his mind. He would age beyond ancient with the specter of his fondest memory eternally before him. Never changing. Never caring. The realization was too much. He pushed the almost Carrington aside and raced toward the nearest exit.

He turned the brass door handle and rushed toward the lobby and his waiting car.

The room was exactly the way he remembered it. The long mahogany bar to his right was polished to a high sheen. The brass rails and sparkling glass and crystal ware reflected in the long mirror behind the bar created the illusion of a huge double bar. And the single bar was plenty large for the room.

The tables were arranged in clusters around a pristine dance floor, recently polished to a high gloss. There were already about fifty couples in various sections of the room. The orchestra played as if there was a New Year's Eve party in full swing. The bandleader threw a two-fingered salute in Lloyd's direction while giving the downbeat for Satin Doll.

"How many in your party sir?"

Lloyd turned to the woman who addressed him. Her platinum hair and fair skin were a perfect contrast to her night black dress.

He could not speak. Undiluted dread clutched his throat with fingers of cold glass bone.

"Sir, will anyone be joining you later?"

He heard a soft click as the door closed behind him.

"Yes."

AUTHOR'S NOTE

THIS BOOK was originally one of, if not **the**, first haunted house novels for the Christian market. Much like James Byron Huggins' book *The Reckoning* (billed as "The first genuine Christian thriller"), it was meant to be something different. A horror novel for the Christian market, but one that reflected the real world a little more realistically and wasn't populated by too good to be true kinds of Christians. I didn't want it to be a *Kum-Ba-Ya, let's-all-hold-hands-and-pray-while-the-bad -thing-goes-away* kind of book. Primarily because that's not how things work in the real world. Also, I wanted to write a horror novel that would speak to the Christian market, but was also a good story that wouldn't turn off people who don't necessarily believe what I believe.

Also, in the early days of Christian fiction, many of the characters and their saccharine, almost naïve, dialogue made me gag. Granted, there are people who talk that way, but too much "First I shall clothe myself in righteousness, put on the armor of God, and prepare myself to do battle" is just off-putting for a lot of people. True, they are valid theological concepts, but it's also disconcerting to those who didn't grow up in the church, or those who have been so hurt by the church that they want nothing to do with it anymore.

They might, however, read, "OK, everybody come over here. First, we're going to pray and get our heads on straight. Then, we're going out there and kick some undead ass."

I would.

When this book first came out, the publisher wasn't quite sure what to do with it or how to market it. It was new territory for them. Consequently, sales were pretty bad. It's not an unheard of story in the publishing world. However, I won't mention the name of the publisher because they did the best they knew to do at the time, and you can't fault someone for that.

Besides, now it's with a publisher who knows exactly what to do with it.

I have tried to fix the spots where the book's age was showing (fax machines, etc.) and have rewritten a few sections that needed to be updated. But I have also tried to keep the original vibe as much as I can.

So, for those out there who are believers, here's a little different kind of story than t you're possibly used to. But theologically, this dog will hunt. So enjoy.

And for those who don't believe like I do, you're especially welcome here. Because I'm a firm believer that stories are for all of us. And even if you skim through the "religious parts" I hope you can also say, "Hey, I'm not so sure about that prayer thing, but that scene with the bat and the window pane was creepy as hell." Because the Jesus I'm familiar with basically said, *This is my message to you and my truth. And if you want to talk about it, I am always ready and willing. But I believe I smell fresh bread ready to come out of the tanur, and we don't want to miss that. By the way, I heard a funny joke on the way here…*and then he hung out with everybody and let every one of them know that they were somebody important and that they were loved.

So, if you read this and get a sense of a greater theological truth, I'm happy for you.

And if you read this and your final reaction is, "hey, that was a pretty good story," thank you. I'm glad you had fun with it.

It has been great hanging out with you. But I think I smell bread baking, and we don't want to miss that…

ABOUT THE AUTHOR

THOMAS SMITH is an award-winning writer, newspaper reporter, TV news producer, playwright, and essayist. His print and multi-media work has been published by Borderlands Press, Group Publishing, Chronicle Books, Grinning Skull Press, Cemetery Dance, Pocket Books, Tor Books, Barnes and Noble Books, and Tales to Terrify. He is probably the only writer in captivity to be included in collections with Stephen King and the Rev. Rick Warren in the same week.

www.ingramcontent.com/pod-product-compliance
Lightning Source LLC
Chambersburg PA
CBHW030642020726
47493CB00006B/1840